✝ARNISHED PULPIT

Also by Marcia M. Cham

You Mean I Have to Look at the Body?!
Stories of Dying and Living

"Gertie's Sisters" & "Leapfroggin' Turtles"
in
High Country Headwaters
an anthology by High Country Writers

†ARNISHED PULPIT

Marcia M Cham

a novel

Marcia M. Cham

This is a work of fiction. Names, characters, places, and incidents are either a product of the author's imagination or are used fictitiously, and any resemblance to actual persons living or dead is entirely coincidental.

Cover Illustration & Design by Adam Tiller
Text Design by Luci Mott

www.marciamcham.com

ISBN-13: 978-0615741734

ISBN-10: 0615741738

Acknowledgments

My GRATITUDE goes to the members of the High Country Writers of Boone, North Carolina, who offered encouragement and suggestions as I struggled to write my work of fiction. Their wise counsel was invaluable. Thanks for the perseverance and laughter with my two writing groups: Fellowship of the Rose and the Monday Critique Group. Thanks to my neighbors, friends, and family who labored with me and read the many drafts. My deepest gratitude goes to my editor, Sandra Horton, who spent hours reading, critiquing, suggesting and encouraging. She is the best at digging in and nudging me to become a better writer. Special thanks to Amy Cham for her inspiration, to Joe Lineberger for the title, and to my husband, Ken, my favorite cheerleader.

Dedication

To my parents, William Mark Mitchell and Evelyn Mills Mitchell,
who brought me up in the church knowing its pitfalls and gifts.

Tarnished Pulpit

Part 1
Genesis
In the Beginning

CHAPTER 1

8 a.m.
May 19, 1967

IRENE imperceptibly parted the lace curtains for a better look. He held a claw hammer in his right hand and a sign attached to a long stake in his left. He was short—only a bit over five feet—shoulders squared in a black suit. She watched as he scanned the front of the white clapboard church. Tilting his head upward his gaze lingered for several minutes on the loose shingles, patched roof, and peeling paint. He lowered his head and surveyed the weed infested green.

Walking along the edge of the green, he paused at each house: Thayer's 1781 saltbox, dilapidated from years of neglect; the Hill's 1890 authentic Cape Cod cottage; the Phillips newly renovated historic log cabin. Irene drew back from the glass and hid in the shadows when his glance came to rest on her house. an aging Victorian. When his gaze moved on, she stepped closer to the window. From her vantage point, she observed him as he whisked past the stately Alden House and stopped to stare at the Deal's tired Dutch colonial on the corner.

To Irene, his inspection was not casual. His precise movements and pivots were regimented and purposeful. When he reached the corner and turned, she drew in a breath. She exhaled and gasped when he stopped at the edge of the green across from her house. He jammed the bottom end of the stake into the ground. It fell over. Again he poked it into the soil and, this time, took a tighter grip with his left hand and pounded away with the hammer in his right.

Splinters of wood scattered this way and that as his haphazard aim chewed the top of the stake. His glasses slipped down his nose. He nudged them up with the back of his hand. Satisfied that the sign was secure, he stepped back, brushed off his suit, and crossed the narrow street onto the edge of Irene's yard. Squaring his shoulders he admired the sign.

Keep Off the Green!
Only Use by Permission Of
The Reverend Matthew Henry Stiles,
President of First Parish Unitarian Church
Ironton Corner

"Well, I'll be. Keep off the green and President ..." Irene moved from the window and stomped to the door. She shoved the screen open, hugged the front of her bathrobe, and charged down her steps. With a few determined strides, she stood next to him. She grabbed the man's shoulder. "What are you doing? What right do you have to post that sign? That's not the way we do things around here." She saw the man's lip curl, but he appeared to think better and flashed a slight smile instead.

"I'm the new pastor ... Mr. Matthew Henry Stiles, and you are?" He paused, but seeing the rage in her eyes, he backed away, turned one hundred and eighty degrees, and quick-stepped to the church some fifty yards away. He grabbed both brass handles of the tall white front double-doors, flung them open, and retreated inside.

Irene Keene, a sturdy New Englander with a personality honed by ancestral pride, ripped the sign off the stake. "Keep off the green—I'll show him."

She dashed through the green with crabgrass tickling her feet through her open-toed slippers and followed him through the double doors, past the sanctuary, and down the hall to the church offices. She nodded to the secretary with the sign at her side.

Stiles poised to unlock the door to his study, dropped the key, and froze. He looked at her in disbelief. Irene towered over him. Her teased auburn hair added three inches to her five-foot-seven inch frame. "Here's your card board sign." She tore it into pieces and dropped them on the floor.

Hands on her hips, she proceeded to give this little Napoleon a history lesson. "In 1867 when the church became sole owner of the green, Pastor Bradford Ellis pledged to care for the green and never allow it to be fenced off from the general public. You will not deny it to the community."

The secretary gasped when Irene jabbed her finger into Stiles' shoulder. "And furthermore you can't be our pastor. We have no money for a pastor. As for being president, we have a president, Arthur Blankenship."

"Please come into my office, Mrs. ...?" He pushed an unruly curl of his black hair off his forehead, straightened his jacket, and finished unlocking the door. He stepped into the narrow doorway.

Irene tightened the belt on her blue chenille bathrobe and attempted to squeeze by him. She snagged her elbow on his jacket lapel and disturbed the white handkerchief in his breast pocket. He fumbled with the handkerchief, straightening it, and glared up at Irene. The glare did not unnerve her as she matched it with a long steady stare of her own.

"I'd be the first to know if we hired a pastor." She rose up on her toes and looked down into his eyes. "Is this one of those things the central office does without our permission? Sends us a pastor and expects us to like it?"

"Please sit and let me explain, Mrs. ...?" Stiles eased into an oak swivel desk chair. He began tapping his ring against its arm.

She dropped onto the stiff-backed chair across from him, the same chair she'd taken many times before when she needed to keep a pastor in line. "For your information, I'm Irene Lawrence Keene. My family refurbished the sanctuary forty years ago and added the educational wing in the late 50s. I've been a member of this church longer than you've been on this earth." She raised one eyebrow and focused on his tapping finger. "By the way, you can stop tapping your ring. I've seen plenty of Harvard rings, and they don't impress me."

"Mrs. Keene, Arthur Blankenship told me about your *History of Ironton Corner*. I've read it. It's brilliant. You quote from the personal journals of the former pastors. I hope you'll share them with me. Like you, I understand that knowing the past will make me a better pastor and you a better church."

His knowledge surprised her, and she relaxed a little and lowered her voice. "You can't be our pastor. I would have known."

"Arthur Blankenship told me he'd explain ..."

"Arthur?"

"Yes, Arthur hired me." His face hardened. "He's approved my plans."

"Plans?"

"By fall, brick pathways will circle the war memorial and fan out like a web connecting all corners of the green to the center. The church building, or as you New Englander's say, the meeting house, will be renovated inside and out." He paused. "To celebrate the renewal of the green, a concert will be held on Labor Day weekend in the new bandstand."

"And who's paying for all this?" Irene's dark eyes glared like a dog ready to strike.

"I am." His gray-green eyes held hers for a moment.

Irene jumped from her chair and bumped into a pile of pictures stacked haphazardly on the corner of Stiles' desk. They teetered. She steadied them, but didn't lose any of her ire. "We don't take hand-outs, young man."

She kicked at the boxes. "Don't go unpacking those boxes until I speak with Arthur."

Stiles stood and moved around his desk. "Mrs. Keene, I've read in the newsletters that you have held this church together for years. You've prevented this historic meeting house from being demolished. Believe me I'm on your side. I empathize with your desire for this church to become, as you say in your book, 'a symbol of the strength of this community.' " He paused and lowered his head as if offering a prayer. After a suitable time, he raised his eyes and met Irene's. "I've learned that your husband had the responsibility of closing the last factory in town."

Irene's speech slowed, remembering those difficult days. "Yes, Kenny was depressed for many months. Our schools suffered from the loss of taxes. Our church carried on even with the relocation of people and the reduction of financial commitments. Each year since 1959, the church membership voted to demolish the old building. Each year, I led a campaign to put the destruction on hold. I urged the members to tap the endowments and trusts to save the building, but they refused."

For a moment her voice trailed off, but then she noisily sucked in a deep breath and charged on. "To keep ourselves from deeper despair, Kenny and I did what we could. He patched up windows. My friend Maida and I helped my brother clean and add a little fresh paint to the Sunday school rooms for the dozen or so children who continued to attend every Sunday. Arthur Blankenship funded student pastors to do the preaching and a few other pastoral duties. Delbert Martin, the treasurer, doles out the little money we have for electricity and water and other monthly bills. And now, our secretary, Joyce Lang, continues to work two mornings a week to keep up the appearance that we still have a church."

She stopped and studied the young man standing in front of her. She stood towering over Stiles and put her hands on her hips. "And now you come around and say with your money, you're going to do all this. What's the catch? I want to hear what Arthur has to say about you."

"Yes, you need to ask Arthur. At the end of a couple of years, you'll be congratulating me on the growth and changes in the church and the community." He flicked a tiny piece of lint off his lapels.

Irene got the message. She stormed out, tightening the belt of her robe as it flapped against her stout legs. Halfway across the green, she shouted, "I'll be damned if I'm going to be pushed aside."

CHAPTER 2

9 a.m.
May 19, 1967

MAIDA had her hands in dishwater when Irene barged into her house, her face red and voice quivering with rage. "Maida, Arthur's hired a pastor."

"I know. Your brother told me." Maida dried her hands, grabbed a couple of potholders, and pulled a pot of beans from the oven, and placed it on a cooling rack next to the stove.

"My brother?"

"Yes. Over dinner at the Tavern on the Pond."

"Wait. George knew, and you had dinner with George and he told you and not me." Irene looked down into the eyes of her life-long friend. "George knew about the pastor?"

"Yes, George met the young man about six months ago. Mr. Stiles learned from the Unitarian office that we were about to close. Since he wanted a church before he graduated, they suggested that he come here and look around. The young fellow impressed George so much, he arranged for him to meet Arthur. Irene, we haven't had a young energetic pastor since Pastor Paul. And that was when we were young brides. Remember him, Irene? Pastor Paul was twenty-six, just like Mr. Stiles."

"That aside, Maida, why didn't George tell me?"

"Confidentiality." Maida's eyes sparkled through her glasses.

"I didn't know that George ever kept a secret."

"He's kept another one from you." Maida fussed with the lace trim around the pocket of her kitchen apron. "George and I have been seeing each other."

"You have?" Irene bit her tongue to hold back a laugh. "My brother hasn't looked at a woman for the past ten years. Not since

14

Ruth died."

Maida blushed. With a finger on each temple of her glasses, she set them right on her pug nose. "I'm enjoying his company."

"Is that why you're dressed up this time of the morning? Is he coming over? Are you going somewhere?"

"No. The fact is George has arranged for Mr. Stiles to come here for lunch."

"For lunch, I'll be." Irene poured a cup of coffee from the pot that Maida kept hot until lunch. She slid into a chair at the kitchen table. "Well, Maida, I met Mr. Stiles this morning, and we've had our first run in."

"Irene, in your robe and on his first day on the job, you didn't. You know how quick you are to judge." Maida juggled her hot cup and saucer as she sat.

"I'm not like you, blindly accepting everyone you meet." Irene huffed and sipped her coffee.

Maida stirred hers and smiled to herself. She knew Irene well. She remembered when she and Irene met in college and how they enjoyed weekends at Maida's family home on the Cape. She recalled their sharing lesson plans during their teaching days and their sadness when neither was successful in having children. Their friendship filled that empty space in their hearts that even the intimacy of their husbands could not satisfy.

Maida studied Irene's robe. She replayed her friend's reaction years ago when the mayor announced the name of the new fire chief. "Jeff isn't old enough for the job. Next thing you know we'll have women on the fire department. I won't have it." Maida's heart warmed remembering how Irene learned to trust Jeff

So Maida understood Irene. At every break from the traditional ways in Ironton Corner, Irene ranted and raved. She let everyone know her opinion, but eventually put the best interests of her loved ones and the community ahead of everything else. Maida, on the other hand, allowed things to settle and looked for the best in each new situation.

"Maida," Irene touched her friend's sleeve, "you've drifted off. You're going to stir the little painted flowers off the inside of your cup if you're not careful."

Maida lifted a spoonful of coffee to her lips and sipped. She watched the irritation work its way over Irene's face. "What happened this morning?"

"He posted a sign."

"A sign? What did it say?"

"Keep Off the Green! Use by permission of The Reverend Matthew Henry Stiles, President of First Parish Unitarian Church of Ironton Corner."

"Irene, you must be wrong. Why would he do that? Are you sure that is what it said?"

"I have eyes. I can read. That's what it said. Plain and simple."

"The man, according to George, is not a Reverend yet." Maida's eyebrows knitted together. "That's curious—he has another year to complete his Master of Divinity degree."

"I'm not wrong. I ran out, confronted him, pulled up the sign, and dashed to the church office and tore it to pieces right in front of him."

"Irene."

"In his office he told me his plans. I pretty much said, 'over my dead body.' " Irene gulped her coffee and made a face, the coffee now cold.

"I'm sure you did. Irene, you must have this all wrong. Pastors don't come here and take charge." Maida pulled the hem of her dress down over her knees. "There must be some reason for the sign. Have you talked to Arthur?"

"I'm on my way to see him now."

"In your robe?"

"Of course not."

Maida followed her friend to the front door. A minute later, she heard Irene shout from next door, "Kenny, apparently we have a new pastor."

CHAPTER 3

11 a.m.
May 19, 1967

STILES stood at the window in his office and watched Irene slam her front door. He called the home law office of Arthur Blankenship. "You're lagging behind on our agreed time table. I need to meet with you ... thirty minutes at the diner ... don't be late."

The new pastor stepped out of the church office, turned right, and passed the Town Cemetery. He squinted to check the pickup times on the mailbox outside the post office.

"They pick up here only once a day. It's better to go inside."

Stiles turned and a police officer extended his hairy-knuckled hand. "I'm Chief John Bird of the Ironton Corner Police Department."

Stiles reviewed in his photographic mind the knowledge he'd collected about Chief John Bird. He'd served as chief for eight years. As an officer, Bird held the enthusiastic teenagers accountable, handled the cases of petty theft, and took a hard line on DUI offenders. Bird was only thirty-two years old at the time of the former chief's untimely death. The town fathers wanted him to be chief, but worried that he didn't have enough experience to manage the two unsolved murders his predecessor left on the books. They were proved wrong and learned quickly that Bird had exceptional investigative skills.

Stiles threw his shoulders back. "I'm Matthew Henry Stiles, the new pastor of the First Parish Unitarian Church of Ironton Corner."

"Pastor? Last I heard they were going to tear down that old meeting house. And here you are."

"Yes, I'm here to turn it around."

"I hope so and soon. The town council is concerned about the safety of the building. If they don't fix it up, they'll have me hang a condemned sign on the door."

"That won't be necessary. By fall, the building will be in much better condition."

Stiles watched with disgust as Bird hitched his pants under his sagging belly.

"Speaking of condition, I'm going to be wearing suspenders before long if I don't lose some weight. I remember watching older officers putting on a few pounds here and there, never thought it would be me. Maybe I'll set a goal to lose a few. You don't look like you have any trouble with your weight."

"I'm late for an appointment." Stiles took pride in his trim figure, but he didn't want to get into a long discussion. He didn't have time for people with no self-control.

"Before you go, Pastor, I want you to know that I observed your encounter with Irene Keene earlier. She darts around town as if she has some official authority, especially when it comes to the green and that church. Beneath it all she's a good person. She takes plenty of our teasing about her need-to-know everything." Bird adjusted his cap. "We only tease the folks we care about, you know."

Stiles winced. He didn't tease because his father didn't tease and his mother didn't dare. Instead, his father castigated Matthew. When his curly hair hung down on his forehead, his father rebuked him, called him a girly girl, and made him wear a skirt for a day. Then his father took it out on Matthew's mother.

Bird touched his cap as if saluting. "Welcome, Mr. Matthew Henry Stiles. I'll be around if you need anything."

I bet you will, Stiles thought, giving a small wave to the chief while crossing the street.

Inside the diner a balding man with ruddy complexion and a thin red mustache, waved at Stiles as he did to all customers. "Coffee?"

Stiles nodded and took a booth in the back. He studied the assortment of bowling trophies and Irish memorabilia, not the kind of décor he'd lived with as the only son of wealthy parents.

Minutes later, a familiar voice called out as the front door slammed shut. "Chet, get us two warmed Jordan Marsh blueberry muffins with butter on the side and coffee. You're serving the new pastor of First Parish Unitarian Church of Ironton Corner." Arthur Blankenship, a local lawyer, dressed in casual black slacks and collared knit shirt, folded his lanky body into the chair opposite the pastor.

Chet brought a pot and two mugs. He set the mugs on the table, filled them, and placed the pot out of the way on the next table. Wiping his hands on the ever-present flour sack towel tucked into his belt, he offered his hand. "I'm Chet O'Brian. I've been around this place for about twenty years. If you don't know Jordan Marsh, it's one of the department stores in Boston. My dad made muffins for them for thirty years. He passed the recipe on to me when I opened this place. Come around anytime, I'll take care of you. Are you a bowler?"

"Not for a long time. Not since grade school." Stiles emptied three creams in his cup. He remembered how the smell of sweaty bowling alleys upset his stomach.

Chet nodded towards Arthur. "Maybe you can get my friend back to the alleys. He's avoided the place lately."

"Chet, you know I had to give up bowling due to my back."

"If we let you use one of those light balls they have for the kids, do you suppose you could bowl then?" Chet laughed and his eyes sparkled. "I'll get those muffins."

The muffins came. Arthur cut his in two, slathered butter on both halves, watching it soak into the warm muffin. Stiles sliced his muffin into four sections and then cut each of those in half. He carefully put each piece in his mouth leaving no mess.

Stiles folded his napkin, and laid it across his plate. "I ran into your Irene Keene this morning."

"What do you mean?"

"She tore down my sign."

"Your what?" Arthur's body stiffened.

"My sign that read, 'Keep off the Green! Use by permission of The Reverend Matthew Henry Stiles, President of First Parish Unitarian Church of Ironton Corner.' I told you I'd be putting up the signs."

"You said no such thing. You said you'd be informing the children who use the green that it would be closed to them during your first project. You didn't say you were posting signs ... besides you are not 'The Reverend Matthew Henry Stiles' or 'President.' The honor of 'The Reverend' comes when you've proven yourself and when the Unitarian office gives its official okay to ordain you. For now, you are Mr. Stiles. And as for you being president, that's never going to happen. We've never done it that way before."

Stiles leaned back in his chair and mimicked Arthur. "We've never done it that way before. Listen to you." He sat forward and waved his index finger at Arthur. "You've already put aside the bylaws by hiring me."

"You forced me." Arthur's face flushed.

"Calm down. You'll be pleased with our agreement by Labor Day. I promise you. Do you have my check?"

Arthur fished in his side coat pocket, pulled out a check, unfolded it, and looked at the amount. He slid the check across the table. Stiles picked up the check and grinned at the figure. He noticed beads of sweat forming along Arthur's hairline as he flashed a grin and tucked the check inside the pocket of his jacket. He rose from the table. "Remember I'm protecting your wife, your Barbara's stellar reputation.' "

At the cash register he handed three dollars to Chet. "That's for both Arthur and me. Keep the change."

"Thanks." Chet rang up the order. He put the extra six cents in the tip jar. He turned to joke with Arthur about the new pastor's generous tip, but stopped when he noticed Arthur wiping sweat from his face with his napkin.

CHAPTER 4

ARTHUR folded the napkin in his lap, took a few deep breaths to regain his composure and nodded to Chet to freshen his coffee.

"You okay, Arthur?" Chet said pouring the coffee.

"I'll be fine."

Chet watched Arthur so closely that he didn't hear Irene come into the diner. When she tapped Chet's hand, he jumped and nodded at Arthur. She tiptoed over. "Mind if I join you?"

Lost in thought, Arthur jerked his head up and clumsily struggled to his feet. He held the chair for Irene.

Chet delivered her usual black coffee, the only non-New England thing about Irene. She claimed something about her mother and cream and sugar and weight.

"Fresh from the beauty parlor, I see." Chet sniffed. "Boy, that hair spray smells strong. How do you women stand it?"

Irene touched the sides of her hair. "If you think it smells strong, you should feel it. It's like having a helmet on your head."

Chet flashed an impish smile at Arthur, waiting for his line about what kind of bird she kept there, but not this time. Chet drifted away from their table with a concerned look on his face for his friend.

Irene studied Arthur. She had known him for many years; he was more like a brother to her. Even during their college years, they weren't far apart. He attended Brown University in Providence and she went to the University of Rhode Island, an hour's drive away. Irene would have had Arthur as the 'man of honor' at her wedding if she had not been a stickler for tradition. Arthur had remained single until ten years ago. She was overjoyed at his marriage to Barbara, fifteen years his junior.

This morning Arthur's eyes looked troubled. Irene folded her hands and waited. When Arthur had something important or difficult to say, he left long silences between sentences. The practice probably came from his work as a lawyer, waiting for some piece of evidence or some statement to sink into the minds of the jurors.

Arthur dropped his eyes. "I hear you've had a run-in with our new pastor. I'm sorry."

Irene stirred her coffee.

Arthur stretched his long arms and played with the napkin dispenser. "Your brother met him first. He told me about an energetic young man he found wandering around the church. I took the man's name and contacted Harvard and the Unitarian office to check his credentials. Harvard sent me glowing reports and the Unitarian officials said they were pleased with his work thus far. They felt he'd be able to bring new life to First Parish."

"At my first meeting with him, he swept me up with his energy and enthusiasm. At later appointments, he showed me plans he'd designed to revitalize the church and our community. Irene, we've never had a pastor want to come here except to get his ticket punched to move on to a bigger place. He says he wants to stay and see his dreams come to life. He may not abide by our traditions, but in his eyes, the end justifies the means. But I ..."

Irene waited for Arthur to finish the sentence. His eyes rolled upward and his body pitched forward face first on the table. Irene jumped up and shook his shoulder. "Arthur, Arthur." He didn't respond. She yelled to Chet, "Call an ambulance."

Within minutes Chief Bird and the medics raced into the diner.

The medics ran through their list before attempting to move Arthur. Once they verified that it wasn't a stroke or heart attack, they moved him to a gurney. "With your history, Mr. Blankenship, we're going to run you to the hospital to be safe." Arthur raised his hand as if in agreement.

While the medics took Arthur out, Chief Bird stayed behind. "Irene, what happened?"

"When I joined him at his table, he looked pale and frightened."

Bird turned to Chet. "Did you notice anything?"

"I heard Arthur raise his voice at the new pastor, and then watched that red mottling work its way up the back of his neck. After the pastor left, he asked for more coffee and popped a pill. He stayed quiet until Irene came in."

"Thanks." Bird left thinking about the new pastor in his town.

* * *

Joyce Lang, Stiles' inherited secretary, heard him knock on the door even though she was tapping away on her typewriter. She paused with her fingers still on the keys. "What do you want?"

"I'm sorry to interrupt you. We haven't had a chance to talk." She watched him as he let a smile spread over his face and let his eyes soften. She knew the kind. She'd lived with an alcoholic husband who sweet talked her for far too long.

"Right. You've avoided me the past two weeks—bringing your stuff in at night, ordering me not to follow the movers into your private rooms upstairs, and leaving these piles of articles that you expect me to have ready for you on your time schedule." Joyce picked up the pile of papers and slammed them on the desk.

Stiles stepped back. "Maybe we could start over."

"Start over?" Joyce mused to herself. A month before Joyce's divorce was final, her ex-husband stopped by her house and pleaded "for the sake of the boys" to consider starting over. She had said, "Hell no," and continued her job search. First Parish Church interviewed her for the open secretary position. When she was offered the job, she asked her mother to help out with the boys. Her mother agreed. The hourly rate helped her finances, but, more than that, the compliments and affirmations about her abilities as an efficient secretary and compassionate listener bolstered her self-esteem. She'd been at the church for six years and recently added another part-time job at the Law Offices of Clyde Weaver. She wasn't going to be put down or ordered around anymore.

Stiles noticed a photo of two boys on her desk. "May I?" He reached to pick it up. "Your boys?"

She nodded. "Bob and Rich."

"They are handsome. I see by their uniforms they are Scouts."

"Yes, they're part of the troop here at the church. I hope you get to know them."

He set the photo back on her desk. "I will. I remember being their age and the problems of adolescence. I'll enjoy being around them and helping them when and where I can. May I sit down? I would like to discuss your work schedule and what we can expect of each other."

Joyce turned away from the typewriter and motioned for him to sit. "You need to get the weekly bulletin to me on Wednesday, and if you are going to have a newsletter, I need the articles five days before you want to send it out."

"I'll be happy to meet your schedule. I have three expectations: one, you keep any business that goes on here in the office confidential; two, you knock on my door when you want to see me; and three, you never go into my office without my permission."

She smiled to herself as he tried to keep a demanding tone out of his voice like her husband did. She paused and stared through his glasses into his eyes. "I have a question. Why has Arthur Blankenship kept you a secret from the congregation?"

Stiles stiffened and stood. He brushed by the corner of her desk knocking the photo onto the floor. As he picked it up, he noticed the glass had cracked. "I'll get you a new piece of glass."

Setting the photo on her desk, he backed out of her office. As she stared at the empty space where he had stood, she heard his office door close and the clicking of his typewriter keys a few minutes later. Visions of the other pastors and a parade of student pastors jogged through her mind. One carried every little concern in his heart, another tried to be everything to everybody, and the students ... they amused her with their wild ideas and long, long sermons. She loved each of them and knew they respected her. This one she hadn't pegged yet.

* * *

Stiles picked up a heavy satchel from the floor and placed it on the chair next to his desk. He fumbled for the key in his pocket, placed the key in the brass lock, unlocked it, and flipped the lock flap back. He fanned through the black leather binders:

1. Walkways and Bandstand
2. Renovations of the Meeting House

3. Raising a New Steeple
4. Pool Complex
5. The Museums of Ironton Corner
6. Memorial for Vietnam
7. The Vietnamese Hut
8. The Historic Wall
9. The History of Arthur and Barbara Blankenship

He touched two unnamed binders. "You are for projects I might have to implement, but since I've planned so well, I doubt I'll need you. These others," he ran his finger down the spine of binders, "show my work and planning over the past six months. Ironton Corner will be another Williamsburg once my plans unfold and the church will be a model for the future. Other church leaders will come to seek my counsel and advice."

He pulled out the "Walkways and Bandstand" binder and read through it, checking each detail. He reached for the phone and called the contractor. After being assured that the project would be ready in three weeks, he smiled. Before closing the binder, he studied the design of the walkways. "Matthew, you have created a masterpiece." He returned the binder to the satchel, and locked it, being sure to return the key to his pocket. He lifted the satchel from the chair and stored it in the kneehole of his desk, out of sight but only an arm's length away.

Stiles stretched over his typewriter, flexed his fingers three times, raised his arms to the ceiling twice, and fed in a fresh sheet of paper. He centered the title and date.

The Chronicle of Matthew Henry Stiles
May 19, 1967

My projects will build my reputation. I'll be more of a success than my father. My call to the ministry and my role as God's servant will endear me to others. The Unitarian office has recommended me.

The folks of Ironton Corner are easy. I know what is best for these people—I may have to patronize them to get them to accept my choices, but in the end, they will see that I am right. They will understand that God has chosen me to make the decisions that are necessary to bring new life to their church.

George was an easy target. Arthur has taken a little convincing, but he is crucial for my plans to work. He sees the value of my mission or he wouldn't have agreed to follow my instructions. He wants to save his church and his wife.

Someday I'll be the most important person in the history of the First Parish Unitarian Church of Ironton Corner. I'll have my empire.

It will give me great joy when my father discovers the identity of my mentor. After the years of history between the two men, father might even threaten to kill him. I'll enjoy that encounter, even the thought of it. Oh my, it is rising.

He looked down and watched the bulge grow in his pants. Enjoying the pleasure, he slowly typed. "I need to find Frederic to witness my work."

He cracked his knuckles again. Like a secretary being tested on the number of words per minute, his speed increased.

Here on my first official day, I've irritated Irene Keene. I've met Chief John Quincy Bird. Reading his body language, I know he will keep an eye on me. Chet will be an ally even if I never bowl with him. When I get Joyce's boys involved in my plans for the Boy Scouts, she'll change her tune. Now I'm off to meet Maida Hobart Alden.

He rolled the paper out and laid it flat on his desk. He rose and counted three steps to his filing cabinet before he reached for the handle on the top drawer. He opened it less than an inch and softly closed it three times before he finally pulled out a folder. He carried it to his desk.

He sat down, opened the top drawer and pulled out a ruler. With the straight edge as a guide, he printed, *The Chronicle of Matthew Henry Stiles* on the front of the folder. After blowing the ink dry, he placed the page inside the folder, counted the three precise steps to the file cabinet, and opened the drawer less than an inch three times before he placed the folder inside. He straightened his suit and crossed the hall to Joyce's office.

Pushing her door open a little, he observed her. He watched her flip her jet black hair back away from her slim face, fan her fingers and check her nail polish. She found a couple of marks on one of her nails, reached in her drawer, brought out the fire engine red polish, touched up the spots, and returned the small bottle to its place.

Disgust chewed in his gut. Her vain habits reminded him of the nosy woman who rented him an apartment during his first year of college. She promised, "I won't tell a soul about your real love—those pictures of you I saw in your top bureau drawer—if you're nice to me." He hated the memory of the woman insisting that he come to her apartment every week. She kissed his ears and with her painted fingernails pulled at his zipper exposing his limp member. Purring like a cat, she stroked him, leaning forward as her hair blocked his view. As she leaned closer, he could feel her breath on him. His breath quickened as she suddenly pulled her head up and smiled at him. She stripped and demanded his tongue, then sent him on his way. He stumbled out of her apartment and made it across the hall to his room before he threw up. He showered her foul smell away along with her words, "You are nothing but a limp little wimp." The sound of her stiletto heels on the linoleum reminded him that he had no power over her. She exerted a power, and he could do nothing, but obey.

Straightening his tie, he tapped on Joyce's door and pushed it further open. "Joyce, George Lawrence has arranged for me to meet Maida Alden for lunch."

"Oh, you'll love her. She's such a gentle spirit. She accepts everyone." Joyce paused with her hands on the typewriter and studied Stiles. "You look like you're going to a funeral. Why don't you loosen your tie and relax a little? You'll get closer to the people if you aren't so formal."

Her attitude grated on him, but he held back his frosty tone. "I hope you'll have the Sunday bulletin ready for me to proofread when I return."

"By the way, I'd use a little less of your aftershave or change it if I were you. It's too pungent," Joyce advised.

Stiles ground his teeth.

Chapter 5

1:30 p.m.
May 19, 1967

MAIDA watched him through her front window. He stood on the short cement sidewalk staring at the brass marker. She opened the door and broke his trance. "Mr. Stiles? The Harvey Mann Alden 1844. Sounds stiff and formal, doesn't it? Believe me I'm not, come on in. It's not often I have a young man visit me."

He climbed the steps and once inside gazed to his right through the archway into the parlor. "Mrs. Alden ..."

"Pastor, call me Maida."

"Well, then, Maida, what a handsome room." Stiles looked around with a satisfied smile.

Maida crossed over to a portrait that hung between two green velvet Queen Anne chairs. With joy in her eyes, she pointed at the picture. "This somber looking gentleman is William's great grandfather, Harvey Mann Alden."

Mr. Stiles stepped closer to admire the painting. "William?" From his studies of the congregation, he knew her husband's name and Maida's situation, but he didn't want to let on.

"My late husband."

The pastor extended his hand and almost touched her shoulder. "Have you been widowed long?"

"Five years." She played with the ring adorned with diamonds and emeralds on her left hand.

He locked his hands behind his back. He whispered. "Lovely ring, lovely house, lovely. ..."

"Yes, it is." Maida walked over to the window and let the light make the ring's facets dance. "William's grandfather found it on his travels to Europe. I wear it for special occasions like meeting our new pastor. Otherwise it's locked away."

Stiles shifted his eyes from the ring to the Oriental rug and traced the design with his foot.

"Mr. Stiles, are you okay?"

"I'm sorry, Maida. This rug reminds me of my grandmother's home. She had a similar one." He took a few steps to a Chippendale slant front desk and rubbed his hands over the finish.

"William's father worked late into the night at that desk. And William proposed to me on that divan." She crossed the room and rubbed the corner of the camelback sofa. The hall clock chimed. He followed her to the hall.

"It's a hand-hewn tall clock. We haven't been able to date it, but the best guess is the late 1700s or early in the 1800s. Let me open the front for you." She released the clasp and opened the glass front.

"Handsome." He peeked into the interior. His eyes caught on a small drawer hidden inside.

"My house … It's a little museum, isn't it?"

"Oh, yes. It speaks of wealth and good breeding." He didn't move. His eyes intently focused on the interior workings of the clock.

After a few minutes, Maida cleared her throat. "Mr. Stiles, let's move to the kitchen. That's where I spend most of my time." He stepped back from the clock and closed the door, adjusting the clasp.

Maida led the way to the kitchen through the formal dining room. As she turned to speak to him, she realized he'd stopped to study another clock located on the sideboard. "Mr. Stiles …"

He adjusted his glasses. "I'm sorry. That clock caught my eye."

"It's the oldest in the house. It has wooden movements." She continued to the kitchen with him following and pointed toward the Windsor rockers that sat in the bay window at the end of her long kitchen. "Have a seat."

He did as instructed. Maida adjusted the pad on her rocker and sat down gently. His eyes surveyed the gardens that stretched to a far tree line. "Maida, your gardens are like the ones in the *Horticulture Magazine*."

"My hobby." She straightened the pile of magazines on the small table that stood between the rockers. "I've studied and visited gardens all my life. My family—the Hobarts—lived near the shore."

She leaned her head back. "There's something about summer flowers by the shore. They vibrate with color. Maybe it's the salt air or the bleached wood of the houses that make them so vivid. I don't know. If you haven't seen the Cape, you should take time and go."

"I haven't had time to visit the Cape, but I see a Canadian influence in your gardens."

"William and I toured a special garden almost every year during our marriage. My favorites are in Quebec City and Longwood Gardens near Philadelphia."

"So you are well traveled?"

"Yes, but since his death, I've felt tied down not wanting to travel by myself. Many of my friends in Ironton Corner never venture out of the town limits, let alone out of the county or the state." She paused. "Traveling offers so many opportunities to learn, don't you agree?"

"I do. Because of my father's work, we traveled to South Africa, the Middle East, and Europe many times."

A black curl fell down on his forehead. He pushed it back. "I've learned more from travel than from any book. Maida, I was twelve when I started a collection of African tribal art. Now my collection includes pieces from Europe and the Middle East. I have plans to display them in the sanctuary."

"In the sanctuary?" She stopped rocking.

"Yes, I feel the sanctuary should look more like a living room or like your parlor with art pieces, sculptures, and collections to enhance our study and to stimulate reflection."

Memories of William filled her thoughts. He loved the plain interior of the church and the glistening light through the windows.

Stiles reached his arm over the table and tapped her sleeve. "Maida, are you all right?"

"I'm fine. Just pondering your idea." She pulled a handkerchief from the sleeve of her olive green dress and wiped at her eyes. "George says you have dreams for the church and the community."

"Oh, they are not just dreams, Maida. A bandstand is going to be built this summer. The first band concert will be on Labor Day. And then next summer I've arranged for a series of eight concerts including the U.S. Navy Band."

"Band concerts. We had them in Yarmouth where I grew up. They sure brought the community together."

"That is my hope for Ironton Corner to return to the early New England sense of community and traditions." He paused. "I have plans to renovate Doc Thayer's house. It will be an apothecary museum to honor Doc and what he did for Ironton Corner."

"For a young man, you have a quite a connection to my generation. That's refreshing."

"And Maida, I'd like us to replace the steeple that came down in ..."

"... the hurricane of 1938. William and I huddled in our fruit cellar at the end of the yard. You can almost see the cellar from here. It's buried in that hillside in the rear. Do you see where I mean?" She stretched her arm toward the window and pointed. He responded by nodding his head.

"At the first warnings, William and I bottled water in old cider jugs, boxed up candles, put dry matches in a waterproof container, packed food in metal crates, and gathered our extra blankets. We hauled them to the cold cellar where we knew we'd be safe from flying glass and rubble, and the roof wouldn't collapse on us. A day later the radio announced for all to seek shelter and we headed to the cold cellar."

"How long did you stay in the shelter?"

"Eighteen long hours. First came the howling winds, banging metal, breaking tree limbs, and then, the silence terrified us. When we came out, the house still stood, but roof shingles, broken porch furniture, dented trash cans, and debris from the neighbors' houses filled the back yard. We found the wringer washer that Irene Keene kept on her back porch leaning against our gardening shed." She took a deep breath.

"The trunk of our neighbor's century old maple blocked our driveway, and its crown covered our entire front yard and porch. William and I held onto each other. We were saddened by the loss of the tree, but when we saw the church we were horrified. I have a picture of it here."

She opened the drawer in the small table, rustled around and pulled out a yellowed newspaper clipping, and handed it to Stiles.

"See, the gusts of wind tore the steeple off the roof. Another gust turned the steeple upside down in the air." She paused as if the scene was too hard to discuss. "The steeple rammed itself through the gaping hole in the roof. It ended up—do you see it there in the photo—balanced on its tip among the pews of the sanctuary."

"I've never seen anything like it." Stiles studied the paper more closely. "How long did it take to remove the steeple and cover the roof?"

"It wasn't all that long. Many of the men in Ironton Corner work construction and have cousins or uncles with heavy equipment. Before we knew it, cranes, steam shovels and heavy equipment of all kinds came. I wish I had pictures of them pulling that steeple out of the roof. It was something to see. Once they got it out, the steeple lay on the green for a long time. It made me sad to see it lying there on its side all broken up.

"On bad days I use to look at that steeple and see it as a sign of hope as it pointed to something beyond. But for years now it's been gone, and the roof is again in disrepair." She fiddled with the sleeve of her dress. "We shared worship in the Methodist Church for almost a year. That's what communities like Ironton Corner did. We helped each other. Now that's changed."

She heard the clock chime again. "I'm going to fix you one of my famous egg sandwiches for lunch. I'll add a few spoonfuls of my baked beans to your plate. They're the best in town. You make yourself at home and look around while I get everything together."

He helped her up from the rocker before he walked back through the dining room.

She picked her apron off the hook next to the refrigerator, pulled it over her head, and tied it around her waist. Ten minutes later the smell of egg sandwiches traveled through the house. Maida heard Stiles coming down the stairs from the second floor. "Maida, this house is truly a historical gem. The antique clocks ..."

"They're lovely, and I love my house." She sighed. "But with my fixed income, the taxes, monthly bills, and constant upkeep, I wonder how long I'm going to be able to keep it." She set the sandwiches on the table.

"I understand." He consumed the sandwich, devoured the

beans, and wiped his mouth. "I read in the minutes from a parish meeting a few years ago that the Evelyn Mills Trust Fund assists elderly women. Maybe that could be of help to you."

"I'd sell my antiques before I'd accept that kind of help." Maida shoved her chair back and busied herself gathering the luncheon plates and setting them on the counter next to the sink.

Stiles let the moment pass and looked at his watch. "Maida, I must be on my way. I have some boxes to unpack."

She walked him to the door. "Before you leave, I have a question."

He stood with his hand on the knob.

"About the sign you posted this morning?"

"What sign?"

Maida felt his discomfort and changed the subject. "Oh, nothing. Don't forget the picnic tomorrow."

After he left, she parted the white organdy curtains that hung over the window and watched him make his way back to the church. Straightening the curtain, she took a few steps and reached for the banister. After climbing the stairs to the second floor, she rested on the bed she had shared with William for thirty-nine years. She touched the picture of her husband on the night stand. "What do you think? What would you have to say about our new pastor?"

She changed from her good dress to one of her everyday house dresses and headed downstairs to tackle the lunch dishes.

* * *

Stiles returned to the office. Just as he opened the door, Joyce called to him. "Arthur Blankenship has been hospitalized."

"What? When? I had breakfast with him a few hours ago."

"He must have had a spell right after you left. Chet called the medics to the diner, and they ran him to the hospital. His wife is there with him."

* * *

Barbara Blankenship saw someone in the hallway when she walked out of Arthur's room. She focused her eyes in the dim corridor. "Oh, it's you."

Stiles turned to look at her.

She gritted her teeth. She remembered how she had controlled her anger when her husband introduced her to Stiles over dinner a few months ago. Stiles sat there with his haughty attitude and his condescending tone. She had been a successful executive in her father's business for many years. She knew that successful men did not talk down to others. They listened and then talked.

"I came here out of concern for Arthur. How is he?" He didn't move a muscle as he waited for her to respond.

"Arthur is fine. It was another of his episodes. He'll be released in a few hours." She brushed him aside and walked with her usual control to a window in the hall. Stiles followed a few steps behind.

As she turned, the heels on her pumps struck the corridor floor with a staccato sound that reverberated in the empty hall. Stiles flinched at the sharp click on the hard surface as if remembering something unsettling. He stepped back and adjusted his glasses. Barbara enjoyed the apparent discomfort he showed around her.

"What is the cause of his episodes?"

"Arthur takes a number of medications and sometimes they interfere with each other. It's really nothing for you to worry about." Barbara's slim sheath dress moved with her arms as she tucked her hair behind her ears.

Stepping close to him, her blue eyes met his. "Arthur loves the church. The thought of it closing has almost destroyed him. He believes the church will prosper under your leadership. I hope he's right."

When Stiles tried to back away from her, he tripped over his own feet. "May I see him?"

"He needs a little more rest, and then I'll be taking him home. He'll be his old self by morning."

"Let me know if there is anything I can do for Arthur."

"Trust me you have done enough." No smile crossed Barbara's lips.

As he turned, he mouthed the word, "Bitch."

Her lips formed a smile as she watched him walk down the hall.

Chapter 6

THE reminder in the community section of the *Ironton Corner Daily News* read,

Don't forget
The Annual End of School Year and Beginning of Summer Picnic
Today: Saturday, May 20, 4 p.m.
At the Elias Howard Meadow
Burgers, Dogs, Buns, and Strawberries are provided.
Bring a favorite dish to share

At the entry to the meadow, Kenny directed parking. Irene, complete with an orange and white reflective vest, instructed men loaded with webbed aluminum folding chairs, and canvas stools to an open area. George Lawrence, with the assistance of Boy Scout Troop 44, arranged the banquet tables. The women placed their side dishes of beans, gelatin molds, potato salads, brownies, cookies, and cream pies on the tables according to Irene's well-labeled instructions.

Somers' Meat Packing van and Easley's Fresh Produce Farm truck drove into the driveway of the meadow. The driver of the van yelled from his open window, "Kenny, where do we park, our usual spot?"

Kenny poked his head in the window of the Somers' van. "Yes, Frank. Hi, Jimmy. Where's Carol?"

"She's home. The last treatment left her weaker than usual. That cancer has a real hold on her this time."

After a few words of concern, Kenny waved Frank forward. Somers' Meat Packing had been in Ironton Corner for two generations. When Frank's dad died, Frank and Carol moved from western Connecticut to take over the business with their adopted son, Jimmy. When the only grocery store in town closed seven years ago, Somers added a much-needed retail section to their business. The market provided the burgers and hot dogs for the yearly picnic.

Bruce Easley pulled the Easley Fresh Produce truck forward and saluted Kenny. "We have flats of strawberries in the back."

"By the looks of this crowd, we'll need them. Take them over to Maida and Irene. They'll help you unload."

Bruce backed his panel truck in the designated spot. With their two sons in tow, Bruce and Sarah Easley had left Maine to come to Ironton Corner to farm. Sarah, an artist with design experience, renovated their farm house to its original style. Bruce was known for the biggest, juiciest strawberries in the area. Sarah jumped down from the truck and joined Maida and Irene. Together they lined up like an old-fashioned fire brigade to unload the berries.

Over samples of the strawberries, Irene looked over at Maida's dessert. "Maida, are you sure you made enough shortcakes for this crowd?"

"I sure hope I did." Maida unveiled her largest tray piled high with shortcakes.

Out of the corner of her eye, Irene noticed a black foreign-made convertible pulling into the parking lot. "My stars."

Maida put her arm around Irene and hushed her.

The children and teenagers crowded around the car. Stiles, dressed in a maroon-colored sweatshirt with Harvard in big letters across the front, jumped out of the shiny car. One of the Easley boys rubbed his hand over the finish. "Cool car! Can I sit in it?"

"Sure." Stiles opened the door, and the boy slid in. The other Easley boy shouted, "If it needs a shine, just call me."

Two girls came up behind Stiles. "We're Sally and Amy Pinckard. Who are you?"

Arthur walked up in time to hear the question. "This is the new pastor of First Parish Unitarian Church of Ironton Corner, Mr. Matthew Henry Stiles."

The children huddled around the car and whispered. "Cool." "Gosh, he's not old." "The car's a Porsche, you know."

Hearing their comments, color rose in Stiles' face. Ten-year-old Becky Davis, dressed in jeans and a baseball shirt, grabbed his hand. "Mr. Stiles, we play ball before and after the picnic. Come and join us."

"I'll be happy to join you, but ..." He grimaced.

Before Stiles could finish his sentence, Arthur interrupted. "Kids, he'll join you later. Now I want to introduce him to the adults." Arthur pushed through the crowd of children, and Stiles followed.

Irene sounded the dinner bell. Friends and neighbors lined up at picnic tables. "Before we dig in," Arthur said, "first a big thanks to Irene Keene for again arranging this celebration." Enthusiastic applause broke out.

Arthur motioned to hush the crowd. "And I want to introduce the new pastor of our church, Matthew Henry Stiles." A spattering of polite applause came from here and there. The uninformed church members stood in an awkward silence; this was news to them. Seeing the disappointed expression on Arthur's face and understanding the surprised looks of the members of the church, Kenny applauded and the others followed.

After Stiles filled his plate, he found an empty chair and joined a table of six others. A woman next to him announced, "Pastor, we're Methodists. You may want to sit over there with your flock." She laughed and pointed to three tables over.

"Oh, I don't mind Methodists as long as you don't mind Unitarians." Stiles put on the charm.

"We don't mind, do we?" She looked around the table. All nodded in approval.

An older man over six feet tall rose and came to stand next to Stiles. "In fact, as you are getting settled if you need anything, don't hesitate to call on us. By the way, I'm Charlie Pierce, the one they," he swept his long arms over three tables, "call their pastor." The two men shook hands.

"Sitting at those tables under the only tree are the Catholics." Charlie waved at a table near the ball field. "Those small groups near the parking lot are the Presbyterians." He grinned. "Irene encourages us to mix up at these gatherings, but we don't, probably to tease her. You see, we love her and what she does for the town, but you know how it is, she's an easy target." He paused. "Her family saved this town more than once."

Stiles remained quiet, stifling a comment.

The Reverend Pierce gave Stiles a hardy pat on the back. "Mr. Stiles, if you don't mind hanging around older clergy, join us for our monthly luncheons at Chet's Diner. If you come, you'll lower the average age of Ironton Corner clergy by a good fifteen years or more."

Stiles stayed with the Methodists and ate.

Kenny motioned for Frank to sit next to him. "Thanks for supplying the dogs and burgers again."

"We are pleased to do it. The townspeople support our store. It's good to give back." Frank winked at Kenny and leaned close to Irene who had just loaded her fork with potato salad. "Say, Irene, what would you have to say if our new pastor lives in the two small rooms above the church office?"

"What? Why, when we have a perfectly fine parsonage? Where did that idea come from? Frank Somers, you're just trying to get my dander up." She shook her hand and some of her potato salad flew onto Kenny's plate. With no fuss, Kenny picked up the wad with his finger, pushed it in his mouth and swallowed it.

Frank loved to tease Irene. "Why not, there's that bedroom, bath, and kitchenette up there. You know the one we added for that couple from Cambodia until they found work. Remember?"

"Yes, I remember, but a pastor living in the church?" She shook her head at the idea of it.

Picnic dinner over, each family scraped their scraps into a tub, to be used later for compost at the Easley farm. The women packed their plates and silverware in the handmade drawstring totes and special baskets made for church socials.

Becky Davis appeared at Stiles' side. She grabbed his hand. "Come on, Pastor, it's time for you to play ball with us." She pulled him through the crowd to the make-shift ball field.

Jimmy Somers handed him a bat. "Let's see what you can do, Pastor."

The adults watched the game until it began to get dark and

the mosquitoes started to bite. At dusk a stream of cars left the meadow. Kenny leaned into Irene. "Count this up as another fine time, my dear."

"Tonight was our thirty-first year, but who's counting." She grinned, gave him a quick kiss, and laced her arm through his.

* * *

Stiles drove back to the church and climbed the stairs to the rooms above the office. He folded his dirty clothes and laid them carefully in a tall laundry basket. Standing in front of a floor length mirror, his hand moved over his chest and down to his stomach. He surveyed his body from head to toe before reaching for his blue tailored cotton pajamas with an "S" monogrammed on the pocket.

Hurriedly pushing his arms into a matching robe, he headed back downstairs. He uncovered his typewriter and rolled in a sheet of paper. He stretched over the typewriter, flexed his finger three times, and raised his arms two times before poising them over the keys.

The Chronicle of Matthew Henry Stiles
May 20, 1967

Baseball. Picnics. T-shirts. Crowds of children. Getting dirty. Mosquitoes. Weed infested field. I impressed them, but no more of those sweaty, mundane activities.

The sweatshirt was okay for tonight, but that's it. Others may think one's wardrobe is of little consequence, but I'll heed my father's advice—impeccable dress shows confidence and a sober passion for the job and tasks at hand. My dark suit, white shirt, tie and neatly folded handkerchief will be my constant uniform—the uniform of power and success—the power of God.

Maida is such a sweet woman, and her antiques are spectacular. She likes me, and she's naive. Her trust will serve me well.

Irene avoided me tonight. It is just possible that my flashy car aggravated her. She spoke to Maida about the sign after my run-in with her, but Maida, poor soul, didn't have the heart to discuss it with me. After the inauguration tomorrow, Irene will know I have been touched by God and sent on this mission.

He rolled the paper out of his typewriter, stood straight, and counted three steps to the file. He reached for the handle on the top drawer, opened it less than one inch, and softly closed it three times before reaching in and placing the page into the folder he'd labeled earlier. He counted three steps back to his desk and pulled the cover back over the machine. As he marched out of his office, he mumbled, "I must unpack Frederic."

CHAPTER 7

8 a.m.
May 21, 1967

THE rooster two streets over woke Kenny and Irene before the first light. Kenny turned to his wife of forty years and admired her body. He ran his hands over her soft skin and noticed her arousal. Kenny reached behind him and pulled open the drawer in the bedside stand. He handed her an oversized glossy paperback book that he had bought when they spent a few days in Provincetown on the Cape.

Thumbing through The *Joy of Love Making*, she laughed. "Look at this one." With their heads together, they studied the couple.

"If we tried that, we may have to call 911 to get us apart," said Kenny.

"I'm game." With the book on the bed they worked themselves into the pretzel-like position and satisfied one another. Irene studied the next page.

"Now don't get any ideas of another position this morning, you sex-devil. That exhausted me." Kenny stretched over her, brushing his arm over her breasts, and reached over to the bedside table and turned on the radio.

They caught the tail end of an announcement about an event at First Parish Unitarian Church of Ironton Corner. Irene rolled over. "What was that they said ... an inauguration at our church?"

"You didn't hear wrong." Kenny sat on the edge of the bed waiting for the flurry of questions that came whenever something was happening in town or at the church that Irene didn't know about.

"Of what? Of whom? That Stiles man referred to being president on that sign. Is that it? We've had installations of new pastors, but never an inauguration. Is that what you heard Kenny, an inauguration?"

"Yes. We'll find out more in a few hours." They pulled on robes and made their way down the squeaky stairs of their eighty-year-old house. Kenny put the kettle on.

Irene stirred leftover oatmeal. "I'm telling you, if Arthur has another one of those spells after being with that man, I'm going straight to him and ask questions." Irene filled the bowls and carried them to the table.

"But you said Arthur's excited about this guy." Kenny dug into his oatmeal.

"He is, but I ..."

"One of your feelings, I bet. I liked watching him play baseball with the kids at the picnic yesterday." Kenny laughed. "But I'd bet he's never picked up a bat before."

"Why on earth did he drive that fancy car a few hundred feet to the Howard Meadow?"

"I guess for two reasons. One to attract girls and two ..."

"... to get the attention of the kids. Did you see how they hung onto him? He put on as if he liked it." Irene stuffed a spoonful of oatmeal in her mouth.

"Now Irene, he may very well like children."

"I'll tell you, Kenny Keene, he's a chameleon. He changes his voice and body movements to suit him. He's a well-practiced con-niver."

"Give him a chance, Irene. He may have been nervous after you had your run-in with him. He's young and inexperienced."

"He's not inexperienced. He's been well trained if you ask me."

Kenny moved to the stove, picked up the kettle, and poured hot water onto the Maxwell House Instant Coffee granules. They finished their breakfast in silence. Kenny cleared his bowl and headed to the shower.

Irene heard their cat scratching on the front door. Opening the door, she looked out and spotted a freshly mown green with a large white circle chalked on it.

Picking up the cat, she said, "Stella, what do you think that's all about?" Stella meowed and stretched full length in her arms.

"You ready for breakfast?" Stella jumped down and ran to the hall and licked her empty dish. "Just a minute. I'll be right there." Irene filled Stella's dish before she made her way to the shower.

Disrobing in the cramped room, Irene fantasized about the day they'd be able to add a bathroom upstairs. Before Kenny closed the plant, they'd had the plans and workers lined up to do the job. But Kenny didn't find work for a year. His job now as the super-intendent of the Town Cemetery brought in far less money. She shrugged knowing that the interest from her small inheritance and the fact that they had no mortgage kept them from financial ruin. She turned on the water and enjoyed thinking about how many things she was thankful for.

Dressed in her navy suit, white blouse, and navy and white pumps, Irene found Kenny standing by the front door waiting for her.

"You look lovely, my lady."

"My usual Sunday outfit." She adjusted the shoulders of his jacket. Kenny reached for her arms and pulled them around him.

"You are going to wrinkle my blouse." Irene pulled away.

"I'd like to do more than that."

"You old lech." She gave him a light poke in his belly. Kenny opened the door for his bride and with arms linked they made their way across the green to the inauguration.

Pickup trucks and cars filled the parking spots along Union Street and the nearby streets and alleys. Kids raced around the war memorial. Friends, neighbors, and strangers greeted each other with hellos and hugs.

At 9:45 a.m., Wally Harris, a photographer and reporter from the *Ironton Corner Daily News*, stepped out of his car. He stationed himself at the edge of the chalked circle. A hush hung over the members of the parish and the curious neighbors and strangers who must have heard the radio announcement.

Wally pointed his camera skyward. Every person followed the camera, heads bent back and eyes shaded. A yellow-and-red-striped hot air balloon came into sight. It hovered for a well-timed five minutes then, descended with two persons in the basket.

The basket hit the ground and bounced once and settled into

the middle of the chalked circle. The crowd stepped back. A man with a replica of the balloon on his hat steadied the balloon. The other shouted, "I'm Matthew Henry Stiles, your new pastor. This is the day of new beginnings for First Parish Unitarian Church of Ironton Corner. Children come and take a look."

For a moment the only sound you could hear was the pilot adjusting the balloon's burner. The children stared, remaining stuck in their shoes. At the encouragement of their parents, they ran toward the basket and reached for the new pastor. Irene shouted into Kenny's ear. "What kind of stunt is this? The parish council needs to meet. A hot air balloon and in the newspaper ... we'll be a laughingstock."

Six uniformed trumpeters appeared on the church steps, playing the trumpet fanfare from "God of our Fathers." Mr. Stiles reached out and released the clasp on the basket door. He stepped to the ground, and with hand gestures encouraged the children to follow behind him and the trumpeters into the church. Uneasy grins and shrugged shoulders passed from adult to adult before they followed and found their usual seats inside. The strangers and curious dispersed with the tales they'd share about this unusual event on their lips.

Arthur, as was the custom, lit the flaming chalice. "May the lighting of this flame bring peace and light to this worship. And may our new young pastor bring us the strength we need to rebuild this church so that we are never in the position to have to think about closing again." Arthur continued with the announcements and introduced the first hymn. The forty people stood and sang words by Louis Untermeyer,

"May nothing evil cross this door, and may ill fortune
never pry about these windows; may the roar of rain go by.
By faith made strong, the rafters will withstand
the battering of the storm.
Though these sheltering walls are thin,
may they be strong to keep hate out and hold love in."

And, as their custom, the congregation repeated their mission statement.

"We, the members of First Parish Unitarian Church of Ironton Corner, are in a free and responsible exploration for truth and meaning. We are unified by a shared search for spiritual growth. We promote social justice and human rights. We use many sources of wisdom to challenge us to grow. We live in an interdependent relationship with all humanity and creation. All life is sacred."

Arthur invited those with joys and concerns to come forward and light a candle and say a few words. Jimmy Somers, a skinny twelve-year-old, leaped up and lit a candle. "Please remember my mom in your prayers. She's really sick."

Bruce Easley came forward. Holding his lighted candle said, "This light is to acknowledge Arthur's surprise of a new pastor for us. May Mr. Stiles' wisdom be sound and his leadership fair and honest." Others lined up with more personal prayers.

Mr. Stiles climbed to the pulpit. "The adventure begins. Are you ready? I'm ready. Forget the idea of closing your church. Start believing in yourselves. I'm the man to make you new. Trust me.

"Trust him ... you are saying to yourselves. He's so young, how does he know how to run a church?

"I have studied and read about the church of the 60s waking up and making its way out of the tunnel vision of the 50s. Just look at what Pope John XXIII is doing with the Catholic Church. He's changing its direction ... getting rid of the dust and creating something new. The Pope is not suggesting changes for change's sake, but to breathe life into a stagnant institution.

"I come from a long line of change makers. My grandfathers started new businesses. My father continues to bring innovative ideas to tire making. He doesn't sit behind the desk as president of the Stiles Tire Company in Akron. No, he's out there leading and stimulating new ideas so his business will continue to be strong in the market. My mother is spear-heading the work to restore her original home, a Tudor of twenty-five rooms. They work hard, they jump in. They are behind me and my new venture. It is the example of their talents of visioning and rebuilding I bring along with me to this place.

"People, when you read the Bible, you discover over and over stories of humanity losing heart and wanting to give up. But then God sends someone to save them. Here I am! The changes begin now."

When he finished, stillness pervaded the room. Irene jumped up and shouted. "Who do you think you are ... God?" Kenny pulled her down and hushed her.

After another silence, applause rang through the old meeting house. Mr. Stiles bowed and descended from the pulpit. He offered a benediction with his arms high in the air and a solemn face. "Be with us, God of the Universe, as we meet the challenges of these times. Grant this church new life. Encourage them to trust me."

He dropped his arms and smiled. "The pilot of the hot air balloon is offering tethered rides for anyone interested."

Children tugged at their parents with the question, "Can I?" The trumpeters led the crowd out the double white doors and onto the green.

Irene squeezed Kenny's hand. "What a showman. We're going to pay for this."

Kenny hugged Irene. "Come on, enjoy. Don't be so suspicious. Shall we get in line for a ride?" She punched him in the side.

The sound of the burner hissed as the balloon ascended and descended. Yells of excitement permeated the air as the children took their turns. Stiles worked the crowd.

By noon, the green was again silent except for the sound of the Methodist Church bells clanging the hour. A whiff of late spring lilacs permeated the air.

CHAPTER 8

STILES sat down on the steps that surrounded the war memorial. Pushing his wire-rim glasses up on the bridge of his nose, he stared at the church. He puffed out his chest, filled with pride at the mark of the beginning of his ministry. A young boy spotted him and rode over on his bike. "Mr. Stiles thanks for the balloon rides."

Stiles smiled remembering he was one of the boys from the ball game the day before and the young man who lit a candle for his mother. Stiles smiled. "Hi. Jimmy, isn't it?"

"Yes sir. What a great time this morning. The other guys and I loved the air balloon rides. We hope you do it again sometime." Jimmy parked his bike and fooled with a baseball glove.

"I will. I'm sorry about your mother."

"Yeah, she's been sick for a long time ... cancer." Jimmy made a fist and dug it into the pocket of his mitt.

Watching Jimmy's frustration, Stiles searched for the appropriate words. "As soon as I get settled, I'll drop by and see her."

"You will?"

The infectious smile of the boy warmed him. "By the way, Jimmy, during several of my visits here, I watched boys and girls riding bikes through the green on their way to school."

"Makes a great short cut."

"And one Saturday, I noticed you and five or six others playing some sort of game."

"Yeah! Bike tag. If I'm 'it,' I have a Red Sox pennant and I count to ten and the other guys scatter. I chase them and try to tag their bikes with the pennant." Jimmy took a breath and hurried on. "When the weeds get too high, we leave our bikes against the memorial steps. Then we hide among the weeds." He stopped and grinned. "Of course, our mothers yell at us for getting stains on our clothes."

"Jimmy, I need to ask a favor from you and your friends."

"Really. From us?"

"I've arranged for some changes to the green. During that time, I'd appreciate it if you'd stay off the green, so I don't have to worry about you boys getting hurt."

"Will we still get to ride our bikes and play tag when it's done?"

"Yes, and if all goes as I've planned, I'm going to need the help of you and your friends over Labor Day weekend."

"You're gonna' need our help?" Jimmy tossed his glove in the air and caught it.

"Yes. Are you surprised?"

"Well, yeah. Kids aren't included in church stuff except for that boring Sunday School class."

Stiles laughed. "That's about to change."

"I'll tell the others about the bikes and let them know to save time on Labor Day to help you. Mr. Stiles, do you have time for a little catch?"

"Maybe another time. I have an appointment."

"Okay, I'll remind you." Jimmy pedaled away giving a hardy wave at Stiles.

Stiles watched Jimmy ride away and thought, boys are so malleable. Just the right words and you have them hooked. Stiles stood, brushed off the seat of his pants, and walked to his car. Exhilarated from the morning, he lowered the top, jumped over the closed door and landed on the front seat. He revved the engine three times before backing out of his parking spot next to the church office.

While shifting gears, he noticed Chief Bird's cruiser parked in the cemetery driveway. He thought this is an opportunity to appear friendly. Turning in, he parked alongside the cruiser. "Afternoon Chief, did you enjoy our morning celebration?"

"I'm afraid I couldn't make it. But I see you're making friends with Jimmy Somers, a fine boy. Not like the ones that leave their cans, bottles, and other unmentionables on the graves in the back of the cemetery. When I was in high school," the Chief laughed to himself, "we had sense enough to clean up after ourselves. I bet you didn't do such things, did you?"

"I knew better. My father lectured me on the importance of reputation. He said if I did something wrong, it would reflect on him and the dynasty he'd built and on his business ethics and his reputation." Stiles stopped abruptly. Discussing his father's expectations always led to anger, and he didn't want to say too much. "I've got to go." Stiles' left eye began to twitch. He turned his head quickly, hoping the Chief hadn't noticed. He restarted the engine and drove thirty miles to the ocean enjoying the sense of power and control as he changed gears on the curvy ocean-side roads.

Revived, he returned to his office. He flipped on the lights, and faced the stacks of dusty boxes that covered the floor. About to open the first box, Stiles heard footsteps overhead. He ripped open his door tripped over his feet, cursed, and fell into the hall. Righting himself, he fumbled with the knob on the door leading to the upstairs to his rooms. Throwing it open, he yelled, "Who's there?"

Silence. He climbed the steps.

"It's only me." Stiles recognized the voice of George Lawrence, the church custodian.

"What are you doing up here, George? These are my private rooms. I told you that." He snapped at George, who had cardboard tucked under his long arms.

With a casual shrug, George said, "I don't hear orders so well." He grinned and chewed on his cigar. "If you could have talked to my wife, she'd have told you I never heard one of hers." He paused. "Mr. Stiles, you mentioned the empty boxes cluttering your living quarters, so I thought I'd do you a favor and gather them up."

Stiles tapped his foot to simmer his anger. "Why, thank you. I didn't mean to sound angry, but pastors have very little privacy. I wanted to claim a place for myself. Do you understand?"

"I know all about privacy. With my wife gone, I have more than I need or want." George descended the steps with the pastor behind him.

With his hand on the door knob to his office, Stiles said,

"George, as long as you're here, will you help me hang a few things?"

"Well, I was about to clean. That crowd this morning left paper towels in the sinks and I don't know what-all on the floors."

"That can wait. I'd rather have you do this now." He moved into his office. "Please get a hammer and a box of nails and give me a hand."

George put his half-chewed cigar in the front pocket of his khaki work shirt. "They're in the cellar. I'll go find them."

Stiles looked through a pile of framed pictures and documents on the floor. He opened a small wooden crate and, with great care, pulled out a black mantel clock. After winding it, he placed the clock on a shelf behind his desk. Running his hands over the finish reminded him of the day his grandmother gave him this family treasure.

Her love came easily. His mother's, by contrast, came scattered from here and there when his father wasn't around. His father didn't show love, only judgment and instructions. He frowned when he recalled his father's repeated message. "Shape up! You'll be the master of your destiny if you listen to me and do as I say."

He whispered in the empty room, "Buck up, Matthew. God has given you a plan to prove that you can build something bigger and better than your father."

Half an hour later, George returned to the office with hammer and nails in hand. Stiles looked at George in exasperation, "Where have you been?"

"I found a few boxes out of place. So I straightened them."

"You said you only had to get a hammer ..."

"As long as I was down there, I thought I'd save myself another trip and tidy up a little."

"While I was here waiting."

"Yes. Where'd you get this stuff?" George surveyed the boxes and pulled the hammer from his back pocket.

"Some of the boxes are mine, but the rest are filled with church history that I found in the basement. Didn't you ever notice the boxes stacked behind the furnace?"

"Can't say that I have."

Stiles pointed and George hammered. Soon the walls of the office were covered with the history of the church.

"I don't know why you let all this history live in boxes piled in the corners in the basement. Don't you people value your heritage?" Stiles straightened the edge of a portrait of the first pastor, The Reverend B. J. Brimfield.

"I never thought much about our heritage." George pulled the cigar from his pocket and slid it between his lips and continued talking. "We go from pastor to pastor and day to day."

"Maybe that's why you haven't had a pastor stay more than two years in the last century." Stiles pulled out the desk chair, sat, and turned his back to George.

George leaned on the door jamb. "Oh, it's not that we don't care. It's that we don't get bothered by much. A few honest words from the pulpit and money enough to pay the bills, and we're just fine and dandy."

George picked up his hammer from the top of the bookshelf. "I'll be going now. I'll get to the cleaning tomorrow. By the way, that's one handsome clock. I hope you have it insured. If not, I'd nail it down, if I were you." George grinned, the cigar in his mouth danced, and he closed the door behind him.

Stiles unlocked one of the windows in his office and waved the smell of George and his cigar out into the evening air. He pulled out a sheet of typing paper, rolled it into position, and began to create a letterhead. The 'i' key stuck. He stared at the word he had just typed "Untaran."

He tore the sheet out of the typewriter. He flipped the key up, checked it, let it flip back in position. Threading another sheet into his typewriter, he went through his ritual, his trinity, a second and third time before he centered the three lines.

Mr. Matthew Henry Stiles.
First Parish Unitarian Church of Ironton Corner.
Ironton Corner, Massachusetts.

He pushed the return lever and skipped down three lines. With the paper centered, he typed in capital letters. "ONLY ONE AMBITION!!" After typing a few paragraphs, he rolled the sheet out and reviewed his words. Satisfied, he wrote "for the newsletter" across the top, walked into the hall, and slipped it under Joyce's door.

Returning to his office, he opened the last box. Stiles' eyes filled with delight as he lifted his scholarly friend, Frederic, from the carton. Climbing on a chair, he reached up and hung Frederic on the ceiling hook he had connected to the right of his desk earlier in the day. He played with Frederic, raising and lowering him with the pulley. He let the skeleton down to his level and smiled into his empty eye sockets. "Welcome to our new home. Do you think anyone in this town will know that medieval scholars hung skeletons in their offices as a symbol of their superior knowledge?" With great reverence, he raised Frederic to the ceiling.

Stiles stepped down from the chair and opened the record player that he'd placed in easy reach on a shelf behind his desk. Sitting in his chair, he spun Frederic around and flipped the switch on the record player. Chopin's Funeral March began to play.

When the record finished, the stylus returned to its holder and the record player cut off. Now completely set for his ministry, he turned off the lights, caressed Frederic's bony hand, and opened the door. As he shut it behind him, he heard Frederic's bones rattling. He smiled.

* * *

George ambled across the green to the Keenes' house. Sniffing the lilacs near the door, he plucked a small branch. He walked in the door without knocking and found Irene and Kenny seated at the kitchen table. He reached down and hugged Irene. "Flowers for the lady of the house."

"Hey there, brother, are you looking for your Sunday night sandwich?"

"Sure am." He took the chair next to Kenny. George had eaten at their house most Sunday nights for the last ten years since his wife died.

Irene put the lilac in a small vase on the table and set tall glasses of milk before each of the men. "George, what did you think of the inaugural event?"

"I missed it. The fish called me over at the pond, and with the day being pretty and all ... Kenny, what did you think of it?"

"Pretty showy, but the crowds loved it. Wally Harris showed up and snapped I don't know how many pictures." Kenny drank his milk and wiped his mouth on his sleeve.

"Mr. Stiles is one strange bird," said George.

"Why so?" Kenny asked.

"He's hung portraits of every dour-faced pastor of the church in his office."

Irene cut the sandwiches. "Why, in heaven's name? Those portraits have been in storage for years."

"To appreciate our history, don't you know?" George pinched his nose and raised it in the air. "We're supposed to value our heritage, not stuff it in the basement." He mimicked Stiles, pushing imaginary curls off his face. Irene set the sandwiches on the table in front of the men.

"Thanks," said George. "He hung all the historical papers, too. Looks like the President's oval office, if you ask me."

"There's that 'president' word again," Irene said. "What do we really know about him? He referred to Akron this morning. You and Ruth lived in Akron for five years or so."

"What about it?"

"Have you heard of Stiles Tire Company?"

"Oh, sure. The papers were always full of stories and interviews about Henry Stiles." George tapped the side of his head. "Are they father and son?"

Irene nodded. "How about contacting some of Ruth's relatives and see what you can find out about the family, especially Matthew in his early years. Now, what's this about you and Maida?"

Before George opened his mouth, they heard footsteps on the front porch and a slamming of the screen door against the frame. Delbert Martin, the church treasurer, barged into the kitchen. "Who paid for that ... that event ... that hot air balloon? For that matter who is paying for that man? Does he have a salary?"

"Delbert," George said scooting his chair back, "take my chair before you have a heart attack."

"Who arranged his hiring? Does he have a contract? I saw lights in the apartment over the church office. What's that about?"

George pointed Delbert into his chair. "I have to be going."

Kenny opened the cabinet above the refrigerator. "Let me get you a little something, Delbert." He pulled down a bottle of Canadian Club.

"I don't need a drink. I need explanations. I told you something like this would happen when Arthur said that the parish council did not need to meet."

"Arthur didn't decide that Delbert. We all made the decision. We didn't need meeting after meeting to remind us that we were dying." Irene reached for Delbert's hand, but he brushed it away.

"Well, we need a meeting now. I want an explanation. You need to make the calls. You are still the secretary to the council, aren't you?"

"I'll make the arrangements," Irene said.

CHAPTER 9

ARTHUR and Barbara Blankenship walked into the church parlor at four o'clock the next afternoon and stopped in their tracks. Barbara threw her purse on the table. Arthur dropped his brief case. "Irene, what do you think you're doing?" They steadied the chair Irene was balancing on to reach the light fixture hanging over the center of the massive table.

"Dusting. It looked like Halloween in here with a layer of dust covering the table, and cobwebs hanging from this light fixture. Pastor Hobart must have been turning in his grave at the state of his room. As I tried to reach the webs with this broom, I felt the chair start to tip. I'm grateful you came in when you did. Otherwise I might have been sprawled over the top of the table like an awkward bird that had a bad landing. Help me down."

Once down, Irene adjusted her dress that had become twisted as she worked. Arthur placed his brief case on the table and snapped it open. Barbara hung her purse over the back of a chair and ran her hands across the top of the chestnut table. "Hobart, he's the one who made this, isn't he?"

Irene fussed with her slightly disheveled hair. "Yes, he worked part-time at the lumber company. He built it and gave it to the church in 1815 with the message that he hoped it was sturdy enough to handle all the arguments and disagreements that came before the council."

"We'll see if it can handle this meeting." Barbara pulled out the chair to the left of Arthur and brushed more dust off the seat before she sat down.

Arthur adjusted his papers. Four council members arrived,

each with a copy of the *Ironton Corner Daily News* and a packet of papers, either tucked in a pocket or under an arm. While waiting for the meeting to start, they enjoyed Wally Harris' photos of the inauguration. "Those trumpeters were great." "See the expectant expressions on the faces of the crowd." "Look at Stiles."

When Delbert Martin marched in, quiet fell across the room. The council, almost in one accord, laid the newspapers aside, opened their packets, and piled the papers flat on the table in front of them.

As Delbert took his seat, Stiles stepped into the room. The pungent smell of his aftershave trailed after him to the opposite end of the table where he found the ornately carved oak chair reserved for the pastor. He looked around and saw papers in front of each member. "Arthur, I see that everyone has a stack of papers. Did you forget to make a copy for me?"

Flustered, Arthur reached in his brief case. The council members on the right side of the table passed the packet down the row to Stiles. Stiles opened the packet and placed the papers in front of him. "There now, you can begin, Arthur."

"Barbara delivered this to you early this morning." Arthur held up the papers. "When I met Matthew Stiles six months ago, I saw an opportunity to save our church. I wanted to ..." He coughed. "I was going to explain earlier, but ..."

"Arthur, let me," Stiles said. "I heard about your church, came on my own initiative to see it, and met George Lawrence. God whispered to me, 'They need you.' "

Delbert jumped to his feet. "That's B.S." Delbert waved his packet, "In this packet, Arthur apologizes and apologizes. He tells us about meeting you, Matthew Henry Stiles. He details his search into your background. Then he says, and I quote, 'In my excitement, I hired him.' Arthur, we have worked together over the church budget and finances for years. You are not an impulsive person. What isn't in this report?"

Arthur's eyes met each of the council members. They saw fear bordering on panic in their friend's eyes.

"And now, because of Arthur's excitement, he expects us to vote on the contract that he and this stranger," Delbert pointed to

Stiles, "have created. Vote, phooey. Instead we should be asking for your resignation as president of the council, Arthur." Delbert ran his fingers through his thin graying hair and sat.

Irene spoke up. "Delbert, if we ask Arthur to resign, each of us needs to resign including you. All of us are guilty of giving up on the church ... losing faith. And as much as I hate to admit it, I'd begun to lose my zest to save the building."

"Irene, on my first visit when I walked into the church, I felt its pain. That's why I am here. Those of you who are exhausted from holding the church together need me and my personal trust fund." Stiles glued his stare on Delbert.

"Your personal funds ..." Delbert tried to return the stare, but detecting darkness in the pastor's face, he lowered his eyes.

"I'm following in my father's footsteps." Stiles placed his hands on the table and straightened in his chair. "My father, a giant in the tire industry in Akron, said if he wasn't willing to take a financial risk on his first business, it would have failed. I don't plan to fail at building you a church to be proud of, a church that will put Ironton Corner on the map. I understand your questions and doubts about a newcomer, but I have only your interests in mind." Stiles held his head high.

After a pause, Frank Somers looked from Arthur to Stiles. "My Jimmy met Mr. Stiles on the green. He ran home full of enthusiasm because Mr. Stiles wanted to include the Boy Scouts in his plans. Mr. Stiles told Jimmy that he would come to visit Carol. That would be a first. Even when we had settled pastors, not one of them came to see her when she was struggling with one of her cancer treatments." Frank paused and wiped at his eyes. "And, oh, the fact he's willing to jump start us with his money ... well, if my father hadn't had seed money from his father, Somers Meat Packing wouldn't have made it."

"Mr. Stiles, I'm Sarah Easley. The hot air balloon and the press coverage was a nice touch. But I found your words on Sunday a bit over the top. I am, by nature, a skeptic and unless you think you are God, I don't see how you are going to reach your goal in our present situation."

The man sitting next to her chimed in, "One thing about my

wife is that you know where she stands. I'm Bruce Easley. My wife and I run the Easley Produce Farm. We met briefly on Sunday. Since the decline of the church, we are one of the few families that still attend. Our boys enjoy the Boy Scout Troop that has been kept alive by George Lawrence.

"I am sad and troubled that Arthur did not include our parish council in the negotiations with you, Mr. Stiles. And, if I read this material right," Bruce held up the papers, "Mr. Stiles has another year to complete his Masters of Divinity. Why are we hiring him before he's completed his degree?"

"Well ..." Arthur started.

"Wait, let me explain." Stiles interrupted and threw Arthur a glance. The heads of the council members turned toward Arthur and then to Stiles. "Even though I have one more year to complete my degree, other churches are contacting me. Arthur wanted to hire the best out of Harvard. And he has."

Raised eyebrows and stunned glances crisscrossed the table. Barbara mouthed "bullshit" in Arthur's direction.

Bruce, vice-president of the council, scooted his chair back and stood. "Mr. Stiles, will you leave us, please?"

Stiles pushed back his chair and, by placing his hands on the table, pushed his body out of the chair. He walked behind Frank Somers and Barbara. As he passed Arthur's chair his fingers lightly ran across the collar of Arthur's shirt. He exited through the door.

Bruce remained standing. "Now that I've read the contract, you are giving Stiles a great deal of power. Sarah and I left a church where all the power was in the hands of the pastor. I don't want that to be the case here."

"Arthur," said Irene, "Stiles says you got the best from Harvard. None of the pastors in our history declared themselves to be the best. What aren't you telling us?"

Arthur coughed, and red splotches moved up his neck. The room filled with a concerned silence. Barbara moved over and checked his pulse as she regularly did when the spots appeared.

After a few moments, Arthur looked stronger. Maida, on his left, patted Arthur's hand. "Mr. Stiles came to my house for lunch. He is interested in replacing the steeple. Wouldn't that be wonderful?" Maida didn't like conflict. When it arose, her habit was to try to neutralize the conversation.

Delbert slammed a fist on the table. "With whose money? His or ours?"

Maida looked up, startled by Delbert's outburst. "Delbert, we need to give him a chance." She pulled at the left sleeve of her dress with the fingers of her right hand.

The council members looked at each other, trying to decide what to do.

Barbara stood. "May I assume the contract you made is a binding contract at least for the next year?"

Arthur nodded in the affirmative.

"And it would take a financial settlement with Mr. Stiles to break the contract?" Arthur nodded again.

In a monotone voice, Arthur said, "I do love this church, and I ask you to trust me."

Barbara, still standing, walked behind her husband's chair. "Arthur's action has been totally unorthodox from a business point of view, but all of us around this table know of his attachment to this church." She placed her hands on his shoulders. "I move we support Arthur's decision and the contract that he's drawn up to hire Mr. Stiles, but when the contract comes up for renewal, that we state clearly it can't be renewed without the approval of the council." She returned to her chair.

Bruce called for a vote. "All in favor of Barbara's motion raise your hand."

All of the members raised their hands except Delbert. "You are going to regret this decision." Delbert slammed the documents against the table to punctuate his words.

"I'll ask Mr. Stiles to come back in." Bruce walked to the door and opened it. "Come join us."

Stiles returned to his seat.

"Mr. Stiles, the council has approved your contract for the year that you and Arthur agreed upon. We added a sentence. It read—"

Stiles interrupted. "That you reserve the right to review the contract at the end of the year to determine if it will be renewed." Stiles smiled, looking youthful and excited. "You'll renew it."

Arthur sat back in his chair and took a deep breath. "Mr. Stiles has another item to discuss."

"I've been spoiled with housekeepers and servants. Managing a place the size of the parsonage when I have so much else to do just doesn't seem wise. And the parsonage needs considerable work." He studied the faces. "It's against my ethics to spend church money on that neglected house only for me. So, I've moved my personal things into the rooms above the church office. Since I plan to be pastor here for a long time and won't be living in the parsonage, I suggest you sell it."

"Sell the parsonage? That place is money in the bank for us. If we have an emergency such as the boiler, we can borrow against it. That's a ridiculous idea." Delbert again smoothed his thinning hair.

Irene slapped her hands on the edge of the table. "You think we can just decide to sell the parsonage. A decision like this must go before the membership."

Stiles gestured toward Irene. "I've read your bylaws. They give the council the power to make this type of decision."

A self-conscious quiet filled the room. All eyes looked at Irene expecting her to know the details of the bylaws. Embarrassed by her ignorance, Irene's face colored. She hadn't read the bylaws in years, so even she didn't know if he was right or wrong.

Stiles pressed his fingers into his temples, trying to maintain his composure. "I'll be living in those two rooms. If you decide to repair the parsonage, maybe you'll rent it and use the rental income for needed maintenance in the church."

"You need to wait until we have this straightened out," Delbert said.

"No, I don't. I need to move on with my plans. I'll keep good records. The church, if it wishes, can reimburse me some time in the future." He puffed up. "We need the greater community to know that there is something new happening here in Ironton Corner. That something new begins next week." Stiles shoved his chair back and stood. "I need to tend to the details of my first project." He marched out of the room.

Delbert raged at Arthur. "What have you done, Arthur?"

The others picked their papers off the table and shuffled out of the parlor, unsure about the decisions they had made.

* * *

Stiles went directly to his office. He stretched over the typewriter. His ritual gave him solace as he fed fresh paper into his typewriter.

The Chronicle of Matthew Henry Stiles
May 22, 1967

Excitement fills me. Arthur followed my instructions, and I have the contract I designed. The support of Jimmy's father, Frank Somers, was a bonus. He's well respected around here. When I pay a visit to his wife, Carol, he'll have no doubt of my good intentions.

I embarrassed Irene. Now they all know that she doesn't know it all. Soon they will be turning to me and not her to propel the growth and prosperity of the church, and even the town. She's been their savior, but that will end.

I impressed myself with my argument for living above the Church office. I knew I'd win. The chase excites me. Bankers are so black and white. His kind cannot see a vision like I can. They always have to follow a script. Delbert doesn't know it, but I have a plan for him.

Stiles filed his report and pulled his satchel from the kneehole of his desk. He unlocked it and pulled out an unmarked binder. He labeled it "Delbert Martin." Opening it to the first page, he wrote a few notes.

He turned to Frederic. "That's what we'll do with Delbert Martin if he doesn't cooperate." Returning the binder to the satchel, he removed another marked, "Walkways and Bandstand," settled back in his chair, and read over the notes.

CHAPTER 10

8 a.m.
June 5, 1967

"ROY, hold it. Doggone, whoever dug this plot missed the mid-point. Move the scoop to the right." Kenny made sure he had the backhoe operator's attention before he wiped his brow. Roy maneuvered the backhoe and lifted out a few more scoops of clay soil. Then he backed away from digging.

Kenny eased his heavy six-foot frame down a ladder into the grave. He planted his sturdy legs in the bottom and perfected the corners. Tossing the shovel up, he climbed out, pulling the ladder behind him. He signaled the flatbed driver. Gus pulled a lever and a winch lifted the grey concrete vault up and over the hole. Kenny guided the burial vault square with the hole. Gus lowered the vault and Kenny shouted over the noise, "Perfection." The vault settled in its place.

Gus jumped out of the truck and joined the men leaning on their shovels. Roy lit a cigarette. "Haven't seen you for a while, Kenny, but wanted you to know I read about your new pastor's descent from on high in the *Daily News*. Kind of strange, don't you think?"

"If you looked closely at the photo, you'll see a halo hovering around his head. Isn't that right, Roy?" Gus winked and kicked his work boots against each other. Clods of clay fell from the treads. The two men snickered like school kids.

Kenny, used to their kidding, tossed his toothpick at them. "We'll see if he's our knight in shining armor, or just a man like the others before him." Kenny pulled the sheets of imitation grass carpet from the bed of his truck. The men helped spread the carpet. The sound of heavy equipment reached their ears.

"What's that?" asked Gus.

"Sounds like it's coming from the green," responded Roy.

They hurried to the street and gawked as a parade of trucks carrying heavy equipment and supplies pulled onto the green. Kenny spotted Stiles, Mayor Sims, reporter Wally Harris, and a stranger leaning over the tailgate of a 1967 Ford pick-up. Curious, they joined the group. Kenny faced the pastor. "Mr. Stiles, what the heck is going on?"

"Good morning, Kenny. I'd like you to meet my landscape architect and general contractor. We're looking over the plans for the green. As you can see, the work begins today."

"Plans for the green? You mentioned changes on Sunday, but the green?" Kenny turned to Mayor Sims. "Why is Mayor Sims here?"

Sims clasped his small hands over his chest. He rocked his pear-shaped body on his tiny feet. "Mr. Stiles showed me his plans a couple of months ago. Even though the church owns the green, he wanted to run them by the town council."

"And you all approved?"

"Yes. Kenny, when you see the finished product, you'll be proud of the changes." Sims stepped away from the back of the pick-up on his toothpick legs.

At that moment, Stiles noticed Gus and Roy. He reached his hand over and introduced himself. "I'm Mr. Matthew Henry Stiles. I've been hired here to create a new vision of church. This is your official invitation to come join us."

Gus and Roy exchanged skeptical looks and wiped the dirt from their hands on their pants. They shook hands with Stiles.

Gus fussed with his hat. "Pastor, I've had about all the church I need. I told my wife two years ago I refuse to get trussed up in a suit and tie just to satisfy some fussy old church biddies."

Rather awkwardly, yet with an air of dignity, Stiles climbed into the back of the pick-up. He raised his arms. "I declare The Eleventh Commandment. There shall be no dress code at First Parish Unitarian Church of Ironton Corner." He lowered his arms and smiled down. "What about you, Roy?"

"You don't want me darkening your doors. I'm too much of a

sinner for First Parish."

"Don't let that stop you. We're all sinners in some way or an-other." He raised his arms again. "The Twelfth Commandment ... First Parish Unitarian is for sinners only."

"Hold that pose." Wally Harris crouched in position and snapped away. "I want to record this sacred moment—the revela-tion of the 11th and 12th commandments issued from the back of a 1967 Ford F-100 Ranger, no less."

Nervous laughter spread through the group.

* * *

From her porch, Irene saw and heard Stiles pontificating. She hurried toward the cluster of men and stood next to Kenny with her hands on her hips. "Show off. You're full of more hot air than your inaugural balloon."

Stiles grimaced, and at the same time, a pick-up tooted and parked alongside the green.

"Here come the stars for the photos." Stiles greeted Frank and Jimmy Somers.

Kenny faced Frank. "Tell him this isn't how we do things around here."

Frank stood, ramrod straight. "You're right, Kenny. All we do at parish council is talk and talk and table discussion after dis-cussion and nothing gets done. We have endowment interest available, but we do nothing. We roll from one pastor to another. That's how we do things around here. We don't do anything. The new members want the church to wake up and make a difference in our community and our lives. It's time we let the community know that First Parish is alive."

Kenny shrugged. "We are alive."

"Alive. Phooey. With this rundown building. And no steeple."

"We'll get to those things. Throughout our history we've been slow and deliberate. We've been taught to make do with what we have."

Frank put his hand on Kenny's shoulder. "Not anymore. Mr. Stiles told Jimmy about his plans for the green and asked him to share his dreams with the other boys. They're excited about the walkways and bike paths and the concerts. And they're especially excited that Mr. Stiles has asked them to help. When was the last time we had a pastor that shared interest in our kids?"

All conversation halted. The crows stirred by the ruckus hushed their noise as if they, too, were listening for a response.

Jimmy Somers piped up. "Mr. Stiles, you said you wanted us here for the ground-breaking photos."

"Ground-breaking photos? Well, I'm not listening to any-more of this lunacy. Let's go." Irene kicked at the grass and about knocked Kenny over as she rushed toward her house. Kenny caught up with her.

"Mr. and Mrs. Keene," Jimmy yelled, "aren't you going to stay and watch us get our photos taken? They'll be in the paper, but don't you want to see us in action?"

Kenny drew Irene in close to him and whispered. "How can we not, Irene? We've seen this boy grow up. How can we miss this?"

"You're right. Okay, let's go back for the sake of the boy." Irene and Kenny returned to the group.

Wally Harris lined Jimmy, Frank, and Mayor Sims in front of a yellow backhoe with their shovels poised and snapped the picture.

* * *

Stiles sat in his office twirling Frederic with a yard stick. His thoughts turned to Irene and Delbert. They had no vision. They didn't understand what he had sacrificed—how much he had giv-en to this holy endeavor. His head turned up, his nose pointed to the ceiling, and he sensed an aura of light surrounding his head, like the 4th century Christian depictions of saints. He performed his trinity and fed the paper into the typewriter.

The Chronicle of Matthew Henry Stiles
June 5, 1967

Frederic, did you see me touching those dirty hands and climbing into that truck?

Did you hear the prophetic voice that announced those commandments? I sounded like Jeremiah and Amos.

That wasn't me—it was a sign from God to show Irene

Keene that I'm here on a divine mission.

He rolled the sheet out of the typewriter and reviewed his words. He performed his ritual as he deposited the page into the "Chronicle of Matthew Henry Stiles" file. Instead of precisely taking three steps back to his desk, he grasped Frederic's bony hands, lifted them to his lips three times, and lowered them and let them swing as they settled into place.

* * *

During the months of June and July, crews worked long hours on the pathways, the bandstand, and the peeling paint and broken boards on the church. By the end of July, the church shone with fresh white paint. The brick pathways were almost completed, and the bandstand lacked only a final coat of paint. Stiles finalized the details and schedule for the renovation of the interior of the building.

Twenty more families were drawn to the church by the sermon titles that Wally Harris included in Friday's paper: "Good Wine Makes You Stronger," "Play as a Serious Lifestyle," and "Your Failure at Education."

Maida, the Easleys, and the Somers greeted the newcomers. Jimmy Somers and the Easley boys encouraged the other children to participate in their classes and to play on the green after church. The new families found Stiles' refreshing and his sermons connected with their lives.

Chapter 11

10 a.m.
July 31, 1967

"ONLY ONE AMBITION! You read these words in the July newsletter." Stiles expounded from the elevated pulpit to a crowd of one-hundred-three parishioners on the last Sunday of July. "I am determined to make First Parish Unitarian Fellowship of Ironton Corner the best and most renowned Unitarian Parish in the country. Only death will summon me from Ironton Corner.

"I don't have to guess why you're here. You want energy, passion, and excitement! You are tired of pastors who come for two years, do little to nothing, and then move on to bigger and better opportunities. I'm going to build this church, and my energy will overflow into the community.

"The witness to my commitment is the restored green and the new exterior of this church building. Save Labor Day weekend for a band concert in your new bandstand with fireworks.

"I'm sad that this is our last Sunday before your traditional August break from church. While you're away, this building and the additions will be closed for needed interior renovations. Be ready for its resurrection when we reopen. See the old done away with and the new ready to waken your spirits."

He stepped from the pulpit, wiped his brow, and descended to the floor of the worship room. After the benediction, a number of worshippers, including Irene, made their exit through the side door shaking their heads. Stiles and Maida greeted the others at the front door. After the last person, Maida hugged Stiles. "I'm ready for the ride, Pastor. We haven't had this many in the congregation for years." She paused. "And so many asking you how they could help. This is wonderful."

Mr. Stiles looked embarrassed that she was still holding onto him, but she kept talking unaware of his discomfort. "Two men gave their names: Ted Murray, a local architect, and Harry Paulson, an area sculptor. They want to donate their talents for special projects that you may have in mind."

He disengaged from Maida. "I'm going to call you my right-hand helper, Maida. Is that okay?"

She smiled. He gave her a stiff hug. She handed him a pile of index cards. "Mr. Stiles, here are the cards. They have the names of all of the visitors, and then this one card, as you requested, lists all the Boy Scouts who were present. Were you a Boy Scout?"

"No, but I love that organization."

"Mr. Stiles, have a nice afternoon and relax during your time off." Maida gently touched his arm as she took her leave.

"Thank you, Maida. Your presence makes me think my grandmother is by my side." He stood still, watching Maida until she reached her door. He fanned through the index cards, walked briskly to his office, and placed the cards on his desk. He locked the door and strutted off to the diner pleased with the enthusiasm of the worshippers.

"You drew a crowd again this morning." Chet placed a cup of coffee with three creams in front of Stiles. "My business is growing. If this continues, I'm going to have to get in more supplies."

"Start ordering the supplies. With my plans, someday you will be adding an addition to the diner." Stiles flashed a rare bright smile at Chet.

When he returned to his the office after his lunch, he placed the pile of index cards in the center of the desk. He opened the top drawer and found two unused ones. On one he wrote Ted Murray, architect; on the other he wrote Harry Paulson, sculptor. "Frederic, I'll need these names for two future projects." He placed the two cards under his desk blotter.

He read the file cards, opened a drawer, and placed a box of notepaper on his desk. He wrote the same message to each visitor. "It was such a pleasure to meet you this morning at worship. I'll need your help to build the parish through your time and your money. Be ready to join in on the Labor Day festivities." He signed each note with "The almost Reverend Matthew Henry Stiles." Each time he wrote those words he leaned back and smiled.

Next he wrote to each Boy Scout. "Jimmy Somers informed you about my need for your help on Labor Day Weekend. He says you are excited to lend me a hand. In addition to the plans he's shared with you, I invite you to an overnight the Saturday before Labor Day to prepare the last details for the weekend. Please let Jimmy know if you can participate. I'm counting on you." He signed each note with Mr. Stiles. He stamped each of the notes, pulled on his suit jacket, and dropped them into the mailbox on his way to the home of Frank and Carol Somers.

* * *

"Please join us in the living room." Frank wheeled Carol into the room and took the chair next to her.

Stiles joined Jimmy on the sofa. "Jimmy, thanks for spreading the word with the Boy Scouts."

"Yes, sir. Do you want to see my badges?"

"Of course."

"Come up to my room."

Carol and Frank watched them go upstairs. Carol was the first to speak. "Isn't that nice?"

After a while, they heard Stiles on the stairs. "Fine boy. I hope to get to know him much better as the years go on." He returned to his seat. "He said he's staying upstairs so the adults can talk."

"He gets tired of hearing about my cancer." Carol moved the wheelchair closer to the sofa.

"I was sorry to hear that other pastors have not called on you, Carol. I'll be with you on the journey, whatever it is, wherever it goes." As Stiles held her hand, the cherry tea cart and Windsor chairs on the opposite wall caught his gaze.

"Tell me about Jimmy." He leaned back to listen.

Frank uncrossed his legs and placed his feet squarely on the floor. "We tried to have a baby and then Carol was diagnosed with cancer. The doctors advised against pregnancy for fear of what the drugs might do to a developing baby. We discussed adoption and made the application. The agency told us we'd probably have to wait a year or more." Frank grinned from ear to ear. "But they called a month after our application was accepted and said we have a special baby, would you like to see him? Of course we raced to the hospital. And there was this little one, a month old, with a half closed left eye and missing two fingers on his left hand. We fell in love.

"During pre-school, the children started teasing Jimmy. We talked with the school. They admitted to problems with students harassing those who were different. We researched and visited communities and schools recommended by friends.

"Once we met and talked with the school officials in Ironton Corner, we moved here and haven't regretted the change. Business is good, and the teachers and children treat Jimmy well." Frank leaned back into the sofa.

"And, now, I think if you asked any of the Scouts to describe Jimmy, I bet they'd never mention his physical problems. I don't think anyone notices anymore," Carol said with a proud, but parched voice.

"I haven't noticed his eye," Stiles said.

"He's had surgery, and it's 100% better. After he's fully grown, he can have another surgery to correct the little sag that's left."

Jimmy rushed into the room. "Mr. Stiles, look. I found my first champion pinewood derby. Pretty cool, isn't it?"

The pastor examined the car. "It's just wonderful. I will look forward to next year's derby."

"I'm too old to make a derby now, but I'll help the other kids." Jimmy joined his dad.

"Frank and Carol, I told Jimmy I'm inviting the Scouts to the church for an overnight before the Labor Day Concert. I hope Jimmy can join us."

"He'll be there." Carol began to cough so hard that she couldn't catch her breath. Stiles watched Jimmy and Frank jump up to help her. Sweat broke out on his brow. As they tried to comfort her, he quietly made his way to the door and drove away.

* * *

Stiles unlocked his office, grasped Frederic's feet, and held them for a moment or two. "That was hard, my friend." He let go of Frederic, sat at his typewriter, and executed his trinity. He mumbled Father, Son, and Holy Ghost three times while wiping perspiration from his forehead.

The Chronicle of Matthew Henry Stiles
July 31, 1967
Carol's coughing frightened me. It took me back to my grandmother when she was dying. I don't like being near the seriously ill. They make me feel frightened and insecure. Maybe I can get Maida to do all those calls for me. But, then, I need the community to know I'm serving Jimmy, Frank, and Carol.

Take the stumbling block of the sights and smells of illness and death from me, my God, so I can be attentive to the Somers. I need them to earn favor with Irene and Delbert. You've given me this fear, blot it out!

This morning I felt a ground swell of support. The postcards were a brilliant idea. My plan is just where I want it. Now I have a month on my own. No Irene Keene and no Barbara Blankenship or Sarah Easley.

He stood, took three steps, reached for the handle on the top drawer of his file, and tried to pull it out. It didn't move. Did someone tamper with my files? he thought. He moved back, took three steps, reached for the handle on the top drawer of his file, and tried to pull it out again. It didn't move. He tugged at the drawer. He peered in the crack and found his chronicle file was caught. Filled with anger, he fished his fingers inside, loosened the file, and the drawer slid open. He inserted the new page and slammed the drawer shut.

He hit the skeleton. The fingers on Frederic's right hand snapped back and grazed Stiles' eye. It watered. Stiles reached for Frederic's eye sockets and poked his fingers inside again and again. Abruptly, he stopped. He gently lifted the skeleton's hands and brought them to his lips three times. "I'm sorry. I didn't mean to lose my temper. I have to be in control. I can't lash out. I'll ruin everything."

He locked his office, climbed the stairs to his rooms, and admired his profile in the wall of mirrors he had installed shortly after moving in. As he was forced to do at the detention center years ago, he folded his pants precisely over the hanger and brushed his suit jacket before hanging them in the small closet under the eaves of the room.

Stretching out on the bed, he turned to his book, *Frankenstein*. He mused at how some loved the creative inventor and called him a brave adventurer; others hated him for transgressing all boundaries without concern. "Who in Ironton Corner will call me an adventurer? Who will hate me? I don't really care," he muttered as he turned out the light.

CHAPTER 12

ON Monday morning a covered truck and a nine-passenger van pulled in front of the church. Stiles opened the double doors. Eight men emerged from the van and unloaded ladders and scaffolding. They lugged the equipment into the building.

The crew gathered with Stiles in the sanctuary. "Good morning. I'm paying you a premium rate, so I hope you are ready to work."

The crew boss leaned back on his heels and hooked his thumbs in his back pockets. "This is the best crew around. Your projects will be ready for your inspection in two weeks, just like I promised."

"Each room has my specific instructions printed on easel paper taped to a wall as we discussed. Go, and see if you understand my instructions while I pack."

Stiles folded each garment, then closed and locked his suitcase. He carried it downstairs and placed it near the door. He stepped into his office and picked up his already prepared brief case. Coming out of his office, he met the crew boss in the hall. "Pastor, your instructions are perfect. We know what you expect. Don't worry. You go off to Harvard and enjoy your class."

"I will and thank you." Stiles squeezed his bag in the back seat, backed out of his parking spot, and gunned his car around two corners switching gears as he went. He stopped in front of the Keenes and waved at Irene.

Irene stood up from her rocker, flipped the bird to the back of his car, and slammed the door as she walked inside to call Maida. "Did you see all that? Looks like painters to me."

"Painters?"

"Yes, they carried ladders, cans, drop cloths, and big bundles into the church."

"I hope so. Paint is crumbling off the walls in the sanctuary. And the rest of the building is dingy. Fresh paint will brighten the place. I have some left-over ham. I'll make some sandwiches and take them over." Maida stretched the phone cord and pulled a tray from the refrigerator.

"Good idea. Find out what's going on, and where he's gone."

Around noon, Maida carried her basket across the green and up the steps to the front doors of the church. She knocked. Eventually, the crew chief answered.

"I'm Maida Alden. I live across the green. I've brought you some sandwiches for your lunch."

"Why thank you." The man removed his hat. "But Mr. Stiles has arranged for our room and board."

"He has?"

"Yes, we brought our sleeping bags. We're bedding down in the church and we're eating at the diner. He's given us permission to use his bathroom for showers. I looked in the kitchen and he has enough bags of coffee stacked up to keep us alert for months, let alone the two weeks for this job."

"What is the job?"

"I can't say, ma'am" The man shuffled his work boots.

Maida shook her head and started down the steps.

"Lady, we appreciate your interest and your offer. I don't want you to think we're not friendly, we really are. Your pastor has asked us not to associate with the townspeople and not to talk about the work." He shrugged and replaced his hat.

Maida carried her basket to Irene's. She walked in the door and found Irene in the kitchen. "The man says that Stiles has made plans for all their needs." She left out the part about not associating with the locals. Irene needed no more fuel for the fire.

Irene stood with hands on hips and eyebrows raised. "So he's planned for everything. And we're to go along for the ride. He's off, and no one knows where. Fine. Not what you expect of a real pastor. "

Maida unpacked two sandwiches and laid them on the counter. "Irene, I have ironing to do. See you later."

* * *

Two weeks later, the truck and van pulled around the church and parked in front. The men made several trips to load their equipment. They sat on the steps and waited.

Stiles' car streaked around the corner and jerked to a stop in front of the truck. He jumped out and raced up the steps. Without so much as a handshake, the men followed Stiles inside. They tagged behind as he inspected the sanctuary, the stairwells, the kitchen, the Fellowship Hall, the parlor, and all of the church school rooms. "Great job, boys. You followed my instructions to the last detail."

"Thanks." The van driver tugged on his belt loops and puffed up a little.

"Did Chet treat you well over at the diner?"

"Hot breakfast. Packed lunches. Complete dinners. Chet couldn't have done any better." The boss smiled with satisfaction on his face.

One of the workers rubbed his belly. "Home cooked meals on a job. Now that's something, Pastor."

"The regulars at the diner eyed us every day, but we kept silent as you requested. Chet said they gossiped about the lights on in the church buildings day and night."

Back on the steps, the driver turned to Mr. Stiles. "Thanks for the use of your shower. You'll find your bathroom as you left it, spotless."

"About the wall of mirrors ..." The short guy commented.

"I closed my eyes. I didn't want to see this old body." The pudgy worker shifted his feet and poked the others, grinning.

Stiles smirked.

The workers headed for the truck and van. The driver remained with Stiles on the steps. Stiles reached into his jacket pocket. "Here's the cash for the workers and an envelope for you—for the special work you did for me."

"It was a bit tricky installing the equipment in this old building," the driver admitted, "but it tested out. There's a strong signal so you shouldn't have any trouble checking for any unwanted visitors in the restroom in the basement or strangers going into your office. Can't be too safe these days, can we?

"No, we can't. And thanks for your assistance. Safe travels."

Once the truck and van rounded the corner, Stiles reached into his car and lifted out his suitcase. Irene leaned forward and pushed herself up from the rocker on her porch. She opened the screen door and let it slam. Stiles heard it, raised his eyebrows, turned sharply on the steps, and headed to his office.

Irene returned to the kitchen and sliced onions for the casserole she planned for dinner. She placed them in a bowl, covered it with a new plastic wrap she was trying. She felt the coffee pot. Finding the coffee still warm, she poured a cup, opened *Ladies Home Journal*, and read her favorite column, "Can this marriage be saved?"

When she heard Maida's car pull in her driveway, she gave her friend a little time to unload her groceries and then called. "He's back?"

"I saw his car, and, Irene, I don't know where he's been."

"I thought George might have found out."

"Since you asked me yesterday? Irene, you know as well as I that he requested the council not to bother him this month."

"I know, but what if we needed him?"

"Well, we didn't, and now he's back. Trust him."

Irene mumbled. "The workers ate three times a day at the diner. Closed mouthed, too, according to Chet."

"Irene, you've questioned Chet."

"I certainly did. I don't like suspicious things going on in my town."

"Irene, it's not just your town." Maida bit her tongue. "And if you're interested, Mr. Stiles is meeting a truck from the Rose Carpet and Tile Company as we speak."

Irene slammed down the receiver. She returned to the porch and watched the workers carry rolls of carpet through the front doors. Her back door opened and closed. She heard Kenny's footsteps. She called, "Kenny, did you see what's happening now?"

Kenny pushed the door open and looked across the green.

"Carpet? Where's the money coming from for that?"

"His trust fund, I suppose."

Kenny settled in the rocker next to Irene. "Well, if that trust fund paid for the bandstand, I'm grateful. Looks nice, doesn't it?"

"Yes, I have to admit it does." Irene smiled. "I even have to say the brick walkways improve the green, makes Ironton Corner look more like an English village."

"Do you think Delbert Martin will find a way to pay him back, so we are not beholden?"

"The council will have to dip into the endowments for that to happen, and you know how the congregation feels about touching those funds." She played with her wedding band. "What do you think about a donut and a cup of warmed-up coffee?"

"Sounds good." Kenny held the door for Irene and patted her bottom as they walked into the house.

The Rose Carpet and Tile truck left at midnight on Tuesday. Wednesday, Mr. Stiles walked through the sanctuary. "Now it's ready for my personal touch." He made many trips to the basement and carried box after box to the sanctuary.

Early the next morning, an old Ford truck pulled up. Three rag-tag young men emerged and knocked on the church door. Stiles greeted them, invited them in, and shut and locked the door behind him.

"Here's the job." Stiles pointed to the piles of framed pictures and stacks of wooden crates. "Unpack the boxes. Line the items along the wall. Study the diagram on the easel. Then, hang the art and place the sculpture. All of them are valuable to collectors. So be careful."

The scruffy young men began their work. Stiles supervised. "Move that to the left." "No, that one goes on the table in front of the pulpit." He grabbed one of the men by the shirt collar and spun him around. "Can't you read? The chart says that one goes in the other corner."

The volume of his voice climbed higher and louder as the day went on. "Wrong way." "Stop your dreaming." "We don't have all day." "I am paying you for eight hours work—so hustle." The clock struck seven and the tallest of the men hung the last picture. Stiles reached into his pocket and unfolded a wad of bills. He handed a few to each man and shoved them out the door.

The workmen looked back as they heard the doors lock behind them. "Crazy duck." "More than crazy ... certifiable."

"At least his money's good." The young men folded the bills and stuffed them in their shirt pockets.

After they left, Stiles touched each picture and ran his hands over the sculptures. He untied the string on a box he had placed on the pew earlier. He opened the doors of the shadow box that the men had hung. He arranged his collection of Boy Scout memorabilia—letters, badges, and handbooks—in the box. "This is the start of the Boy Scout collection. Before long this church will have more Boy Scout documents than anywhere in the world."

He sat with his legs crossed on the carpet, and traced the embossed peace symbol that had been carved into the sky blue carpeting. He turned out the lights and walked up to his rooms.

Stiles stood in front of the mirrors on the wall across from his bed. "My ambitions are coming true. These innovations will bring controversy and new blood. The old will flee. Jesus is proud that I've become a fisher of men." He climbed into bed and picked up two books from his night stand—*Enjoy Planting Your Aquarium* and *Tropical Fresh Water Fish as Pets* and thumbed through the well-marked pages in preparation for tomorrow.

Friday morning, two work vans, Richard's Electric and Miller's Tropical Fish, pulled in front of the church. Wally Harris drove in right behind them. Skip Miller tugged two one-hundred gallon tanks from the back of his van and loaded them on a dolly. Mr. Stiles led the way into the sanctuary. Wally snapped photos of the parade and the lifting of the tanks in place on the shelves at the back of the room. While the others worked, Wally photographed the sculptures, the collections, and the art.

The electrician disappeared into the basement and strung wire through the floor and the walls to connect new receptacles near the tanks. He plugged in the lights and returned to the basement to turn on the electrical power. He shouted, "Mr. Stiles, did the lights come on?"

Stiles checked each tank. "Yes."

Miller returned to his truck and hefted jars of fish, greens, and water onto the dolly. Stiles placed the greens in the tanks. He arranged them just as he'd reviewed in the books the night before. Miller slowly poured the water and fish into the tanks. Wally, snapping pictures, moved with ease gaining the best angle of the operation.

"Now turn on the pump." The electrician said.

"I can't believe it." Stiles shouted with exuberance. "It's wonderful, isn't it?"

Stiles walked from one tank to the other.

The electrician lifted his cap and scratched his head. "Fish tanks in a church sanctuary—a first for me. My dentist has one in his office. I guess to relax us." He hitched up his pants. "Aren't you afraid the folks will get so relaxed they'll fall asleep?"

"If they do, they do." Mr. Stiles paced back and forth admiring the installation from various angles in the room. Wally followed him step-for-step and snapped more photos.

"Mr. Stiles, I'm sure these photographs will bring a two-page spread come Saturday's paper." Optimistic, Wally continued, "And by Sunday, who knows? The AP may pick up the story."

"Wally, that would be wonderful—more of the world should know of the transformation of this old place."

CHAPTER 13

September 3, 1967

STILES crept down the stairs in his pajamas and opened the door a crack. He picked up the *Ironton Corner Daily News* and ran back upstairs to jump into bed. He devoured every word of Wally Harris' article, "New 'old' Meeting House." He studied the detail in every photograph and preened at the one of him in front of the fish tanks. After he dressed, he ran down the stairs, and unlocked his office. He read the article to Frederic and showed him the photographs. "We are on our way, my friend."

He folded the paper under his arm and headed the two blocks toward the diner. In his excitement, he started to skip like a child, but chastised himself, settled his feet, and walked with dignity.

Chet nodded and raised his eyebrows as Stiles entered. He leaned over the counter. "Wally's pictures have generated anger and curiosity among my patrons this fine day."

"Good." Stiles took his regular stool at the counter.

"Good?" Chet poured Stiles' coffee and dropped three cream cups next to the pastor's mug.

Stiles drank. He watched the diners in the mirror on the wall behind the counter. In a loud whisper, he said to Chet. "A little controversy is good for the folks. As Jesus demonstrated when he drove the moneychangers out of the temple, we are to comfort the afflicted and afflict the comfortable." Conversations at the tables and booths paused. Along with their surprise over the photos and article, quoting Jesus in a diner in New England where any mention of Jesus was done in private, if at all, shocked them. Stiles marched back to his office.

He unlocked the door and heard the phone ring. After the

sixth ring, he grabbed the phone. "Hello."

"Stiles, what have you done?"

"What do you mean?"

"You know what I'm speaking about. The photos in the paper. We never talked about you doing anything like what is pictured ... fish tanks and statues ... some nude I'm told."

"Arthur, slow down. I created something new like John writes in Revelation, 'A new heaven and a new earth.' "

"You have the whole town talking."

"I'm sure." Still standing, Stiles adjusted a pulley that lowered Frederic to his level. He placed Frederic's arms on his shoulders. They twirled round and round as far as the phone cord and Frederic's hook allowed. The skeleton came alive in Stiles' arms. "Arthur, wait until Sunday morning before you judge. You'll be pleased. I need to go. I have to prepare for the ten scouts coming for an overnight."

Stiles bowed to his partner and adjusted the pulley. Frederic's bones settled back into place, he appeared lifeless and hollow again as he hovered three feet off the floor of Stiles' office.

* * *

The commotion began at five Saturday afternoon when the ten scouts arrived. The boys unrolled their sleeping bags on the floor of Fellowship Hall. They scrambled to the tables and devoured the pizza and coke. They inflated balloons and made bags of confetti; others decorated popcorn bags for the concert on Monday. Still others folded the programs for Sunday and the band concert on Monday. Stiles removed his suit jacket, loosened his tie, and joined in on the fun. He encouraged the boys with soft pats on their shoulders.

Later, Stiles lined them up outside the sanctuary. "I have a surprise for you." He opened the door and led them in.

The boys said in unison. "What? When did all this happen? It's cool."

"Go explore. Touch and feel. Watch the fish." Stiles observed with delight.

One boy stopped in front of the Boy Scout memorabilia. "Feel

free to open the doors and touch the badges and read the letters."
He held his hands about an inch off the boy's shoulders; his fingers
twitching.

Two others ran to the fish tanks. "Real fish and snails. And not
just gold fish, some strange ones. Mr. Stiles, over here." One of the
boys pointed to several unusual fish. "What are those?"

"They are exotic guppies."

"They can't be. Guppies are always plain and gray."

Stiles showed Joyce's oldest boy, Bob, the All about Fish book
that lay next to the tanks. "Look in here. You will discover the
amazing varieties of guppies." Stiles brushed his arm over the boy's
shoulder.

Three other boys yelled. "Come over here. See this statue." The
Scouts gathered around the marble woman. Their eyes bulged and
they looked down, afraid to make eye contact with each other,
since the statue had one breast showing.

"She's the Greek goddess of wisdom, Athena. I'll tell you more
about her when we study Greek culture and religion."

"What do you see in that painting?" Stiles pointed to his left.

"A black Jesus," Jimmy said.

"What do you think others will say about it?" Stiles asked. The
boys turned to Jimmy and waited for his answer. Jimmy was the
one who paid attention during their Sunday school lessons and he
might know how to respond.

"Mr. Stiles, even though we learned that Jesus had olive skin
like others from the Middle East, I think the old people will say
you are trying to start trouble."

"They sure will." Joyce said as she and her mother stepped into
the room. "The room looks like a ..."

"Mom," shouted Bob.

"And Grandma," groaned Rich, Joyce's youngest. "Why are you
two here?"

"This is your first overnight in the church. We wanted to check
and see how it was going."

Bob walked toward his mother. "Mom, it is going fine. We're
having fun."

"And we think the room is just great." Rich chimed in.

"We all do, Mrs. Lang." The Scouts said in unison. "The room is no longer boring." Bob added, "Mom and Grandma, please go home. You are embarrassing us."

"Wait." Stiles had recovered from the unexpected visitors. "Boys and ladies take a seat on the front pew and let me explain."

Hiding his irritation, Stiles gave details. "I'm not trying to start trouble. I'm trying to stimulate your imaginations. Open your minds to original thoughts. Encourage you to ask questions. Take you away from sitting in front of the TV. In a couple of years, we will travel together. Seeing and touching other places will broaden your horizons for sure. This is a start ... art, sculpture, and fish from all around the world."

Joyce swallowed her reaction to Stiles' explanation.

Stiles glanced at his watch. "Okay, it's time for bed. One last thing, we need to be at Chet's diner at eight in the morning and then back here for worship at ten. Get some sleep. I'll leave a light on, so you can find my rooms if you need me."

Stiles took Joyce's elbow. "I'll talk with you on Monday."

She pulled her arm away from Stiles and regained her composure. She looked at her boys to be sure they were okay before motioning to her mother. The two disappeared as quietly as they had arrived.

The boys scrambled to the Fellowship Hall. They herded into the men's room to change their clothes. Returning to the room, they crawled into their sleeping bags. Jimmy Somers whispered, "What do you think? Isn't he cool?"

Comments traveled from bedroll to bedroll. "Cool, but weird. He kept brushing his hand across my shoulder." "Church will be more exciting with all those things to look at." "Yeah, it won't be as boring." "I'm going to insist my parents sit near the aquariums." "The Methodist sanctuary's going to look drab compared to this." "Sorry about your Mom showing up." "It's okay. She's not sure about Mr. Stiles." Slowly the conversation stopped, and a variety of breathing rhythms were heard throughout the room.

In his office, Stiles fell into his desk chair and performed his ritual.

The Chronicle of Matthew Henry Stiles
September 2, 1967

Joyce. She may be more trouble than I thought. Will I have to start a binder on her, too? With the story of her marriage break-up, there must be something I can use to keep her in line.

I am exhausted from being enthusiastic, but I need her boys in my corner. They are excited. I'll be able to mold them with my ideas. By the time they are adults, they will be ambassadors for my empire.

The big weekend is here. Arthur's anxious, but in a day or two, he'll be completely in my pocket. First Parish Unitarian Church of Ironton Corner, can you feel the excitement, the innovation, and the changes coming? You'll be alive again, and it will all be due to me.

He sat back in his desk chair and stretched. He got up from the desk, walked his three steps to the file, opened it less than an inch, carried out his ritual, and filed the entry in the chronicle folder.

CHAPTER 14

9:30 a.m.
September 3, 1967

TRAFFIC and pedestrians jammed the streets around the green. The Boy Scouts ran out of bulletins fifteen minutes before worship. Jimmy Somers craned his neck over the crowd trying to see his dad pushing his mother's wheelchair. When he spotted them, he shouted, "Just wait 'til you see. Just wait 'til you see!"

Jimmy reached his parents and dragged them, pushing others aside, to see their first reactions to the newly decorated sanctuary. "Isn't it wonderful?" He led them by the statues and the collections, right to the fish tanks. "Look, they're alive. The room is alive. Not dead like it used to be."

Frank and Carol stared at each other. What could they say with Jimmy so excited?

The pews filled. As more and more swarmed into the sanctuary, the ushers asked the seated ones to move to the center to make room for more. At ten sharp, the last minute arrivals crowded around the sides and back. Trumpets blared from the balcony. The organist pulled out all the stops and stepped on the pedals as she played the "Hallelujah Chorus." The Scouts untied bags of red balloons which bounced their way to the ceiling with long, colorful ribbons trailing behind. A hired twenty-five voice choir entered from the rear and tossed confetti high in the air while singing, "Hallelujah! Hallelujah! And he shall reign forever and ever. King of kings! Lord of lords! Hallelujah! Hallelujah!" Wally Harris snapped picture after picture of the festivities.

Arthur Blankenship and the church council, dressed in their Sunday best—men in dark suits, white shirts, and ties; women in navy suits, white blouses, hose, and heels—crowded the pulpit with Matthew Henry Stiles. Arthur's eyes scanned the crowd. Here and there he spotted a familiar face, but mostly he saw strangers, happy and excited strangers amazed at the spectacle. He watched their faces light up as the confetti settled on their shoulders. Following the gaze of the children as they watched the balloons play on the ceilings, he almost laughed when a few children jumped to catch the ribbons hanging from the balloons.

Stiles stepped to the lectern. The assembly quieted. Like a TV Evangelist, he spoke into the microphone. "Welcome to this revitalized house of worship!" He raised his arms and his voice. "A new spirit is moving. The old is passing away. The new is occupying this historical space. A new generation of church is being born in your midst. Hallelujah. Hallelujah."

He turned and surveyed the bewildered, yet expectant, faces of the church council who sat behind him. He motioned to Arthur.

Arthur, walking as if in a daze, shook hands with Stiles and halted frozen for a moment in front of the lectern. His eyes scanned the art and statues and row after row of members and guests. Momentarily, the scene took his breath away. Then with his arms spread like an awkward bird, he began speaking softly and built to a shout.

"If I wasn't witnessing this with my own eyes, I, for sure, would think I was dreaming. Can you old timers believe it? This old sanctuary," his arms fluttered faster and faster, "this church that only a year ago we thought we'd have to close, today is overflowing with people and something new everywhere. And it's been only a few short months since Mr. Stiles descended to us from a hot air balloon. Just look around at what he's accomplished."

He did a final swoop with his arms and turned to Stiles. He reached for his hand shaking it vigorously. "Congratulations, Mr. Stiles!" Applause broke out. Arthur held Stiles' arm in the air as if the pastor had just defeated the world boxing champion.

Stiles returned to the microphone. He cleared his throat and pushed his glasses up on his nose. "You've heard the music. You are surrounded by art, statues, aquariums, and collections—all from the son of a wealthy family. Is he showing off his inheritance by doing this for you? No." He shook his head, and his eyes swept the room.

"Why am I committed to providing you stirring music each and every Sunday? Why is the room decorated with statues? Why the aquariums and collections? Why have the other rooms in this church building been colorfully painted and new light fixtures installed?" He glanced over the crowd.

"All of this," he rose on the balls of his feet bouncing a little, "is to stimulate your imaginations, to discover new ideas, to dig deep and search and act on our commitment to this church and to the social ills of this country. By this time next year, this room and the other rooms of the church building will be filled twenty-four hours a day with artists, potters and painters, dancers, musicians, reading clubs, and philosophical discussion groups. This old meeting house will return to what it was in the 1800s when all the community activities of Ironton Corner centered in this building. Isn't that right, Irene?" Stiles turned and looked at Irene seated in one of the chairs behind him. She didn't answer—only stared through him.

"This is not just another church." He pushed his glasses up on his nose and spread his arms. "This is the beginning of a new paradigm of church. We are emerging from the self-satisfied and inward-looking church of the fifties to an experiment in what religion will become. Our programs will be unique. Hundreds will come here to witness what we are doing.

"It may be that all the usual language for religion, God, and prayer will have to be thrown out because it has been overused and misused to the point where nobody understands what it means." He threw his shoulders back and squared his body. "We will stand on love, friendship, truth, and beauty. We will celebrate creativity and ingenuity as we delve into the depths of life."

At that, most of the crowd jumped to their feet, and applause rang out. The throng followed as Mr. Stiles led the band and the choir out to the green playing and singing his revised words to "Go Tell it on the Mountain."

"Go tell it on the mountain,
over the green and everywhere.
Go tell it on the mountain
that we will rise again."

Stiles climbed the steps of the new bandstand, placed his hands on the railing, and said, "Don't forget to bring your picnic and enjoy the Labor Day concert. I'll be here ready to meet you and the friends you plan to invite. Now turn to someone you don't know and greet them."

At his instructions, handshaking and greetings traveled from one family to another. Kids began games of Mother May I? and statue tag. The atmosphere danced with joy.

Jimmy Somers jumped up on the bandstand. He hugged Stiles, grinning from ear to ear. "This is just great, just great." Stiles squeezed Jimmy against his chest.

Irene and Kenny held court with Joyce, Delbert, and the Blankenships near the Civil War Memorial. "Did you check on the boys during their overnight?" Irene asked.

Joyce stood tall, squared her shoulders, and pivoted. "Yes, and Mr. Stiles wants to talk with me first thing on Monday." They laughed at her impersonation of Stiles.

"I definitely unnerved him, but the boys didn't notice. They're fawning all over him. I don't like it." Joyce grumped with her arms folded across her chest.

"And I don't like the amount of money he spent ... aquariums, nude statues, and, of all things, pictures of a colored Jesus. We'll be the laughing stock of the town," Irene added.

Delbert joined the conversation. "I'm keeping an eye on our accounts. Every time I stop in to collect receipts for his expenses so we can pay him back, he dodges my request. Before I know it, he has me discussing the latest bridge hands in the morning paper. He's a real manipulator. Don't worry though. I'll get the receipts."

"Delbert, if you need my help, just let me know." Barbara Blankenship tapped her heels on the cement, impatient to know more about Stiles.

"All this aside, wasn't it something to have the church full and to have great music?" Arthur noted.

Irene hooked her arm through Kenny's. "The test will be if the crowd comes back next week and the next—and if they get involved. Or are they coming to be entertained like the herds that go in bus loads to the Cathedral of Tomorrow over in Ohio. That charismatic Rex Hubbard had an elephant come down the aisle last New Year's Eve."

"Where did you hear that, Irene?"

"On *the Tonight Show*, of course. Johnny Carson did his entire monologue on that man one night."

"Well, that won't happen here."

They crossed the green on one of the new brick pathways.

* * *

Stiles sat in his office still glowing from the morning. He placed a call and shoved his satchel in the back of his car.

Within forty minutes, Stiles reached a two-room cottage tucked under a canopy of pines near the entrance to the Revere Forest Reserve between Ironton Corner and Providence, Rhode Island. He parked. With his head down and lugging the satchel, he moved sporadically over the stone pathway avoiding every crack. He lifted each foot gingerly and pointed his toe as if putting his full weight on the stone would break it. He reached the door and before he knocked, a man opened it.

The man blinked his crocodilian green eyes at Stiles as if he were prey. Stiles lowered his eyes. A feeling of shame swept over him. He waited for chastisement. The man bowed and stood aside. Stiles entered the room. "You are no longer a child, grow up. Stop that tiptoe routine."

"Leroy, you made me start that, or don't you remember? You said that it would help me control my emotions. That by negotiating something as small as the cracks in the sidewalk it would empower me to face my father. I haven't needed to do it in years, but now with our plans, the anticipation overwhelms me. I need to use that crutch to contain my excitement."

"Matthew," Leroy reached out and squeezed Stiles' shoulder with his long bony fingers. "The plans are perfect. Don't become preoccupied with each one. They will unfold in time. Relax. I helped you step-by-step through the mess you made in high school, and I'm here to help you now."

"You helped me, yes, but you know too much about my life." Stiles shook his head to block out his memories of a green-walled recreation room in the detention center where a counselor sexually abused him.

Leroy's eyelids fluttered. Stiles pushed Leroy's hand off his shoulder and marched with a constant beat across the room, heaving his satchel onto Leroy's scratched harvest table.

"Relax, Matthew. When you called six months ago, you said you needed my contacts and support. You've drawn me into your dreams with your enthusiasm. I am here to be of whatever service you need." He took a place on the bench seat at the table.

Stiles removed the binders and sat down beside Leroy. The two men studied and discussed each page and double-checked lists, charts, and graphs.

His mentor got up, pulled a notebook from the bookshelf and placed it on the table. "A surprise ... the original plans for the development of Williamsburg and Sturbridge Village. I know your plans aren't that big, but I thought they'd be a guide for you." Leroy remained standing, patting his hands together like a child waiting for a pat on the back.

"Your contacts amaze me."

Stiles studied a page and turned to the next. Leroy watched Matthew getting lost in the details, imagining his new creations for Ironton Corner. He stepped to the counter and poured them each a glass of wine.

Stiles lifted his head and smiled at Leroy. Leroy brought a glass to Stiles. Their glasses touched in a toast.

"These drawings will help with my plans for the museums. Thank you." Stiles tapped his fingers on the stem of the wine glass.

"Now, come move to the sofa and relax and tell me about this morning ... the unveiling of the new meeting house." Leroy patted the sofa and Matthew joined him.

"Arthur couldn't believe it. He was almost speechless. The Boy Scouts ran around pointing out each piece of sculpture and the aquariums to their parents. It all went according to my plan. The bandstand is perfect, and you should have heard the compliments about the design of the brick pathways. I, of course, let them know they were my design."

"Matthew. You'll have your empire before you know it."

Stiles looked at his watch. "It is time for me to go. I'm exhausted."

Leroy helped his protégé to his car with the satchel. "Next time, we'll look more closely at the steeple and pool designs. Meanwhile, I'll be interviewing area contractors."

Matthew drove back to town filled with energy and the assurance of his mentor. Before he knew it, he was inside the town limits and saw a flashing blue light in his rear view window. He pulled over.

Chief Bird lumbered out of his cruiser and knocked on the car window. "What's your hurry, Mr. Stiles?"

"I'm sorry chief. I wasn't thinking."

"Show me your license."

Stiles handed it through the window.

Bird studied it. "Are you on a high from your day?"

"I guess I am. Can you overlook my speed this time?"

Bird smiled to himself at the pleading look on Stiles' face. "Well," his fat fingers thumbed on the side of Stiles' car. "Let's call this a verbal warning."

"Thanks, Chief."

Bird recorded Stiles' license number in his book.

* * *

On Labor Day, the Boy Scouts tied balloons to the trees and bandstand. They popped popcorn. The Navy Band set up and tuned their instruments while families and friends picnicked. Stiles introduced the band and walked to the back of the crowd to watch.

Wally's headlines in the *Ironton Corner Daily News* read, "Hats off to Mr. Stiles, Ironton Corner's Knight in Shining Armor." "Band Concert A Smashing Success." "Town Reinvigorated." "Boy Scouts Praised."

Part 2

The Book of Kings: I Kings and II Kings

Celebration and Deception

Chapter 15

March 17, 1968

THE crowds returned and grew in numbers week after week. By the end of September, classes in dance, water color, pottery, and knitting had been organized. An art appreciation course grew out of a November sermon by Pastor Stiles who told the congregation that art stimulates your religious imagination and opens your vision of God. The younger men formed bowling teams and joined the Sunday night leagues at Sutter's Bowling Alley. Couples and singles formed card clubs, and during the February school break, the aquarium lovers started a club to study marine life.

On St. Patrick's Day, Irene and Kenny met George and Maida at Chet's yearly "Irish Night at the Diner." Green streamers hung from the ceiling, and green helium-filled balloons held in place by a weight bobbled above each table.

"Chet, you sure have the place decked out." Irene clapped her hands in excitement. She picked up a derby hat and handed one to each of the others. Kenny and George put theirs on and engaged in a little Irish jig before the four of them sat down.

"Since Mr. Stiles has rejuvenated Ironton Corner with the band concerts and sprucing up the green and the church, I decided to make some improvements." Chet twirled to show-off his new green jacket complete with sequins on the satin lapels. "Like it?"

"The word 'amazing' comes to my mind." George raised an eyebrow and picked up a small plant from the table. "Real shamrocks, I'm impressed."

Chet filled their frosted mugs with green beer. "Here's the menu—potato and leek soup, followed by corned beef and cabbage, and soda bread. Then, my grandmother's Irish shortbread to dazzle your taste buds."

Kenny fussed with his green bow tie and raised his mug. "Isn't this something?" He looked around. "The whole town's changing. We were going to accept dying a slow death, and now we believe in ourselves again."

"Last year, the church was dark except on Sundays, and now there are meetings and activities to suit anyone's taste and interest." Irene patted her hair adjusting the shamrock she'd pinned above her ear. "Can you believe I'm planning the Saturday dinners?"

Maida buttered her roll, but her attention was focused on Irene. "So, Irene, are you feeling better about Mr. Stiles?"

"I feel good that new people are coming to our church. I like their energy and fresh ideas. But truth be told, I'm still skeptical about Mr. Stiles. There's something not right about him."

George played with the ever present cigar in his shirt pocket. "He participates in the Kitchen Talks. You should join us. I'm learning more about him and hearing fresh perspectives on current events from the others in the group, especially from those outside of Ironton Corner. I'm afraid I have a small view of the world."

Kenny wiped crumbs from the Irish short bread from around his mouth. "Clyde Weaver leads that group, doesn't he?"

"Yes and Mr. Stiles is the reason Clyde and his family are now members of the church." George pulled the cigar from his pocket and began to unwrap it. "For years they commuted to a colored church in Roxbury near Boston. Jimmy Somers told Clyde's children about the youth programs and the family began coming. Clyde told me that Mr. Stiles and the Somers welcomed them with such genuine hospitality that they joined our all white church."

Maida's eyes widened. "George, do you think the community views us as an exclusively all white church?"

"I asked Clyde about that. He said with some of our pastors he wondered if his family would be welcome. And besides, with racial tensions being what they are, he didn't want to create another difficult situation for his children."

"I'm glad they are part of us now. His wife is the best pre-school teacher we've had in the Sunday school for years. You agree with me, don't you Irene?" Maida smiled across the table toward her friend.

* * *

On April 5, 1968, Clyde Weaver welcomed an exceptionally large, but subdued group, to Kitchen Talk. He knew why they were there—the assassination of Martin Luther King, Jr. the night before. Clyde's grief showed in the way his usually tall posture sagged and it showed in the people, as they huddled shoulder to shoulder in the front few pews of the worship room. Mr. Stiles sat off to the side.

Clyde stood and leaned on a portable lectern. "This is a sad day for my people and many of you who've supported the civil rights movement. Those who followed Dr. King know he's had other threats on his life. He said over and over again that he was bound for the Promised Land, but for him to be so cruelly cut down in Memphis is hard ... really hard."

George Lawrence struggled to his feet and quietly joined Clyde. He put one arm over the shoulder of his friend. "I had the privilege of hearing Dr. King's 'I Have a Dream' speech at the Lincoln Memorial in '63. Feeling the spirit of that crowd is indescribable. I believe, even though he's been cut down, his vision will continue."

"It sure will," Clyde affirmed. "Doctor King shared a vision that few of us dared to imagine. His words of inspiration built a fire in my people and many white folks. His marching moved us to action, instead of sitting back and waiting for something to change." Clyde pulled folded newspaper from his pocket. "I've brought a few clippings of his speeches over the years. I'd like to share some with you."

Maida Alden stood up from her front row seat, walked to the front, and hugged Clyde. "You go ahead."

Clyde unfolded the paper and read. Tears and sniffles traveled from mourner to mourner.

George wiped his eyes. "I have a suggestion. How about we bring candles to the green tonight and have a vigil like I hear other towns are doing?"

"That's a great idea." Kenny waved his hand from the second row. "I'll let the schools and the radio stations know. Irene and I will get the candles."

"Mr. Stiles, you'll help us, won't you?" Maida looked over toward the side pews.

Stiles got to his feet, eyes down, and body slack. "I'll certainly help. Tell me what to do." His heavy grief permeated the room.

After dark and in near silence, figures of all sizes made their way to the bandstand. Irene and Kenny passed out candles. Chief Bird and his officers directed the traffic. With the lighting of each candle, a flickering glow pushed away the darkness. Clyde Weaver read again from Dr. King's speeches. His family led the mourners in "Take My Hand, Precious Lord," the piece Dr. King had requested to be sung upon his death.

Mayor Sims joined Clyde's family on the bandstand. "I want to thank the Weavers and First Parish Church for organizing this vigil. Mr. Stiles, your church is making a big difference in our community."

Afterward, many hands helped Stiles hang black bunting over the door of the church and around the pulpit. It remained there for forty days.

The bunting returned in early June after the killing of Robert Kennedy. That Sunday, Stiles stepped from the pulpit to the floor directly in front of the first row of pews. "I realize that some of you were not fans of Robert Kennedy's politics. His convictions concerning the Civil Rights Act, migrant workers, the Middle East, and the war in Vietnam created divisions among people. His view on racial equality in our schools disrupted parts of Boston where some of your families live. Whatever your view, I know all of you agree that this destruction of the lives of our young leaders is an abomination to all who live in a democracy. I've chosen to send you forth today with Robert Kennedy's own words.

"'Each time a man stands up for an ideal or acts to improve the lot of others, or strikes out against injustice, he sends forth a tiny ripple of hope, and crossing each other from a million different centers of energy and daring, those ripples build a current that can sweep down the mightiest walls of oppression and resistance.' "

After a moment of silence, Clyde's baritone voice filled the auditorium from the balcony. "Let there be peace on earth. Let it begin with me. Let there be peace on earth. The peace that was meant to be. Let there be peace on earth. And let it begin with me."

The congregation reached for each other's hands, joined in

the singing, at first singing quietly and then with deep conviction that filled each corner of the room.

Stiles stood stone still while a deep silence settled in the room. "Due to this tragedy, the concert we planned for tonight has been postponed until next week. Tonight you are invited to the green for a vigil in memory of Robert Kennedy. Each light will stand for a ripple of hope. I hope to see all of you there." A solemn Mr. Stiles walked to the front door with Maida to greet the worshipers.

Kenny and Irene walked down the steps and across the green toward their house. Irene pulled Kenny to her side. "He knows how to work the crowd. I feel anger lurking behind his words about understanding those with different opinions from him."

"Irene, haven't you learned anything more about him from the Kitchen Talks where he shares his views?" Kenny guided her across the street to their porch.

She stayed quiet until they were seated. "I hear his words about being open to others, but there is something in the way he says it. He is condescending; his soul is not into it. His lofty ideas are only tools for his ambition to make us the biggest church in the area. Have you noticed how his nostrils flare and he tilts his head up when anyone supports the war in Vietnam?"

"Nostrils?" Kenny rubbed her back.

She turned away. "Yes. When they flare, he tilts his head, and he takes on an air of arrogance that makes him appear on the verge of rage."

"Irene, I've heard it all now. Look. Look at me. What am I saying?" Kenny flared his nostrils and tilted his head.

Irene laughed. "Come on, the roast must be about done."

As soon as they settled down for lunch in the kitchen, George came walking in. "Got enough lunch for me?"

"Where's Maida? Has she dumped you?" Kenny continued cutting his meat as he teased George.

George put his cigar in his shirt pocket. "She's out with one of her friends. She told me I was on my own today." He pulled out a chair and stabbed a piece of roast and placed it on top of a pile of mashed potatoes on his plate. "I'm sure glad Mr. Stiles cancelled the concert tonight. These assassinations are hitting me hard. What's happening to our country?"

Irene stared in the direction of her brother. His face was drawn and tight; his eyes filled with sorrow. "George, I don't know, but I'm in no mood for a concert tonight either. We've had too much sadness. Maybe the flags and patriotic music next week will help us 'be ripples of hope.' "

George relaxed and threw his head back and laughed. "I'm going to write this down; Irene remembered the words of Matthew Stiles."

"They were Robert Kennedy's words." Irene huffed, and the men laughed at her attempt to defend herself.

At dusk, community leaders, concerned citizens and members from all the churches in Ironton Corner gathered for the vigil. Stiles and Clyde shared the leadership with Mayor Sims.

After the vigil, Stiles separated from the dwindling crowd and made his way to his office. As he entered, the urge to confide in Frederic overpowered him. He pinched each of his friend's ten bony toes. "Frederic, you remember that ridiculous 'Drama in Education' course I took for my Master in Education at Harvard, don't you? I hated that professor. Her voice grated on my nerves. I complained and complained about her. Now I wish I could thank her. Maybe I will."

He let go of Frederic's toes and sat at his desk. He reached for his calendar from the top desk drawer. Running his right index finger down the page, he stopped at the date marked with dollar signs. "Frederic, it's that time again. I need my monthly check from Arthur." He returned the calendar to its place. Turning to his typewriter, he loaded a fresh sheet of paper, cracked his knuckles, raised his arms over his head, quietly set his hands in his lap and glanced toward his friend as if expecting a response. Receiving none, he flexed his fingers three times and placed them on the keys. He spoke softly as he typed.

The Chronicle of Matthew Henry Stiles
June 5, 1968
Dr. Pigget, you would have been proud of my performance these past weeks. I would have won the top acting award for radiating humility and compassion.

When they watched me holding my candle or speaking from the pulpit, they thought we were one. Bullshit! We aren't one. They are too weak-minded to understand the politics and manipulation behind those assassinations like I do. They think their little candles will make everything okay. I mesmerized them with my performance. They are beginning to worship me.

All except for Irene. She's still suspicious. She's a rule follower who needs to know it all, but there is more. I see it in her eyes. The way she walks, and the way she wears that hair all stacked up and frozen with spray on top of her head. What is behind her distrust of me? Does she distrust others, too? If I knew, maybe I could use that information for my gain.

Clyde Weaver has been stellar through all this. He's well-spoken and that voice of his reverberates and stirs in every heart. Every day someone comes up to me and thanks me for bringing him to my church. I look down and mumble a quiet "thanks" to show my sincere humility.

Stiles smiled over at Frederic. He walked to the filing cabinet, pulled the drawer in and out three times and placed the page in the chronicle file.

Chapter 16

WALLY Harris jumped around like a jack rabbit taking photos and interviewing the attendees at the summer's first concert and festivities sponsored by the First Parish Church. Red, white, and blue streamers decorated the green for the celebration of Flag Day.

The Methodists, along with Charlie Pierce, congregated on blankets. Others arranged webbed aluminum chairs around small tables laden with food. The Easley boys organized a game of Whiffle ball. Off to the side of the bandstand, Jimmy Somers and Joyce's boys, Bob and Rich, sold popcorn.

When the crowd heard the band tuning their instruments, quiet settled over the crowd. At the tap, tap, tap on the microphone, all heads focused on the bandstand. "I am Mr. Matthew Henry Stiles, pastor of First Parish Church. Welcome to the first summer concert of 1968. The U.S. Navy Band is here to stir us, even in these tough days. We are the land of the free. Let's welcome the band with a generous round of applause."

The band played and the Boy Scouts handed out little American flags to all the children. During the last number, "Stars and Stripes Forever," Stiles marched with the children through the crowds. After an encore and standing ovation, the attendees made their way to their cars leaving the green empty except for a renewed spirit enveloping the red, white, and blue streamers hanging from the trees.

The next morning, the Keenes ambled to the diner as was their custom. As they opened the door, they heard Chet reading the *Ironton Corner Daily News* to a captive audience.

Several hundred locals and families from as far away as Providence and Fall River filled the First Parish green with lawn chairs and picnic baskets. The scene was as exciting as Mohammed Ali defending his World Boxing Association Title in '65 and '66.

The audience groaned at Wally's hyperbole. Chet continued.

The U. S. Navy Band played patriotic numbers and familiar sing-along tunes. The Boy Scouts handed out programs and sold popcorn to raise money for a future trip to the Scout Museum in England.

When asked how he felt about the concert, Matthew Stiles, pastor of First Parish Unitarian Church of Ironton Corner said, "It exceeded my expectations, but this is only a beginning. Next summer the concerts will return on Flag Day and finish with an even bigger Labor Day extravaganza. And the community can expect more attractions on the green."

Mayor Sims, when asked how he felt about the evening, responded, "Ironton Corner hasn't seen a night like this since the celebration for the end of World War II. Mr. Stiles has my support."

Kenny pushed his plate aside and spread the *Boston Globe* in front of him. A broad smile came over his face. "Hey folks." He stood up. "We made the Community News in the *Globe*." He handed the paper around. Some got up and read the piece over the shoulder of others; some talked loudly from table to table. The excitement dimmed when Arthur Blankenship and Delbert Martin entered the diner together. Delbert's unhappiness with Stiles had traveled through the rumor mill.

Chet grabbed the paper and shoved it at Delbert. "See what Mr. Stiles is doing. Good publicity instead of the usual gossip about the invasion of Asians to the communities surrounding Ironton Corner."

Delbert read the piece and handed it to Arthur. "Chet, can we get a table in the back?"

Chet scanned the room. "I'll clear the window table. Be just a minute." Delbert and Arthur waited standing apart like two strangers. They nodded greetings to Irene and Kenny as they threaded through the tables to the back.

Irene put her coffee down. "Was that a cold greeting or what? I wonder what's up with them."

Chet poured coffee for the two men. He hoped it would warm up the icy atmosphere. "What can I get for you?"

"I'll have Chet's Special." Arthur laid the paper on the table and took the seat looking at the back wall filled with Chet's bowling trophies.

"The Special for me, too." Delbert sat where he could see over tables to the front door. Arthur handed him a section of the *Boston Globe*. They read the paper until Chet interrupted them with their meals—two eggs over easy, two pancakes, three sausage links, hash browns, two slices of Chet's frosted homemade raisin bread and bottomless cups of coffee.

The men ate in silence until Delbert laid his utensils across his plate. "Arthur, we can't let the pastor support us with his own money. We have to stop him. I need a record of his spending." Delbert tried to keep his voice down.

"He wants that private. He says he doesn't want any repayment, or maybe he just realizes that we don't have the money to repay him right now."

"Well, we will repay him—it's our church, not his. He could leave us for another church at any time. We need to know what we owe and have some say in the money that he is spending. You know this could come back to haunt us." Delbert motioned to Chet to refill his cup.

Arthur pressed his hands together. "Delbert, give him a little space."

"Why? What do we owe him?" Delbert brushed his hand through his thinning hair—Delbert's method of controlling his frustrations.

"Just leave it alone, Delbert."

"Arthur, what promises have you made to him?" Delbert stared at his friend.

Arthur avoided Delbert's eyes and focused on the bowling

trophies. "He has me in a bind." Red splotches began to appear on his neck.

"Arthur, what kind of bind?"

"I can't say."

Delbert hunched over the table. "We've been friends for a long time. You can share any problems with me."

"I know, Delbert, but I can't share this." Arthur's shoulders slumped.

"Whatever it is, how did he find out?" Delbert lowered his voice.

Arthur shrugged. "Someone who knew someone—you know how it is."

"Is he blackmailing you?"

"That's not what he calls it." Arthur hung his head.

"Damn it. Arthur, how could you let him use you and the church like this? If we don't have a conversation with him and straighten this out, I'll be the one who demands that we get rid of him, contract or no contract." Delbert stood and threw his napkin on the table.

"I'll arrange the meeting, but I need you to promise that you won't question him about the hold he has on me."

Delbert looked down and caught the desperate look in his friend's eyes. "I won't."

Arthur shoved his chair back and stood. The two men walked toward the front of the diner together.

Irene mumbled. "Arthur looks like an old man, and Delbert looks like he's after a bear." Irene fanned her face with the menu. Even the air conditioning couldn't keep up with the humidity of this early summer heat.

* * *

Delbert and Lois Martin awoke at their usual time, 6:30 a.m. on a beautiful crisp fall day. Dressed in sport clothes, they settled their dog, Daisy, into her spot in the backseat of their car. They drove to Findlay Park for their daily two-mile walk through a forest of pines, white oaks, and sumac that had already turned deep red due to an early cold snap. At the half-way point, Lois stopped in mid-stride and turned to Delbert. "You seem distracted this morning."

"I am. I'm sorry. I'm finally having the face-to-face meeting with Mr. Stiles that I asked for months ago. I feel like I'm failing the church by not knowing how much we owe him for the work he's done on the building and the green and the concerts."

"I remember you telling me the church council earmarked the profits from selling the parsonage to settle up with Mr. Stiles."

"They did, but I haven't seen the receipts. Each time I bring it up, Mr. Stiles changes the subject. I'm concerned."

"So this morning, you're thinking about your approach to Mr. Stiles."

"I am and I'm planning to be firm and get those receipts."

"You'll do fine. Remember the time you confronted a couple of trustees at the bank with similar personalities."

"You mean those two who were convinced they were God's gift to the bank like Stiles feels he is to the church."

"Right."

"Thanks for reminding me." Delbert wrapped his arm around Lois. The couple strolled arm in arm with Daisy barking at their heels for the remainder of their walk.

At 10 a.m., Delbert and Arthur met in front of the church. Arthur stooped down, picked up a red maple leaf, and twirled it between his fingers, "The green looks spectacular, doesn't it, Delbert?"

"All of New England takes on a special beauty this time of year." Delbert breathed in deeply while opening the door to the church office. The two men stepped inside. Seeing Joyce at her desk, they stopped to wave.

Joyce waved back. "Did I see you both at the football game on Friday?"

They nodded, and Arthur said, "Good game. Your son is developing into quite a player."

"Thanks, Arthur. Mr. Stiles is waiting for you in his office." She noticed Delbert grimace and Arthur's posture sag when she mentioned Stiles. "Are you guys okay?"

"Oh, sure." Arthur attempted a smile.

Stiles' door opened. "Good morning, Delbert. Arthur. Pardon me if I am a little disheveled. I just this minute returned from taking a battery of tests in Boston. The Ecclesiastical Council of the Unitarian Universalists requires candidates to take them. They determine if we are suited for ministry. Come in."

The men stopped abruptly to avoid colliding with a skeleton twisting on a wire attached to the ceiling.

"What's with the skeleton?" Arthur asked.

Stiles stood tall and adjusted his handkerchief. "All medieval scholars of any merit had one. His name is Frederic. Just as a skeleton inspired Chopin to compose the Funeral March in his Sonata No. 2 in B-flat minor, Op. 35 for piano, Frederic inspires me."

Both men shrugged and pulled up chairs to the front of the desk.

Delbert started in with his practiced first statement. "As church treasurer, I need the receipts from the work that has been done on the church and the green."

"Delbert, let's talk about the bridge game at your house before we get to that. You and your wife are my type of players, sharp and—"

"No. Stop. Enough of your malarkey. I want to get this money situation cleared up." Delbert threw his shoulders back and straightened his posture.

Stiles twirled a pencil between the thumb and index finger of his right hand. "You've worked at First Bank of Ironton your entire career."

"Yes, I've been with them for about twenty-nine years."

Stiles continued fingering the pencil. Time suspended as Delbert and Arthur waited. The only sound was the ticking of Stiles' grandmother's clock. "And they hold parish trust accounts."

"Yes, the bank has handled the accounts since before my time as treasurer."

"And you've acted as treasurer for what, almost twenty-five years?" Stiles cocked his head to the left and finally stared at Delbert.

"Right. Not everyone is interested in the parish accounts and trusts as I am. I follow them closely and make suggestions to the church council for ways we can make our endowments grow."

Stiles waited as the clock chimed the half-hour. He opened a folder on his desk. "You've provided me with copies of the endowments, but not with any accounting of the weekly offerings from the church members."

"Right, you don't have access to the contributions of the church members. They're locked up." Beads of perspiration collected on Delbert's forehead.

Stiles noticed Delbert's resolve fraying. With clenched teeth, he asked, "And why do you keep the files locked?"

"To protect the members," Arthur interjected.

"What kind of protection do they need?" Stiles stood. His hand edged instinctively toward Frederic. He pulled his arm to his side and turned toward Arthur.

Arthur met Stiles' eyes. "We've always held that the amount the members pledge to the church is confidential. The treasurer is the only one who knows their giving level."

"Why shouldn't I know what people are giving?" Stiles demanded.

Delbert started to run his fingers through his hair, but dropped his hand to his side. "Mr. Stiles, our thought is that if the pastor knows what each member gives, he might have favorites and neglect the others."

Stiles twisted one of the buttons on his jacket, as he lowered his body to his chair. He brushed the curl from his forehead. "I'm sorry I raised my voice, but I love this church and ..."

"Stop. I'm not going to fall for your 'I love this Church' and 'I've been called here by God' routine. I want the receipts and from now on the council needs to approve all expenditures." Delbert held Stiles' gaze.

Stiles opened his top desk drawer. "Here are the receipts." He placed a pile on the corner of his desk.

Delbert reached for them. "I'll study these and make a plan to reimburse you, Mr. Stiles."

"I'm sure that over the next few months we'll come to the best financial arrangement for the future good of the church. And," Stiles adjusted the knot on his necktie, "since we have settled that messy detail, I'd like to move away from business. I enjoy you and your wife at the Bridge Club, but we don't get time to talk. I'd like you both to join me at the Tavern on the Pond for dinner one of these nights."

"We don't usually—"

"It will be my treat. Speaking of treats, I've completed my plan for the funding of the new steeple." Stiles reached in his top desk drawer.

Delbert, with Arthur looking over his shoulder, studied Stiles' plan. "Now this makes sense, I'm pleased that you are now sharing your plans with us."

"I understand." Stiles softened his eyes and forced a smile to spread over his face. He glanced at his watch. "I don't want to rush you, but I have another concerned church member coming in a few minutes."

Stiles opened the office door, shook hands with the men, and closed his door securely before grabbing the skeleton's hands. "Frederic, thank God for Dr. Pigget. I chose the right lines and used the right voice inflections. I've set Delbert up for a surprise." Stiles massaged Frederic's bony fingers, turned on his record player and relaxed for a few minutes before his next appointment.

Chapter 17

"Hello, the Office of the Unitarian Universalist Fellowship. How may I help you?"

"This is Matthew Henry Stiles. I need to talk with President Ackers. I received a letter from his office."

"I'll put you through."

"Matthew, you received the letter from the Ecclesiastical Council?"

"Yes, and I don't understand." Stiles fidgeted with Frederic's fingers. Compulsively he arched his toes and paced as far as the telephone cord would allow him.

"Matthew, as I suggested in the letter, we need to talk about this person to person. When are you available to come into Boston?"

He clutched the receiver in his hand, his knuckles white. "I have time tomorrow."

"Let's say eleven, so you can avoid the rush hour traffic."

"I'll be there." Stiles put down the receiver. He paced three steps stopping in front of Frederic. Grasping Frederic's bony fingers again, he stared into his empty eye sockets. "They can't do this to me."

The next morning at eleven a.m. precisely, Stiles arrived at the Office of the Unitarian Universalist Fellowship. The Reverend Ackers greeted him and introduced him to the Ecclesiastical Council—three men in control of who would be ordained and who would not. They took their seats around a weighty round table. Ackers' assistant brought in coffee. Stiles sat stiff and ill at ease. As he composed himself, he sensed a foggy haze between him and the others as they added cream to their coffee.

Ackers set his coffee aside. "We've followed the newspaper articles about your entry into Ironton Corner. You've created quite a splash of activity and controversy."

"That's right."

"We're proud of what you have accomplished. The growth you've achieved is nothing more than miraculous."

"Thank you."

Ackers nodded to the man to his right. The man cleared his throat betraying his concern for the report he needed to give. "Matthew, we've reviewed your superb scholastic record. We know you did your undergraduate work in three years and completed your Master in Education in record time. The school in Ghana where you taught and reorganized their educational system sent glowing reports. You've completed all the steps we require in the pursuit of ordination." The man caught the eye of his colleagues around the table. "Your work on your Master of Divinity is progressing well. You are, indeed, a scholar. But we've found a problem in your background."

Stiles fought to remain calm. The eyes of the other men bore down on him. "My background? What do you mean? I've had all the privilege anyone could want ... best schools, opportunities, and travel. I'm more prepared to run a church than the other clergy I've met around Ironton Corner or anywhere for that matter. What more do you want of me?"

Ackers fingered a manila folder. "As the final step, two months ago you sat for a battery of psychological tests. When the psychologist shared the results with us, he recommended that we look deeper into your background. With the assistance of experts in psychology, we found some inconsistencies with your personality patterns; some bordered on pathological lying."

"They are fools. How could they single out those characteristics?"

"Matthew, the team of psychologists met with me and walked me through your test results. What they revealed alarmed me, as well as them, about your suitability for ministry at this time."

"At this time—that's bullshit I am already doing it and being successful, as you've already noted. You are worried because my success overshadows those hollow, gutless ministers you've already ordained." Stiles gritted his teeth to hold back another outburst.

"If you recall, when we took you on as a candidate for ordination, you signed an agreement giving us full permission to investigate your background." Ackers pulled a page from the folder.

The color disappeared from Stiles' face. The curl fell onto his forehead. Under the table, his toes drew inward and his feet pointed downward. The fog in the room grew thicker. Stiles rubbed his eyes.

"We found that you have a juvenile record."

"My records are sealed." His voice squeaked at a high pitch.

Ackers held up the file. "Our lawyers presented your signed form to the judge, and the judge gave permission to open your file. We found that you had stolen property and threatened a person with a deadly weapon."

"But I was a teen. My parents made sure I had the best therapists." He placed his hands down on the table and turned to the other men for help. They remained stoic. The fog crystals turned to ice. Hard eyes studied Stiles.

"Mr. Secretary, will you read our formal statement?"

The secretary straightened his posture. "Dear Mr. Stiles, We, the Ecclesiastical Council of the Unitarian Universalist, have studied our bylaws and have determined that we cannot recommend you for ordination." The reader stopped.

Stiles' head dropped. "I can't believe this. I suppose you have sent a copy of your statement to the Church."

"No. Our decision will only appear in our executive minutes, and they are archived. Someday the law may change, and we'll be able to share this kind of private information with those who need to know, but for now our hands are tied. Your past mistakes will be your secret. I trust that through your therapy you've learned from them. I'm sorry, Matthew." Ackers reached over to pat Stiles' shoulder. Stiles jerked away.

The man across from Stiles turned to Ackers. "If I may, I'd like to offer a personal word?" Ackers nodded his approval.

"Mr. Stiles, I find you resourceful and energetic. Your scholarship is outstanding. You have a gift for writing and your ideas for education are sound. Pursue a scholastic career. Delve into history and our fallen culture."

Stiles' face heated and flushed with disbelief and rage. He physically took a deep breath as the color drained from his face. His colorless lips formed a limp smile.

One of the other men spoke. "Matthew, we deliberated for many hours before we came to this decision. We are truly sorry, but with the ethical standards we hold for our pastors—"

"Ethical standards! I'd like to investigate each of you. I'm certain I'd find some questionable business practice or personal flaw."

"Matthew, let's not make this worse." Ackers pounded a gavel.

"Worse?" Stiles slammed his fists on the table. "You can't make it any worse. You've ruined me" He paused and squared his shoulders. "I'll find a way around this. You will not have the last word." He stormed out of the room.

Like a robot, he unlocked the door of his room and slid into bed. Hours later, still not having slept, he crept down to his office. He wrapped his arms around Frederic. "Those bastards. They are afraid of my vision of church. They are looking for ministers that serve only pabulum. Their opinion won't stop me. They will regret their decision when this church is known around the world, and hundreds are coming here to study my example." He clung to Frederic until he found some hidden strength and made his way back to bed.

The next day he called Leroy. "Meet me at the movie theater. I need a diversion."

Stiles hid in the back row of the Plymouth Cinema. Leroy entered while the previews played, and Stiles motioned for him to sit down. Halfway through *The Graduate*, Stiles began to perspire. He jumped out of his seat, tripped over Leroy's feet, steadied himself in the aisle, and ran for the door.

Leroy followed. Outside the theater, he grasped Stiles' shoulder. "What's the matter?"

Stiles slowly turned to look into the eyes of his mentor. Leroy stood silent, watching sweat pour down the sides of Stiles' face.

Stiles struggled for breath. "That movie ... that movie gave me flashbacks."

"Didn't you check to see what movie was showing? Flashbacks to what?"

"To an awful woman who made me have sex with her my freshman year of college."

The marquee lights cast a yellow glow on Stiles' face. "She used me and it made me sick."

"I've not heard this story."

"No, you have not."

"Let's find a place and sit and discuss the movie like we have at other times."

"I don't want to discuss the movie or hear another of your philosophies. I called you because the Unitarians refused to ordain me. They discovered my background. I need to work out a new strategy to be ordained." Stiles moved to a shadowed area in the parking lot of the movie theater.

Leroy followed and leaned against the side of the building. "With that news, you have it all wrong ... we need to talk about how you are going to handle yourself while waiting for the right opportunity to discuss your ordination, so your earlier debacle does not destroy our plans. After the experience of my termination as a pastor, we will not allow small-minded people to destroy your plans as they did mine. I may no longer be a pastor, but we will ensure that you remain in control of your church. I'll see that it happens." Leroy reached his arms toward Matthew. He hesitated for a moment, wondering if Matthew would slap them away. He didn't.

As Leroy placed his gaunt hands on Stiles' shoulders, his eyes locked with Stiles. "Go back to your high school years and focus on your destructive behavior. I helped you learn to manage your raw and runaway emotions. I can't have you ruining this opportunity to prove to yourself that you have what it takes to build a kingdom for God. You must succeed. Together we will show the church's supercilious leaders what our power can create."

"You screwed me up with your crazy philosophies and your movies. I don't need your advice and counsel." Stiles brought his arms up and knocked Leroy's hands from his shoulders.

Leroy took a step back. "That's your disappointment talking, my friend. I've heard that before. I'm not hurt. You needed to yell at someone. I am here for you. There, now, look into my eyes, see my calm spirit, and claim it as your own. You need me, and you know it. Feel that you are going through a fresh incarnation of your spirit."

Stiles breathed deeply from the calm pool in Leroy's eyes like he had done in high school. He shrugged, straightened his posture, and his concern and anger floated away. He flashed a sly grin at Leroy. He linked arms with Leroy and they walked the half mile to the coffee shop.

Over coffee Stiles was fully in touch with his creative spirit. "By the time Advent and Christmas are over and the kings arrive for Epiphany, all the church will know I am the living incarnation of Jesus."

CHAPTER 18

January 12, 1969

STILES expounded from the pulpit. "In less than two years our membership has jumped from forty to one hundred ninety. Some families are traveling over thirty miles to enjoy our fellowship. Along with the artisans and dancers, we have an investment club, an ESP group, an organ club, Whist tournaments, and a monthly gathering of World War II widows. Our current events discussion group grows each week.

"So what's next? Along with the goal to double our membership and activities, the men of the church say we need to shore up the foundation of the building." He studied the crowd. "And that's about as exciting as buying new underwear, isn't it?"

A few chuckles came from the crowd.

"So, how's this? We do the foundation because we have to," he paused for effect, "and replace the steeple because we want to."

A number of yeses and "Let's do it' came from here and there in the room.

"I have taken the liberty to print up pledge cards. I've provided a place for you to check off an amount and a line for your signature to make your commitment to the new steeple. The Boy Scouts will pass out the cards. Pens are in the pew racks. As per a colonial New England tradition, the names of all who give will be installed in the steeple's gold finial."

Irene and Kenny studied the card. Kenny whispered to Irene. "Humph. Look at his suggestions. Ten dollars per inch. One hundred dollars for a whole foot. Maybe the new people have that kind of money, but we don't."

"He likes confetti. I'll just toss this up." Irene pulled the card

116

from Kenny and tore it into tiny bits.

Kenny grabbed her hand and poured the scraps into his side pocket. Irene folded her arms across her bosom. "What else will he come up with?"

The Scouts marched forward with the pledge cards and placed them on a table.

At that moment, George Lawrence walked down the aisle and handed a note to Mr. Stiles. Stiles studied it and appeared to wipe a tear from his eye. Taking a deep breath, he read the note to the congregation. "Carol Somers collapsed early this morning. The doctors worked on her for three hours. Carol died at ten. Arrangements will be announced soon."

He put the note aside and hesitated for just a moment to settle his emotions. "For those who do not know, Carol suffered from cancer for fifteen years. She and her husband Frank came to Ironton Corner to take over the family business, Somers' Meat Packing and Grocery. They have one son, Jimmy. Please hold the family in your hearts."

Friends of the Somers dissolved in grief. They moved in slow motion to the front door of the church. Mr. Stiles touched each shoulder as they passed—some crying softly; others shaking their heads at the news.

***

Maida, Irene, and Kenny settled at the Keenes' kitchen table. "This will be Mr. Stiles' first funeral." Irene poured hot water into three cups.

Kenny swished a tea bag through the hot water while staring vacantly out the window. "He was really broken up."

"Was he? Or were they just words?" Irene wiped at her eyes.

"Irene," Maida spoke softly, "that's your grief talking."

"I'm sorry. We've lived with Carol's illness for a long time, and we knew she was near death, but I wasn't ready." Irene squeezed her eyelids tight. Tears brimmed over and tumbled down her cheeks.

The ring of the phone jarred the grief-laden air. Kenny jumped up. "Hello … Mr. Stiles … Yes, I know their plot … I'll prepare the grave."

Kenny slid his chair back under the table. "I need to go." He reached down and kissed the top of Irene's head.

Over the next few days, Maida arranged food for Jimmy and Frank. Irene gathered a group of women. They arrived at Frank and Carol's and cleaned the house, as was the custom. No one knew when this custom began, but it helped the family, and it gave grieving friends something to do. Frank and Jimmy escaped to the porch while the women worked.

Before the women left, Frank found Irene in the kitchen. "I need to decide what clothes to give the funeral home for Carol. It's the one thing she didn't plan. What would you suggest?"

"She looked smart in her navy suit and red blouse."

"Will you get those for me? I can't go into our bedroom."

Irene could feel Carol's presence as she pushed through the hangers in her closet. She found the suit and blouse. Then her eye caught a sparkly patriotic pin on the dresser. She laid the jacket on the bed and attached the pin to the lapel.

Downstairs she handed the hanger of clothes to Frank. Jimmy caught the glint of the pin. "Mrs. Keene, I gave my mother that pin for Christmas."

"I didn't know." Irene reached out and gently touched Jimmy's shoulder.

Frank cleared his throat. "Driving out to get the paper this morning, I pulled into the cemetery and watched Kenny tending to Carol's grave." He choked back tears. "I thought I'd be ready."

Irene hugged him, knowing there was no need for words.

* * *

Wednesday at 10 a.m., friends, family, townspeople, and customers who shopped at the Somers' market lingered in tight bundles on the church steps due to the cold of this January day. At the sound of the organ, they filed in and filled the pews. A carpet of roses lay over the casket. Baskets and vases of flowers consumed the altar. The High Street Choir sang hymns until the funeral director led Jimmy, Frank, and Mr. Stiles into the sanctuary.

Stiles walked to the microphone. With a voice softer than normal, he led the bereaved through the service. At the end, they joined in singing

"Amazing grace, how sweet the sound,
that saved a wretch like me!

I once was lost, but now I'm found,
was blind but now I see."

The mourners trailed behind the pall bearers to Carol's gravesite. Jimmy and Frank laid red roses on the casket. The Boy Scouts added multicolored Gerbera daisies. Stiles did the same, but knelt and remained kneeling, his shoulders shaking. The funeral director waited before leaning down, and whispering in Stiles' ear. He helped Stiles to his feet.

Stiles walked over to Jimmy and Frank. "I'm sorry. I didn't mean to break down. It was unprofessional of me, but my grandmother ..." Frank and Jimmy hugged Stiles to them, while the funeral director quietly invited everyone to Fellowship Hall to share in lunch and greet Jimmy and Frank. Engaged in hushed conversations, the crowd walked slowly back to the church.

Kenny and his men folded the fake green carpet and placed it in the truck. Kenny leaned against the truck. "This one has taken the stuffing out of me."

Gus lowered the lid of the vault on the casket, and Roy locked it. The three men shoveled the piles of dirt over the casket, tamped it down, and arranged the baskets of flowers over the created hill. Kenny tried to hand each of the men their usual envelope, but they pushed the envelopes away. "Give it to the boy," Roy said.

Gus shoved his hands in his pockets; his shoulders slumped. "I'm going to sure miss Carol at the market. No one made me feel more special than she."

"She was the kindest person I believe I ever met." Roy reached over and squeezed Kenny's shoulder for just a moment.

Kenny pulled a large handkerchief from his back pocket and wiped his eyes. "I'll give you this—Mr. Stiles knows how to handle a funeral."

* * *

After the reception and lunch, Stiles, responding to Frank and Jimmy's invitation, followed them home. They settled around the kitchen table. "Coffee ..." Frank asked.

"No thanks. I had plenty at the reception."

"Mr. Stiles, what you did today for us ... and ... Mom ... well ... it was just great." Jimmy played with his Scout ring.

"I tried to do what I thought you and your dad needed." Stiles pushed his glasses up in position. "Your mother made me think of my grandmother, so it helped me, too."

"What do you mean?" Jimmy asked with a puzzled expression on his face.

"My grandmother showed me the same kind of love your mother showed you and your dad. It felt good to remember."

Frank cleared his throat. "Jimmy and I have been talking about a memorial for Carol. We'd like to contribute to one of your dreams."

Stiles leaned back. "Frank, thank you. What do you have in mind?"

"We'd like you to make a suggestion."

"Last Sunday I kicked off a campaign to replace the steeple. You could contribute to that."

"Yes, I heard, and we will, but we want to—"

Jimmy interrupted. "Do something that would be all our own with my mother's name on it. You know the Carol Somers blah, blah, blah."

"One of my dreams is to have a pool complex in the basement of the church."

"That's a swell idea." Jimmy's eyes sparkled.

Frank pulled at his chin. "A pool? Can an old building like ours have a pool in the basement? Or have you already checked?" Frank looked over the top of his glasses. "You always seem to be miles ahead of us."

"Yes, I've checked. With our town so close to the ocean, I think all of the children need swimming lessons. And if the church could provide this service to the community ..."

"Gr-r-r-eat." Jimmy's voice cracked like the adolescent he was.

"You run with it, and we'll pay for it. But, it'll be our little secret until it's completed. Okay?" Frank reached across the table to shake Mr. Stiles' hand.

"Then we'll have a grand opening, and Dad and I will cut the ribbon and jump in the pool together shouting, 'The Carol Somers Pool Complex ... a gift from Frank and Jimmy Somers.' "

"We'll do it." Stiles pushed his chair back and stood. "I need to go, but we'll do it." He slipped into his coat and started down the front walk.

Frank called after him. "Thanks for everything. We need to get you ordained before some other church comes along and steals you away from us."

Stiles almost skipped to his car. Frank's words about his ordination sparked an idea. He turned on the car radio and tapped his fingers on the wheel as he drove back to the church. He parked his car and walked around the green with his back straight and his chest high. He smiled over at the Keenes' house. "Irene, it's going to happen. I'll be the official savior of the church and community. Are you ready?"

In his office, he danced around with Frederic before opening his satchel and pulling out binder #4 "Pool Complex." He read through it, making a few notes as he read. He replaced "Chopin's Funeral March" with "Handel's Hallelujah Chorus" on the record player, performing his ritual as the music played.

The Chronicle of Matthew Henry Stiles
January 12, 1969

Frank, thank you. Your determined statement about getting me ordained sparked an idea. I will lay the groundwork to adopt the ways of the independent Baptist Churches where each church ordains their own minister without any assistance or recommendations from a higher body. What higher body does the church need? Doesn't it only need the sincere commitment of one of God's servants? We will leave the Unitarians completely out of it. We will be independent. I'll not have to answer to anyone. Independence and industry are highly valued in this New England culture. The idea will be an easy sell.

Frederic, my grief was on full display at the gravesite. I knelt and felt an aura of glory on my head like that of Jesus in the Garden of Gethsemane grieving for his own death. As I straightened, I read in Irene's eyes that I touched her soul. Now I know she is just another female impressed by my presence.

He switched off the lamp and sat in the dark. From the glow of the street lamp outside his office, Stiles stared at the typewriter's keys. Lifting his index finger, he pounded each letter to type the last sentence of his entry.

> They loved me today. They really loved me. I have to ar-
> range a meeting with Arthur.

Stiles rolled the sheet out of the typewriter. He filed it, and fell asleep in his office chair.

A month later, Stiles placed a call to Arthur. "Arthur, we need to talk. When would it be convenient for you to come to my office?"

"Late this afternoon."

"That would be fine. Joyce will be gone, so we won't be inter-rupted.

"Is this serious?"

"Yes."

Stiles hung up the phone and fiddled around his office, mak-ing stacks and dusting shelves. "Matthew, stop it. You have the upper hand. What is making you so nervous? Leroy helped you with your script. Frederic will help me stick to it. I don't want my temper—" Hearing someone enter the church offices, he stopped his dialogue and tossed the dust rag in a drawer. Straightening his jacket, he opened the door.

"Arthur, come in." Before he closed the door, he hung a Do Not Disturb sign on the doorknob in case George came by. "Have a seat."

Two hours later, Stiles wrote in big letters on a legal pad. "First Independent Community Church of Ironton Corner." He tore off the sheet and put it in his chronicle file.

Folding a check from Arthur, he slid it in his pocket. He stared at Frederic. "Frederic, as you heard, Arthur is going to lay the ground work for the church council meeting. You watched him read over the research I'd put together on independent churches. He was amazed at their success stories. When he finally admit-ted how little the denomination had done for this church over the years, I had him. Of course my little threats about slowly revealing Barbara's history helped, didn't they?"

CHAPTER 19

March 17, 1969

CHET prepared the back room of the diner for a meeting of the First Parish Council. As the council members straggled in, he motioned toward the room.

Arthur chaired the meeting. "I sent each one of you a packet of information concerning the ordination of Matthew Henry Stiles. From reading the materials you know that he is asking us to bypass the Unitarians and ordain him ourselves. I've talked with each of you individually and know your questions and concerns. Now it's time to focus our thoughts and opinions and come to an agreement."

"Right, Jimmy and I are ready. We've been ready for a long time. As we told Arthur, we don't want to lose him to another church." Frank punctuated his statement by slapping his hands on the table.

Jimmy Somers, now fourteen and serving as the youth representative to the council, followed his Dad's comments. "He's done so much for the Scouts. And what he did for my mom, I can't tell you ..."

Delbert pushed at his thinning hair. "I'm not ready. He feels there is no need for checks and balances."

Frank said, "Delbert, you worry too much. I like the idea that we ordain him ourselves ... an independent community church, doesn't that sound just like us New Englanders ... independent?"

Delbert set his elbows on the table, rubbing his hand together. "I read that propaganda Arthur sent. Not all of the community churches are successful. Some fall into financial decline very quickly. And with Stiles' stubborn attitude about our church funds, I fear he'd lead us to bankruptcy in a short time."

"But you have control of the money—you write the checks, how can he spend our money without you knowing it?" Frank's face turned red in frustration.

"I've checked with a couple of friends at other churches, and they've ordained pastors." Maida scanned the faces around the table. "Arthur, what kind of support have we received from the Unitarians over the years?"

"They've supplied us with the names of potential pastors and student pastors the past few years," Arthur responded.

"Other than that?" Maida persisted. No one answered Maida's question.

Clyde Weaver pushed his chair back and stood. "Where I lived in Boston, all the local Baptist Churches ordained their own pastors." He let out a hearty laugh. "Yes, all a guy had to do was speak in tongues, swoon a little, and a store-front church opened in his name. Some made it and some didn't, but none of them ever accomplished what Mr. Stiles has accomplished in his short time with us. There are times, people, when we must take a risk, and I believe this is such a time." Clyde returned to his seat.

Arthur waited and after no one offered a comment, he reached in a folder and pulled out some other papers. He passed them around the table. "This is a draft of the contract that Frank, Mr. Stiles, and I have drawn up if we decide to independently ordain him."

A silence hung over the table while they read.

Delbert bellowed. "Hey, wait a minute. President of the Fellowship? That can't be. You realize the president, in the absence of the treasurer, is given the power to handle the church finances —to sign checks and manage our trust funds. We can't let this happen."

"Calm down, Delbert." Bruce Easley leaned back in his chair. "Since your children are grown, you don't know about all of Mr. Stiles' gifts. I know enough to support ordaining him now."

"I will never agree to this." Delbert pushed back his chair, wadded up the paper, and threw it on the table.

The council watched Delbert walk out.

Irene turned to Arthur. "Arthur, don't you remember that pastor, when we were teens, that about led us into bankruptcy?"

Frank interrupted. "I read the reports. The council hired him on the advice of the Unitarians. Later the denomination told us they'd never fully investigated the man. We've known Mr. Stiles for two years, and yes, he's quirky, but he has done so much for us, isn't that enough for you, Irene?" Frank asked.

"Why is his ordination so important to him? Why can't everything stay the way it is?" asked Sarah Easley.

Arthur focused on Sarah. "He'll leave soon if we don't make a move. He wants the title of Reverend."

"And President?" Clyde asked.

"Yes, in name only, he assures me." The blotches appeared on Arthur's neck.

"Well, folks," Clyde cleared his voice. "I read the 1967 agreement that you made with Mr. Stiles when he first came. It indicates that we'd consider ordination within two years. He's proven his abilities by the physical improvements, the growth in membership, activities, and even making it possible for my family to call this church home. I move that we ordain Mr. Matthew Henry Stiles, but I recommend that we add a clause that reads something like, 'upon ordination, Mr. Stiles will give us sixty days' notice if he determines he needs to terminate his contract with us. Likewise, the Parish Council will give Mr. Stiles sixty days' notice if the council finds Mr. Stiles in violation of his contract."

Jimmy shouted out, "I second the motion."

"All those in favor of the motion that's been made and seconded raise your hand." Arthur said. "The motion's been passed. I'll inform Mr. Stiles, and we will work out the details of date and time for the ordination. Jimmy, go out and tell Chet we're ready for our dinner."

Barbara and Arthur walked by the darkened church on their way home from the diner. A voice called from the shadows of the front steps. "What's the news, Arthur?"

"Mr. Stiles, you frightened us." Barbara looked into the dark.

Stiles stepped out of the shadows.

A strong shiver ran up Arthur's spine. "Yes, you will be The Reverend Stiles. I'll call you to work out the details."

"I saw Delbert Martin scurry by the windows from my office. I suppose he doesn't agree."

"He has his concerns, but he'll be fine." Arthur managed to keep his voice even and calm.

"I'll contact Delbert and make amends."

"I think he needs some time, Mr. Stiles." Barbara stepped toward him, her heels clicked on the pavement.

Stiles shrank back from Barbara. He did not know how to deal with her strength and nausea swept over him. "I'll take that under advisement."

"I hope you do." Barbara tugged Arthur's arm, and they walked on.

Chapter 20

April 10, 1969

STILES dialed the number for First Bank of Ironton Corner and asked for Delbert Martin. "Delbert, I want an opportunity to clear up any misunderstanding between us. I'd like you and Lois to join me for dinner tonight at the Tavern on the Pond."

"Unless you are ready to commit ..." Delbert attempted to say.

"Delbert, I have a plan ... a divinely inspired plan. Call Lois and see if you can join me tonight?"

"I'll call her and get back with you." Delbert held the receiver away from his ear thinking, "What's he up to now?" He shrugged and dialed Lois.

"Hi, Honey, Stiles called and wants us to join him for dinner."

"Why? You didn't accept, did you?"

"I told him I'd check with you."

"Why didn't you just tell him no?"

"He says he has a plan."

"Do you really want to meet with that man?"

"If I stay in contact with him, at least I'll know what he's up to."

"Okay, but if it gets uncomfortable, I'll fake a headache or something. You've already had words with him. I'm worried what meeting him face-to-face will do to you."

Stiles finished his workday and drove to the Tavern. As he pulled into the circular driveway, the valet rushed to his car. "Good evening again, Mr. Stiles."

"Chip. How's your restoration project going?"

Chip gestured toward the far corner of the parking lot. "There she is." A lemon-colored 1952 Chevy Bel Air convertible gleamed in the late afternoon sun. "She's a real beauty, isn't she?"

"Sure is." Stiles put his arm over Chip's shoulder. "Next you can work on my 1949 Cadillac that is stored at my parents."

"I don't think I'm ready for a high-priced car." Chip shrugged.

Stiles smiled at the boy, straightened his shoulders, and walked to the door. The maître d' met him. "You're looking sharp tonight, Mr. Stiles." Tony brushed a tiny piece of non-existent lint from Stiles' jacket. "I have the table ready that you requested."

Tony escorted Stiles across the dining room. He pulled out an upholstered chair and held it for Mr. Stiles. Once he was settled, Tony unfolded the white dinner napkin and draped it over Stiles' lap.

Stiles slipped a twenty dollar bill into Tony's hand. "Make sure I get the check, and as soon as they get seated, pour the wine."

"Yes, sir. Is there anything you need before your party arrives?"

"No, nothing. I'll enjoy the quiet." Stiles smiled.

Lois and Delbert pulled up to the valet service of the Tavern. Chip greeted them, helped Lois from the car, and parked their car next to Stiles. The Martins walked arm in arm to the glass doors that opened automatically as they stepped near.

"Welcome, Mr. and Mrs. Martin. Mr. Stiles is already seated. Follow me." The maître d' escorted them to the table.

Stiles stood and greeted Lois with a nod and Delbert with a handshake. "Thanks for joining me." Stiles held Lois' chair and then slipped back into his. "I was sorry to have missed bridge club last month. I needed to see my parents about my pending ordination."

"Is there a date set for your ordination?" Lois asked, unfolding the white damask dinner napkin.

"Not until he understands who is in charge of our finances." Delbert enunciated every syllable of every word.

Stiles laid his hand on Lois'. "I understand, once a dollar and cents man, always one."

Lois pulled her hand away and wiped it on her napkin.

Stiles motioned to their waiter who presented each person with a menu. They made their choices for dinner.

Lois handed her menu to the waiter and turned to talk to Stiles.

"Back to your parents, have they been to Ironton Corner?"

"No, but they've looked up its history. From their investigation, they find it hard to understand why I came to such a small place. They envisioned me in a church in Boston. When they see the potential of Ironton Corner and what I've accomplished, they will understand."

"Why did you come here to Ironton Corner? With your ego, I would have thought you would have wanted the church in Cambridge or Wellesley." Delbert sawed at his pork chops.

"As you know I read about your church, and God said, "Ironton Corner may not have been the place you dreamed of for your ministry, but I want you to go there. It is there that you will build a kingdom for me."

Delbert swallowed the first words that came to his mind and instead said, "If you fail, will you be blaming God, or us, or yourself?"

"Delbert, I will not fail with or without your cooperation."

Lois' fork bounced on her plate. "Mr. Stiles, your success or failure is not dependent on my husband. It is on you being honest and supportive of all the people who come through the church doors."

Stiles stared at her, surprised as he reassessed his opinion of Lois. In previous dealings, he had pegged her for another docile female.

An uncomfortable silence stood over the table.

Stiles touched his napkin to his lips, folded it, and placed it next to his plate. Laying both hands flat on the table on either side of his plate, he addressed Delbert. "The week after my ordination, we will have a ceremony in the church honoring your service as treasurer as you graciously pass the responsibility of the church finances over to me. I've prayed about this and with the help of the Divine, this is the plan. In fact," Stiles reached into his jacket inner pocket, "here is your speech."

Delbert grabbed the card and ripped it in two pieces. "Leave the Divine out of your scheming. You are full of it." Delbert fumed.

Stiles adjusted the white cotton handkerchief in his jacket's breast pocket. "During that service, I will announce that Frank will serve as my assistant. Delbert, this change will be the best for the church." Stiles leaned into Delbert's personal space. "And Arthur supports me all the way."

"Best for the church or best for you? You already have Frank in your pocket. He'd give you permission to do anything you wanted. And you've had Arthur backed into some sort of corner since you arrived. I'm the only one who is strong enough to keep you from destroying our church." Drops of perspiration accumulated on Delbert's forehead.

Stiles snapped to attention. "Frankly, Delbert, during the years that you've been in charge of the church money, you've had a conflict of interest. What, with you working for the bank that holds the church trusts, serving as the treasurer, and keeping the financial records under lock and key in the church office. Delbert, how do we know what's really been going on? During your personal lean years, you might have—"

"Skimmed off the top? You are even more evil than I thought." Delbert rose, pushed back his chair, and helped Lois to her feet. He exploded. "I'll be hanged if I let you have control over the church funds." He fished in his pocket, threw a ten on the table, pushed Lois ahead of him and in his haste bumped into a table of guests. Stiles remained seated at the table.

Outside the front door, Delbert, a little short of breath, demanded, "My car, Chip."

Chip, sensing an emergency, hurried to Delbert's car, swung it into the curved driveway, left the drivers' door open for Delbert and ran around to the other side and held the door for Lois. With a worried look on his face, Chip watched the Martin's car swerve a little as it exited the parking lot.

Inside the maître d' rushed over to Mr. Stiles. "Is everything all right?"

"Just fine. Please bring me a bottle of '64 Inglenook Cabernet Sauvignon," Stiles smiled up at Tony.

"Did your guests enjoy their dinner?"

"They did. They lost track of time. He had a medication he needed to take." Stiles shrugged.

The maître d' brought a clean glass, uncorked the bottle, and poured a little for Stiles to taste. "Wonderful, Tony."

Alone now and moving the glass to his lip, he rolled the wine around in his mouth. A smug look covered his face. He lifted the glass, and offered a toast to his reflection in the window. "Here's to the future president and treasurer of the First Independent Community Church of Ironton Corner."

Stiles finished the last sip of wine and a slow smile spread over his face. He stood and stretched to his full height admiring his reflection in the window as he pulled a tip from his pocket and headed to the front door to settle the rest of the check. Chip ran to get his car. Stiles climbed in and drove to the church.

He wore a half-cocked grin as he unlocked the door to his office. Picking up his satchel, he placed it on his desk. He removed the binder labeled "Delbert Martin." He located the phone number and placed the call.

CHAPTER 21

April 11, 1969

THE Martins couldn't sleep. Lois made tea and they sat together on their worn sofa. Lois broke the silence. "What nerve he had. Everyone knows you're an honest man. What is he insinuating?"

"He's clever. At the council meeting, Arthur presented a contract that Arthur, Frank, and Mr. Stiles created. If agreed to, Stiles would be named president and treasurer of the congregation. I walked out."

Lois set her tea cup down on the coffee table with a bang. "With that sort of contract, that young man would have access to all the church finances. What were Arthur and Frank thinking?"

"I learned a long time ago that some strange arrangement exists between Arthur and Mr. Stiles. I have seen how anxious Arthur becomes whenever Mr. Stiles' name comes up, and I think it is affecting his health, too. Frank is blinded by the attention Mr. Stiles gave to Jimmy and him throughout Carol's illness."

Delbert stopped, studied his tea, and swirled his teaspoon gently in the cup. "Now he accuses me of wrongdoing. Lois, even if he's named president, I'll fight for control over the endowments and savings. He can have the check book. He can't do much with the small balance that we carry. If I insist on a group of us counting the weekly offering then ..." Delbert leaned his head back on the sofa and his entire body relaxed.

Lois reached over and massaged his temples and gave him a lingering kiss. "You are a good man, Delbert Martin."

"I think I can sleep now," he answered. Hand in hand they climbed the stairs.

Settled in bed, Lois reached for her husband and cuddled up to the warmth of his back feeling the comfort that had always existed between them after a crisis.

The next morning Delbert woke and gently unwound from Lois, not wanting to wake her. He showered, dressed, and started breakfast as he did every day.

Lois tiptoed into the kitchen and pressed against Delbert's back, reaching her arms around him while he turned the eggs. "Feel better, honey?"

"Yes, a little. I think I'll take a walk in Findlay State Park for my lunch break."

"That sounds like a good idea. I'll make you a sandwich, so you don't have to waste time picking one up." Lois opened the refrigerator and laid the sandwich makings on the counter.

"Thanks." Delbert plated their breakfast. "You are so good to me." They held each other for a while, reaffirming the love they shared. "Hey." He held her chin up so he could see her eyes. "Tomorrow is our anniversary. What if, we leave after your day at school and get away for a couple of days?"

"Yes, let's do that. I'll get Daisy a dog sitter. She won't miss us for a couple of days. We both could do with some time away from Ironton Corner."

* * *

Late in the day, Chief John Bird received a call from State Police Captain, Dick Rogers. "John, my boys are out at Findlay State Park. A hiker found a body. I'm on my way out there. I'd appreciate it if you could join me."

"Sure, but who's the victim?"

"They think it's Delbert Martin, but I can't believe it. He and Lois had dinner at our house last week for my dad's birthday. I'm hoping that there is some mistake."

John Bird stared at the wall. He leaned back in his chair, pulled a handkerchief from his back pocket, and blew his nose. A bit dazed, he stood in front of his secretary's desk. "That was Dick Rogers. A body has been found in the State Park. I'm going out there."

Blue flashing lights surrounded the park entry. When Bird pulled up, Dick Rogers was getting out of his car. They shook hands and, without a word, walked along a tree-lined path. As they neared the scene, they spotted the yellow crime scene tape and their steps slowed. Bird nodded to a trooper. The trooper lifted the drape from the body.

"I can't believe it." Bird's face drained.

Rogers choked up. "Delbert? Why?"

Their shadows fell across the body. Bird turned away, kicked at the dirt. Rogers fell to his knees alongside Delbert and made the sign of the cross for his cousin.

Rogers struggled up. "There's a gunshot wound to his head, a pistol on the ground. Looks like suicide, but we'll be doing a full investigation. John, will you inform Lois while I finish up here?"

"Are you sure you want to stay with him being family and all?"

"It's my job, John, but thank you."

"I'll contact Mr. Stiles and see if he wants to go with me to inform Lois. Keep in touch." Bird blew his nose.

Rogers grasped Bird's shoulder. "Tell Lois I'm sorry, and I'll stop by tonight. My dad is going to take this hard. Delbert is his only nephew. Dad always bragged that Delbert became a banker because he wanted to be like his uncle."

Back in town, Chief Bird stopped by the church. Tipping his hat to Joyce, he knocked on Stiles' door. He pushed the door open and held his hat in his hands. He ran his fingers around the band, searching for the right words. "A hiker found Delbert Martin dead in Findlay State Park."

"Delbert? What happened?" Stiles stood and leaned against the file.

Bird slumped into a ladder-back chair. "A gunshot wound to his head."

"Suicide?"

Bird straightened. "State Police Captain Dick Rogers is handling the case. He says there'll be a complete investigation."

"What can I do?" Stiles stepped close to Bird and noticed the redness around Bird's eyes.

"Rogers asked me to inform Lois. Since you're her pastor, I thought you'd like to go along with me."

"Why..." Stiles caught himself, and his face colored. "I'm sorry. I'm just shocked by the news. I had dinner with them last night.

Of course, I'll go with you."

"Thanks. I need to check in at the office. I'll meet you at the Martins' house in fifteen minutes."

Bird left.

Stiles snatched a paper from the side drawer of his desk and threaded it in his typewriter. It caught in the roller. He ripped it out, grabbed another sheet, and took a deep breath. He began to type; the keys stuck. He swatted at Frederic and yelled, "Why now? What's wrong with this damned machine?" He pried the keys apart and yanked the paper out, tearing it. Without proofreading his words, he unlocked the file, pulled the drawer out one inch, and rolled the drawer in and out three times, but this time it brought him no peace. He shoved the torn page into the chronicle folder. Stiles slammed the drawer shut. Frederic's bones rattled against the metal. The rattle stopped him in his tracks. He looked into Frederic's eye sockets. "I'm sorry."

* * *

Dressed in a fresh shirt, Stiles pulled in behind the Ironton Corner police cruiser parked in front of Delbert and Lois' tree-shaded gray Cape with white trim. The two men walked up the brick walkway lined with purple and white impatiens to a fire engine red front door. Bird lifted the eagle-shaped knocker and rapped. A few moments passed and he knocked again. Lois opened the door with a wet dog wiggling under her arm.

Bird reached in and scratched Daisy, who twisted and squirmed out of Lois' grasp. Her eyes passed from one man to the other. Bird wrapped his arm around Lois' shoulder and guided her inside to the sofa. Daisy jumped into Lois' apron-covered lap, and Bird squeezed close in at her side. Stiles closed the door and took a chair across from the sofa.

Lois whispered. "What happened? Tell me."

"A hiker found Delbert dead in Findlay State Park—a gunshot wound to his head. I'm sorry."

The color drained from her face. She grasped Bird's arm and took several deep breaths. She leaned into Bird, and her body shook with grief. Daisy huddled closer, her warmth radiating into

Lois. Stiles watched.

She tried to speak between sobs. "Are you sure? Who would shoot Delbert?" Lois gasped and pushed her arms against Bird, so she could see his eyes. "Not suicide. Not suicide. Not my Delbert. He had no reason, nothing to hide. He had no enemies."

She turned. Her eyes focused on Stiles. A cold chill stabbed at her heart. Standing up, an overwhelming anger put her in control for a few moments and energized her to fight against her pain. "I need to call my children."

Stiles crossed the room and reached for Lois' shoulder. She brushed his hand away and snarled between her teeth like a wounded animal. "Don't touch me. Take this man away. I don't want to see him." She walked to the desk with Daisy clutched in her arms.

Bird's eyebrow shot up at the interchange. "Lois, I don't want you to be alone. Do you mind if we wait in the kitchen?"

"Just get him out of my sight and contact Irene and Maida. Ask them to come." Lois sat at her desk.

"Sure." Bird sent Stiles to the kitchen and asked if he could use the phone. After he finished, he went into the kitchen.

Stiles sat at the table. Bird leaned against the counter that was covered with wet towels and dog shampoo. Miserable with grief and looking for something to do, he cleaned up the counter. He heard Lois sob between smatterings of words. "Couldn't be suicide ... a thorough investigation ... Stiles ... treasurer ... your dad ...yes ... I need you." For a few moments the only sound they heard was Daisy whimpering her lament.

After a long silence, Stiles started for the door. Bird stuck out his arm. "Let's give her a few more minutes."

Bird heard the front door open and the voices of Irene and Maida. The men quietly entered the room and found the three women huddled together on the sofa. They watched Daisy climb to the back of the sofa and drape herself against Lois' head.

Lois looked into Stiles' eyes with a cold blank stare. "We'll be taking Delbert to Maine for the services and burial at my parents' church." Her voice strengthened, and she enunciated her words. "Mr. Stiles, we won't need your services."

Stiles did not move a muscle.

Bird knelt in front of Lois. "When the news of this gets out, reporters and TV crews will camp in front of your house. I'll post men twenty-four hours a day to try to keep them a good distance away."

Lois reached out and grasped his hands. "Thanks, John."

Irene smiled into Bird's eyes. "We'll take good care of her. You take care of yourself. I know your job is harder when the tragedy involves friends."

Chief Bird seized Stiles' elbow and walked him to his car. "What was that look she gave you? Her words were cold. What is going on between you two?"

"I have no idea, but you know how grief affects others—people do strange things." Stiles struggled free from Bird's grip.

Bird noted the twitch in Stiles' eye. "I've seen grief affect people in many ways over the years, but her look wasn't anything I've ever seen. It was more than grief. Are you sure you have no idea?"

"I have no idea at all." Stiles straightened his back, turned on his heel, with head held high, climbed into his car, and pulled slowly away from the curb watching the chief through his rear view window.

Bird shook his head at Stiles' attitude, glanced back at the house, and lowered his head in his own grief. After a few moments, he found his strength renewed and returned to the scene of the crime at Findlay State Park.

Chapter 22

STILES sat at the typewriter and attempted to calm himself with his trinity. As he completed each step—Father, Son and Holy Ghost—no sense of peace prevailed. His mind raced as he began to type. He tried to focus on the keys.

>The Chronicle of Matthew Henry Stiles
>April 20, 1969
>Gossip and false reports about the death in the park are swirling through the congregation. A feeling of unease and suspicion is smothering everyone. I need to lift their spirits. The tragedy of Delbert's death will bring more worshippers than usual today.
>After my sermon, I'll descend from the pulpit and speak to the people on their level. I will gather their pain into me just as Dr. Pigget demonstrated in her acting class.
>I don't understand why Lois didn't want to hold Delbert's funeral here. She cannot see the big plan. I cannot expect her to understand that all I do is for my congregation. I am their guide and their comforter. It is I who must make the hard decisions. This morning, although the service will not be an official funeral, I'll be doing my part to soothe the people.

He walked to the file cabinet, pulled the drawer open and shut three times, and filed the entry. Up in his room, he showered and took meticulous care while dressing—crisp shirt, paisley tie, gold eagle cuff links and a newly pressed and cleaned suit. He'd shined his shoes the night before, and they gleamed. He studied his image in his full length mirror and added a monogrammed, white cotton handkerchief with delicate black trim. "Matthew, it's perfect for today—refined but not overdone."

He descended the stairs from his rooms. As he turned through the back hall, he peeked into the sanctuary. It was filled; ushers were squeezing late comers into the pews. After the opening and the lighting of candles, many for Delbert and his family, Stiles climbed up the steps to the pulpit and made eye contact with each person before he began to read,

> Fear not, for I have redeemed you; I have called you by name, you are mine. When you pass through the waters, I will be with you; and through the rivers, they shall not over-whelm you; when you walk through fire you shall not be burned, and the flame shall not consume you. Isaiah 43:1, 2.

He adjusted his glasses. "The death of Delbert Martin has shocked all of us. Fear not. We need to understand that something bigger than us will carry us through these dark and fearful times. I will be with you. Our community will come through this. The fires of the tragedy will not consume us. We will learn from it and grow into stronger people. Fear not, fear not the waters, the fires, I will be with you."

After his sermon, he stepped to the floor of the sanctuary. "Again I say as God would have me say to you, don't let fear consume your lives. Our local police and the State Police are on high alert. They want us to go about our business as usual. I've asked Chief Bird and Captain Rogers to be with us this morning. They will be in Fellowship Hall after worship to answer any questions you may have and dispel some of the vicious gossip that has already started.

"Focus on the barometer that is tracking the collection of money for the steeple. We will have that new steeple by fall. When it's installed, you'll have the sign of hope that's been missing for years.

"And if you're having a tough day, be a sidewalk superintendent. Watch the foundation of the church being stabilized or the construction of the pool complex. Look forward to the annual summer picnic.

"Realize that I am grieving the death of Delbert Martin along with you. I make these suggestions as ways to lift your spirits, even for a moment, along this hard road we have to travel. If I can be of any help to you, don't hesitate to call."

After the service, George and Maida congratulated Stiles on his words and compassion. A small group gathered at the back of the church to meet with Chief Bird and Captain Rogers.

For the rest of the week, Stiles watched others observing the construction and engaging the workers. In their nightly phone calls, Leroy suggested that he go out among his congregation in a hard hat to mingle and visit. He did this frequently and talked with his parishioners. Chief Bird or one of his deputies watched Stiles every action.

* * *

Toward the end of May, Arthur asked Stiles to meet him in his home office. "The last few weeks you have made bold announcements during the worship service. Are you sure we'll have the funds for the steeple? The money's coming in, but I told you we can't afford to have a large debt to meet your schedule." Arthur thumbed his fingers along the wooden spokes of his chair.

"It's all covered. My parents are coming through with the remainder. After, you give me another two thousand."

"I told you."

"And I told you." Stiles pulled an envelope from his brief case, waved it in the air, and then filed it back in the case.

Arthur struggled for breath as he reached into his desk for his checkbook. His hand visibly shook as he wrote the check.

"Get more medications for your anxiety. The struggling for breath and the red rash popping out on your neck are becoming tedious. Get it into your head: you are in this for the long haul. And that wife of yours, she needs—"

"You agreed to leave Barbara out of this."

Stiles turned his eyes away from Arthur and put the check in his pocket. "I will if you continue to cooperate. I have accomplished so much with your monetary support. You need to understand that you will be supporting me for a long time to come. It might even be time to raise the amount of your monthly gift to me."

Barbara knocked and peeked in. "Are you two done with your business?" She felt the tension in the room. "Are you okay?"

"Honey, we just finished. Mr. Stiles had a few complaints, and we were discussing how to approach each situation."

Barbara raised her eyebrows, and then lowered them taking in a soft breath. "Mr. Stiles, won't you join us for cheesecake?"

"I have to meet an old friend." Stiles gathered his brief case and walked out of Arthur's office and toward the front door.

"Too bad, it's delicious," Barbara said as she opened the door.

"I promise the next time I have an appointment with Arthur, I'll stay and have some with you. I'm sorry." Stiles stepped out the door.

Barbara and Arthur watched Stiles walk down the stone path to his car.

"Arthur, look at him."

"It looks like he's doing some kind of tap-tap dance."

She turned her face up to Arthur. "You look exhausted."

"I am. I need to go upstairs."

They climbed the imposing staircase, his breathing labored. She stripped his shirt and rubbed his chest. He stood lifeless as she slid his pants and jockeys down and he stepped out of them. "Lay down. I'll rub your back." He watched as she unbuttoned her blouse, slipped out of her bra and threw them on a chair. She smiled while removing her slacks and silk panties. Opening a bottle of the lotion, she squeezed some out and warmed it in her hands.

She straddled him and began making slow circular motions on his back. Gentle murmuring came from him as his muscles relaxed. After a while, he turned over and with her on top of him, sucked her breasts. He held back as long as he could and then burst. She lay on top of him and ran her fingers through his hair and over his eyes and circled his mouth. They smiled deeply into each other's souls.

"I am so lucky to have you Barbara. The difference in our ages ..."

She put her hand over his mouth. "Arthur, now don't start that talk about our ages. I love you more than you could ever know." Rolling off him, she hugged her pillow and fell asleep tucked up against him. He stayed with his arms locked around her until he heard her slow breathing. Carefully pulling his arms away, he laid back and his mind turned to Stiles. He tossed and turned for an hour before he finally crawled out of bed.

He stood in front of the mirror and murmured to himself, "What have you done?" He reached for his robe and pulled it tight around him as if covering his shame before making his way downstairs to his office.

* * *

Too tired to sleep, Stiles slipped down to his office. "I told Barbara Blankenship that I had a meeting with an old friend tonight. You are my old friend, Frederic."

As he talked to Frederic, he readied himself in front to the typewriter.

The Chronicle of Matthew Henry Stiles
May 20, 1969
Arthur knows I'm holding all the cards. He may break and tell all to that wife of his but the good news is that I'm off tomorrow with the Boy Scouts to New York City.

Frederic, the arrangements are in place for me to meet with Leroy's friend to secure a number of the letters of the founder of the Boy Scouts for The Museums of Ironton Corner.

After he filed this chronicle entry, he opened his satchel and pulled out several binders and placed them on his desk. He checked for any last minutes details for the pool and steeple. Finding that all was in order and everything completed by October, he opened a binder labeled, "Ordination Details."

CHAPTER 23

October 11, 1969

STILES' parents took a late afternoon flight from Akron to Boston and rented a town car to drive the forty-five miles to Ironton Corner. Stiles spotted the black Lincoln and walked out of his office to greet them.

His mother, Alice, dressed in a taupe Cassini shift with matching coat, hugged her son. She pushed him an arm's length away from her. "You look like the job is agreeing with you."

"It is Mother, just wait until you see all that I've accomplished."

She slipped her Gucci handbag over her shoulder. "After your ordination tomorrow, I'll have to call you Reverend."

"I think you can still refer to me as Matthew, Mother. What is Father doing?"

"He's fussing with the rental agreement. He complained all the way out here that he's being overcharged."

Henry came around the car outfitted in a suit that matched Matthew's in style, but more elegant. Father and son shook hands. "How can you make a difference in this off-the-beaten path place?"

"Henry look around, it's lovely." His mother, taller by several inches than Stiles and Henry, took her son's arm.

"What's with the crane and that other mess?" Henry's eyebrows furled as he grabbed his son's other elbow.

Matthew's skin bristled under his suit. He squirmed away from his father's touch and the curl fell onto his forehead. "The crane is for the raising of the new steeple. The other is risers for the dedication of the pool complex."

"Pool complex? You didn't beg me for money for the pool like you did for the steeple."

143

Alice reached up and brushed the curl from Matthew's face. The sleeve of her jacket worked down to her elbow. Matthew noticed a bruise. He leaned close to his mother and whispered. "I see father's lied. He has been at it again."

"Be careful, don't ruffle him. He's been on some kind of tirade for two months since the stockholders of the company voted against his choice for chairman of the board."

Stiles led his parents on a tour around the green, naming the residents, and giving a little history of the town. Coming to Maida's house, he stopped. "And here is where we are having dinner and where you are staying tonight."

"Her fall flowers are spectacular." Alice Stiles leaned close to admire the variety of mums. "She has quite an eye for arrangements, doesn't she?"

"Oh, yes." Stiles assisted his mother up the steps and reached out for the bell when the door swung open.

"Welcome. Welcome." Maida extended her hand to Stiles' parents. "I'm so happy to meet you. Come on in." They stepped into the hall and George came around the corner from the kitchen. "This is my friend George."

George removed his ever-present cigar from his mouth and stuffed it in the pocket of his shirt before greeting the Stiles. "Your son has done wonders with our old church and this tired community. Come in the parlor for a little wine."

"Maida, this room is just as Matthew described. Your antiques are such quality." Alice Stiles slowly walked from piece to piece surveying the details and admiring the finish as she ran a gloved hand over the surface.

"Aren't they amazing, Mother?" Stiles sat next to George on the sofa.

"Let's have a toast to the raising of the steeple, the opening of the pool complex, and to Matthew Henry Stiles who breathed life back into us all." George distributed the already prepared glasses of wine, and they celebrated for a moment, engaging in small talk.

Maida glanced at her watch. "Excuse me. I need to finish up in the kitchen or we'll never eat." She scooted toward the kitchen.

"Maida, if you don't mind, I'll come along with you," Stiles' mother said.

"Come along."

Stiles escorted his mother behind Maida to the kitchen.

George turned to Henry Stiles. "Do you want to step out on the porch with me while I take a couple of puffs on my cigar?"

"Sure. I'll join you if you have another one of those cigars." Henry followed George.

"Matthew speaks highly of you and Maida." Henry wet the end of the cigar and turned to George for a light.

"He's really turned the church around."

"Matthew's been trained to produce."

George focused his eyes across the green to the church. "Mr. Stiles, I trained to be a mechanic at the Great Lakes Naval Station and met a girl from Cleveland. We married and I found work at Goodyear Aircraft in Akron."

"Akron? Now that is a coincidence."

"Yes, we lived there for about seven years before she agreed to move to where I could be near the ocean."

Henry pivoted and studied George.

George continued. "I recall talk about a certain young man who bulldozed his way into the tire business."

"I wouldn't say bulldozed, but I did have a plan, and I pushed forward until it was implemented." Henry puffed on his cigar and smiled.

"I checked and you accomplished your goals with honesty and integrity. I hope your son has the same ethics." George stubbed his cigar against the dock post.

"He's been groomed to be a success." Henry dropped his cigar into Maida's flower bed and pulled a package of mints from his coat pocket.

Swallowing the last of the mint, Henry looped his thumbs around the lapels of his suit jacket. "I have a flawless reputation for ethical business practices. Matthew wouldn't dare tarnish my reputation after I—"

The door opened. "Dinner is served," Maida announced. The men joined the women and Stiles in the dining room.

After dinner, Stiles glanced at his watch. "Maida, dinner was lovely, but I need you to excuse me. I have a few details to go over before tomorrow." He stood. "Thank you for entertaining my parents and allowing them to be guests in your home."

Alice helped Maida with the dishes while Henry made a business call. Standing near the foot of the staircase, Maida gestured. "The guest room is on the right. I'm sorry I have only one bathroom, and it's down here in back of the kitchen."

"No problem." Alice put her hand on the newel post.

"I'll have breakfast ready at nine. Don't want to be late for this special day. We are proud of your son." Maida watched Henry follow Alice upstairs.

* * *

Stiles crossed the green lost in thoughts about his mother. Unlocking the church office door, a voice startled him. "Mr. Stiles."

"Chief Bird, I didn't see you."

Bird moved out of the shadows. "I'm sure you have a lot on your mind with all the festivities tomorrow."

"And my parents are here."

"Maida told me she was entertaining them. So that's one less worry for you."

"Yes, she's been a good friend for me, but I must ..." Stiles pushed on the door.

"Wait. I have some news."

Stiles stopped and focused on the Chief.

"We've had a break in the investigation of Delbert Martin's death."

"You have."

Bird watched Stiles reach down and play with the end of his necktie. "After months of repeated scouring in the woods near the spot of Delbert's death, we found a leather glove and part of a boot print embedded in the mud under a pile of leaves that we'd missed. We sent those to the State Investigation Department. They've sent the results and it will be public information in the morning paper."

"Does the evidence point away from suicide to murder?" Stiles straightened his posture and let go of his tie.

"Definitely. The unusual boot print is the same as ones found at two unsolved murders in Providence."

"A serial killer, then?"

"No. A hired killer."

Stiles stepped into the shadow as his left eye began to twitch. "Not suicide then."

"No, we'll be focusing our investigation along with the FBI, on finding the murderer."

"I'm sure it will be a relief to Lois to know that Delbert did not take his own life."

"I just shared the news with her. She is greatly relieved."

Stiles looked at his watch. "Thanks, Chief. I have a few things to do before I go to bed. Please excuse me."

"Pastor, I didn't mean to interrupt your focus, but I wanted you to know before your big day tomorrow. Good night." The chief tipped his hat and watched Stiles scurry inside.

Stiles switched on a small lamp. He paced and shouted at Frederic. "Sloppy work. How did this happen? I was told it would be a clean shoot. I was told the shooter was an expert at setting the scene for suicide. I can't believe this."

He stopped, breathing in deeply while massaging Frederic's fingers. Feeling soothed, he lowered his voice to a barely audible whisper. "I have nothing to fear. God has called me here. He is looking forward to my ordination tomorrow. I've proved myself. God never lets go of his prophets."

Switching off the lamp, he climbed the stairs to his rooms shaking his head to purge it of unpleasant thoughts concerning Delbert's death.

CHAPTER 24

October 12, 1969

AROUND the breakfast table, the conversation with Alice and Henry turned from pictures of the hurricane to Maida's gardens full of fall mums and late asters.

Alice reached for the jar of blackberry preserves. "Tell me about the 1781 saltbox at the south end of the green."

"That belonged to Doc Thayer. It's been a problem since his death. Family squabbles you know. One son can afford to buy the other out, but he doesn't want it, so it sits. Come to think of it, I haven't seen either of the sons for a couple of years. George mows the grass and rakes the leaves, but other than that it remains an eyesore. I wish I could afford to buy it, but then, I'm not sure they'd sell. Stubborn New Englanders, they are."

"Maybe no one has made the right offer." Boldness flashed in Alice's eyes before she looked down.

"Alice, don't be foolish. A buy in this town is a waste of your money." Henry started to pound his fist on the table, but thought better of it and instead balled up his napkin, tossed it toward Alice, and pushed the chair back away from the table. The chair fell over onto the floor. With jerky angry motions, he bent over and righted the chair. He threw a cold look at his wife and stomped out of the room and up the stairs.

Maida noticed Alice's lips moving, but no sound. "Are you all right?"

A moment later, Alice without explanation asked "Can you suggest a realtor?"

"A realtor? Does that mean you might be interested in the old Thayer place?"

"Yes. It would be fun to have a place close to Matthew. And, of course, I'd enjoy transforming it to its former elegance."

Alice glanced at the clock. "We agreed to meet Matthew in a couple of minutes. I heard Henry upstairs. Would you mind calling him down for me, Maida?"

Maida called up the stairs. "Henry, we need to leave for your son's big day."

Henry Stiles straightened his jacket as he came down the steps. When he reached the bottom, he laid his hand on Maida's resting on the newel post. "Thanks, Maida. I'm sorry I reacted so poorly to my wife's interest in investing in your town. I have so many business concerns—another investment wouldn't be wise at this point in time.

"Don't you worry, Mr. Stiles, I understand the ways of high-powered men. My father was one of those."

* * *

Taking his position on the green, Stiles motioned to his parents. "Come on. Stand here. I want Maida on one side and George on the other side of you." A curious and excited crowd filled the green and the streets.

After the Methodist Church bells rang nine, trumpets blasted. While they played, Stiles climbed into the container of a bucket truck. All eyes watched Stiles being lifted some twenty feet off the ground. "Welcome to this historic day. Since 1938, the church has continued without its symbol of hope ... the steeple. I congratulate the contributors for making this dream come true. I especially want to thank my parents who graciously gave the last $5,000 to complete our fund raising effort. Let's give them a big round of applause."

As previously arranged, Maida raised Alice's arm and George raised Henry's, during the sustained applause. "Graciously, is not the word I would have used—coerced would be a better choice," Henry murmured to his wife.

"And now we raise that vision of hope," Stiles said.

The bucket truck lowered Stiles from twenty feet to ten. Two members of the crane crew steadied the finial. The pastor spoke into a microphone. "Into this finial, I am placing my written history of the church, copies of other historical documents, the names of contributors, and the present membership list of the church."

The crowd cheered as the crane operator swung the steeple up to another team of men already positioned on the roof. Shaded eyes watched every move. The workers raised their arms in victory when they had the steeple temporarily secured. George led the masses in three "hip, hip, hurrahs."

Stiles spread his arms out toward the throng. "Turn your attention to Bob and Rich Lang." Joyce's boys pulled on the ropes that dropped the cover on the new sign above the doors of the church.

"A new name for a new beginning. Welcome to the First Independent Community Church of Ironton Corner." The church council led a cheer that floated in waves through the crowd while the bucket truck lowered Stiles the remaining ten feet to the ground. Lining up behind the Boy Scouts, Stiles marched behind the boys into the church. His parents tagged behind him. Arthur and Stiles climbed the pulpit and stood while the throng found their seats.

Stiles' parents stopped dead at their first view of the sanctuary. Their eyes traveled over the collections and locked onto the fish tanks.

"I can't believe this. What's wrong with our son? This is an embarrassment." Henry reached for Alice's arm and twisted it.

"It's always about you, isn't it?" Alice winced and attempted to pull her arm away.

Barbara spotted the angry exchange. To avoid a further scene, she wiggled between them and guided them into the second pew from the front.

The remainder of the throng found their seats and stood until Arthur approached the microphone and gave the sign for them to sit.

Arthur smiled broadly. "Welcome to this special occasion as the First Independent Community Church of Ironton Corner gathers to ordain Mr. Matthew Henry Stiles as its pastor and president. We are proud of his accomplishments and look forward to his long ministry with us as The Reverend Matthew Henry Stiles." Applause filled the sanctuary. Confetti floated down from the ceiling.

At the laying-on-of-hands, hundreds of the now First Independent members and guests stood and formed one connected unit, extending their arms from one shoulder to the next and connecting them to The Reverend Stiles. Clyde Weaver sang.

"Spirit of the Living God fall afresh on Matthew Henry Stiles.
Spirit of the Living God, fall anew on us.
Fill us with hope to dream our dreams
and courage for Reverend Stiles to guide us through."

The laying-on-of-hands infused the newly ordained with the power of the Holy Spirit needed to carry out the office.

Irene's body shuddered, remembering Lois' voice when she informed Stiles that she would not need his services for the funeral of her husband. She leaned into Kenny, and he walked her back to her seat. "Something isn't right about ordaining Stiles. I feel an evil power filling this room. Maybe it's from reading the news that Delbert was murdered and did not commit suicide."

The now Reverend Matthew Henry Stiles climbed to the pulpit and received a standing ovation. Once the crowd quieted, he came near the microphone.

"Thank you for your affirmation of my ministry at First Independent Community Church of Ironton Corner. I guarantee that I'll be with you until they bury me in the Town Cemetery." Another prolonged applause. He grinned and pointed to Kenny Keene. "And that man will be the one to put me in the ground."

Someone from the back of the church shouted, "Kenny's going to have to live a long time, isn't he?" Laughter rippled through the room. Kenny stood and waved.

The Reverend Stiles stepped down to the floor of the worship room. "Now for the moment many of you have been anticipating—the dedication of the pool complex and the revealing of the names of the donors. Follow the men with the yellow arm bands outside and down into the basement. There is seating for everyone. Be careful on the steps."

Once the assembled group settled on the moveable bleachers, Jimmy and Frank Somers emerged from the rear wearing long coats. They stood on either side of a canvas. At a drum roll, father and son pulled on ropes that uncovered a four-by-six-foot sign reading, "The Carol Somers Pool Complex."

The crowd cheered and tears of happiness traveled down Frank's and Jimmy's faces. Reverend Stiles quieted the gathering. Jimmy stood in front of the microphone at the deep end of the pool. "My dad and I are happy to dedicate the pool in memory of Carol Somers. We loved her very much. We know she'd be proud of this addition to the church and the community."

Jimmy and Frank tore off their long coats, exposing their bathing trunks. In one coordinated motion, they dove in. The crowd went wild. Mayor Sims leaned over and gave them a hand out of the pool. Sims adjusted the microphone for his height. "The town is proud to be connected with this project. On November second the first class of school children will begin their swim lessons. Frank and Jimmy, thank you."

Stiles stepped to the front. "Thank you for making my ordination a day that I'll never forget. Everyone is invited to the Fellowship Hall to enjoy a light lunch prepared by Chet's Diner. Please come. I want to shake the hand of everyone who is here."

All the members and guests were caught up in the excitement at the reception except for Reverend Stiles' parents. Irene and Kenny noticed and went over to join them. "We're Irene and Kenny Keene."

Irene with her usual tact said, "You look lost."

"We're feeling lost," Alice replied. "We've enjoyed the events, but now it is Matthew's time to greet all the well-wishers. We're not sure what to do next."

"Why don't you come over to our house? We live right over there." Kenny began walking toward their house.

"I'll put on the tea kettle, and we can get acquainted," Irene said.

"Thanks." Henry Stiles looked over at the Keenes' house, sizing it up.

Irene fixed them lobster rolls for lunch. Henry caught Kenny laughing. "What's so funny, Kenny?"

"Me burying Reverend Stiles. The truth is, I'm sure, that he'll be saying words over my dead body."

"Let's not talk about dead bodies, Kenny. Have you enjoyed

Ironton Corner, Alice?" Irene laid her hand on Kenny's.

"Oh yes, I find it a quaint New England town. But most of all, I like the people. They are more down to earth than the ones we associate with in Akron."

Henry glanced at Irene. "Matthew sent me a copy of your *History of Ironton Corner*. Histories usually bore me, but your writing style is captivating. I hear you've had your struggles with our son. What will you write about him?"

"Time will tell."

"Speaking of time, we need to go and say goodbye to Matthew before we leave to catch our flight." Alice rose from her chair. "Thanks for your hospitality."

Alice and Henry Stiles rushed across an empty green. Stiles stood like a statue with his arms folded. "Where have you been? You should have been at the reception. You embarrassed me. You don't know how many wanted to meet you."

"Like hell, no one cared about us. I couldn't have gushed over your present path and what you've done to the sanctuary. Don't you have any sense?" His father berated Stiles as they walked toward the office door of the empty church. Do you really think God has appointed you?"

Alice reached for her son's arm. "Matthew, you must understand we felt lost with all of your guests, and when the Keenes invited us to their house, we accepted."

Stiles stepped back from her touch. "The Keenes? They are a thorn in my side. I hope they didn't fill you with their interpretation of my ministry."

Stiles unlocked the door to the offices and allowed his mother to enter first. He flipped on the hall lights, took two steps around his mother, and unlocked the door to his office. Filled with anger, he kicked the door open. Frederic swung in the breeze. His parents froze in their footsteps.

"Why do you still have that?" Henry yelled. "I told you to destroy that thing after Leroy Roach left our church."

"Leroy didn't leave. You had him thrown out."

Henry grabbed the front of Stiles' jacket. "I did it to protect you. He's a pervert who was leading you down a path to more criminal activity. Hadn't you already been in enough trouble with your insane need to be different from me? For your information, I didn't graciously give you the $5,000 for the steeple." Henry pushed his son against the wall.

His mother came to her son's defense, "Henry, leave the boy alone." Henry turned and shot a look at her.

"Woman, leave him and me alone." Henry's face grew redder as he continued to push and slap his son.

Stiles forced his body to go limp to interrupt his father's rage as he'd seen his mother do on many occasions. "Let me go. I am no longer a product for you to manage." His father loosened his grip. "And, Father, you lied when you said you kept your hands off Mother."

They heard a knock at the door. "Who's there?"

"Reverend Stiles, it's George. Are you all right?"

"Yes, I fell over a box."

"Okay." They listened for George's footsteps to fade.

Alice reached for her son. He turned away. "Mother, when will—"

"She never will." Henry held his head high as if he'd won a battled before he exited the office and disappeared into the driver's side of their rental car. Alice scurried behind her husband. Stiles caught up to his mother and opened the car door. He held the door as she slid into her seat. He closed the door and stepped back studying his mother. He knew that during the drive to the airport and for many weeks to come, there'd be silence between his parents—his father's weapon of choice until she crawled back to him.

Switching on a small light in his office, he stretched over his typewriter, cracked his fingers, raised his arms to the ceiling three times, and fed a fresh sheet of paper into the typewriter. He centered the title and date.

The Chronicle of The <u>Reverend</u> Matthew Henry Stiles
October 12, 1969

I have the church and the town just where I want them. I felt their admiration and power surging through my body during the laying-on-of-hands. The power was the kind that could only originate from God. He has me in place to continue to save the church and continue to shape me for further success.

Then there are my parents. What a waste they are. I'll play along and keep them informed to receive the remainder of my trust money and any other money I can get from my mother for taking her side. I do love her, but at the same time she sickens me with her weak backbone. Why does she take it from him? I'd have more respect for her if she told him where to go and walked out. I wonder if she ever will.

It's time to finalize the plans for the museums. Good night, Frederic, and good night to me,

The Reverend Matthew Henry Stiles.

He rolled the paper out and reverently performed each step of his sacrament. Turning to switch off the lamp, he heard a knock at his door. The door opened a crack and Leroy's eye appeared in the space. "I want to congratulate you on your day, The Reverend Matthew Henry Stiles."

"Did you see everything—the steeple and the pool?"

"Yes. You were wonderful. The crowds were in awe. I heard many comment on how much you've accomplished in such a short time."

"Come on in. I've been going over the museum plans."

"Can't you relax and enjoy today?" Leroy reached out his hand and touched Stiles' hair. He lightly touched the curve in Stiles' cheek with the back of his hand before settling both hands on the knot of his tie, unloosening it.

Stiles enjoyed the physical touch, but then grabbed Leroy's hands. "No."

"Come on, Matthew. Every time I approach you, you ..."

"I'm in charge of my life now."

"Matthew, Matthew in some ways you are such an innocent. You haven't been in charge of your own life since high school. Remember I rescued you from the adult guards that wanted you in the detention center. Don't I deserve a little gratitude?"

"No. Now help me decipher your notes on the government artifacts. I need to understand the details of the borrowing agreement."

Chapter 25

The Chronicle of The <u>Reverend</u> Matthew Henry Stiles
February 2, 1970 7 a.m.
Groundhog Day

A new phase of my plan begins today.

This part of my plan for First Independent Community Church of Ironton Corner has nearly exhausted me. Months of work are completed and the papers signed for three of the homes around the green. The Museums of Ironton Corner will be a reality by the fall.

The Hills were an easy target with Ed Hill needing full time nursing care. In the agreement, their children will clean out the house, and then it becomes The Ironton Corner Boy Scout Museum. I haven't asked George yet, but I'm sure he'll build the shelves and cabinets that I'm going to need for the collections.

I've chosen to name the art museum, The Alice and Henry Stiles Museum. You do know why, don't you, Frederic? You guessed it ... to lead the church to think that it's my parents' money that has purchased the house. The Deals who own, no, who owned the house were delighted when my realtor approached them. They are now able to purchase their dream house in Florida. I have a bid out for Alice and Henry to purchase the collection of maritime paintings by William S. Barrett.

I had a hard time obtaining Doc Thayer's 1781 Saltbox for the Old Time Doc and Apothecary Museum. Another party countered my offers. I paid more than I wanted, but

I won. That property needs the most attention. The crew should arrive today to begin the gutting and new construction. You know who will be on their porch filled with curiosity, don't you?

The Albert Howard family is considering my offer to buy the property next to the church for a playground and to develop trails to the river for fishing and recreation. I know none of those are my interests, but my new paradigm for church includes activities for everyone.

And last, the U.S. Government Services Administration has agreed to lend me twelve historic clocks to display in what I hope will be, The Maida Hobart Alden Clock Museum. I'm on my way to see her this afternoon.

He did not want to be late for his meeting with Maida, but he took the time to perform his trinity and file the entry. Stiles climbed the stairs to his rooms, showered, and dressed. He stuffed his sketch of the three-fold brochure and other drawings for the museums in his inside jacket pocket, then pulled on his heavy winter coat.

When he walked out the door at 10 a.m., just as he had planned, trash and debris were flying out the windows of Doc Thayer's 1781 saltbox into a dumpster. As he predicted, he spotted Irene and Kenny huddled on their porch under a wool blanket.

By the time The Reverend Stiles rang Maida's bell, he knew that Maida would have finished her laundry, primped her hair, and changed into her favorite skirt and blouse. She took his coat, hung it in the closet as she directed him into the parlor where she had tea laid out.

Maida poured two cups and handed one to Stiles. He held the china with gentle hands. "I love the Bellefleur pattern. Haviland, isn't it?"

"Yes. I'm glad you like it. It belonged to my grandmother. Matthew, I was surprised to wake this morning to crashing sounds and seeing a swarm of men attacking Doc's house. Are you aware that your mother asked me about Doc's place the weekend of your ordination?"

"No." He raised his eyebrows registering real surprise, wondering if it had been his mother bidding against him.

"Your father told her it was a poor investment to buy in Ironton Corner. Do you suppose she went ahead and bought the place?"

"That would be like her, especially if my father had strong feeling against it. She has an inheritance of her own and sometimes to defy him, she makes large purchases. And sometimes ..." he hesitated before continuing, "... she pays dearly for her rash spending as he calls it." Stiles pulled the mock-up brochure from his pocket. He handed it to her, leaned back against the sofa, and watched.

"Museums and a park? How?"

"Because of the changes I've made in Ironton Corner, several private investors contacted me and wanted to see my complete plans." He pointed to the brochure.

"The Alice and Henry Stiles Museum and—" she stopped and adjusted her glasses. "The Maida Hobart Alden Clock Museum."

"Yes, that's why I wanted to talk with you." He scooted to the edge of the sofa. "The General Services Administration of the U.S. Government has agreed to loan me a dozen antique clocks." He handed her several more sketches.

"This is ..." she shuffled through the other drawings, "these are the rooms in my house with all my antiques noted."

"Maida, I've seen photos of the government clocks. If they are set among your antiques, their beauty will be enhanced." He reached out for her hand. "I'm here to ask you to open your home on a limited basis for tours of the Maida Hobart Alden Clock Museum."

"I don't know what to say."

He let go of her hand and stood. "I'll go out in the hall and leave you to think for a while."

Stiles walked to the hallway. He watched her reflection in the hall mirror. She stood and straightened her dress. Her face mirrored doubt as she crossed the room to her husband's desk. She sat down in her husband's chair and picked up the photo of William taken a year before his death. She touched the glass gently and shut her eyes.

When she looked up, Matthew was closing the front of the tall clock. He looked lost in thought. She whispered, "Poor thing," under her breath and walked into the hall. She touched his arm.

Startled he said, "Oh, Maida." He stuffed his left hand in his pocket.

"I'll contact my insurance company to check on my liability. Then we'll talk again."

"Thank you. You are dear. I'll get my coat."

Stiles made his way to Doc Thayer's. He approached a worker who was leaning against the dumpster having a cigarette and drinking hot coffee from a thermos. "I'm The Reverend Matthew Stiles. You look to be in charge."

"I'm not in charge, but I'll be onsite every day." He set the thermos down. "If the winter weather cooperates and the spring rains don't cause delays, we'll have it ready for decorating and furnishings by early summer." He dropped his cigarette and mashed it with his foot. "If we get the work done on time, the boss told me the owner is offering a bonus. By the way, we found an unusual old clock in a closet in the Doc's attic. Do you know who we should talk to?"

"I'll find out, but may I see it?"

The worker went inside and returned with a package. He removed the faded newspaper wrappings. "See." The clock was indeed unusual—a greenish marble base with four short black columns that supported another piece of marble on which stood an elegant clock face on one end and a correctly proportioned statue on the other.

The man ran his fingers over the statue. "Looks like one of those mythical creatures to me, how about you, Rev?"

"Indeed, Aesculapius, the Roman god of medicine and healing. The Romans built temples in his name that became places of healing. The staff of Aesculapius, the rod with a serpent coiled around it, became the symbol for medicine. According to the legend Zeus struck him down with a thunder bolt, but to appease Apollo, Zeus turned him into a constellation ... Ophiuchus, the Serpent Holder." Stiles touched it.

"You must really be smart to be able to spout off all that information. I see that it certainly fits old Doc Thayer."

"Did you know Doc?"

"No, but I attended school here, and we all heard the stories about Doc. Seems he didn't have a bad bone in his body." The man scratched at his beard. "We don't want the clock to get tossed out. Say, we're looking for a safe place to keep it. Since you're a reverend and all, will you keep it until the boss notifies the owner?"

"Sure."

He handed the wrappings and clock to Stiles.

Stiles carried the clock into his office. He cleared a space on his book case and arranged it between two antique vases. He stepped back to admire it. "Frederic, this clock must be a sign ... a good sign."

He reached into his pocket and held Maida's diamond-emerald ring up to the light. "Frederic, I hated to do this to Maida, but business is business, isn't it?" He opened the back of the clock and set the ring inside, a safe place until he needed it.

* * *

Maida laid the three-fold sketch in front of Irene on the kitchen table. "What the—" Irene said.

Kenny leaned over and read the title. "The Museums of Ironton Corner."

"I can't believe that Doc's boys stopped their feuding long enough to sell the place." Irene turned the sketch over.

"And the Hills and the Deals. I wonder who ..." Kenny said.

"He says some investors," Maida informed them.

"One must be his parents."

"Looks like it with one of the museums named after them."

"The gossip mill sure missed this one." Irene walked to the stove and turned the gas on under the kettle.

"I'll bet the money from my next burial, he'll have all of us involved in this project by Labor Day."

"Not me." Irene reached into the cabinet and set three cups on the table.

CHAPTER 26

September 5, 1970

CHET'S Diner buzzed with a standing room only crowd on the Friday before Labor Day Weekend. The hungry mob cleaned Chet out of muffins, and he was down to his last dozen eggs.

Twelve folks huddled around the center table. "Can you believe this spread? The whole paper is about us," Irene bragged.

Kenny teased. "My photograph shows my best side, don't you think?"

"I'm not sure you have a best side." George gave Kenny a slap on the back.

"Hey, everyone." Chet yelled above the crowd. "My wife called a minute ago and Wally Harris is on WBZ-TV Boston. They're interviewing him about the article. And she said they're sending a crew down for the opening of the museums."

Excitement rose in the packed diner. "Let's raise our cups to Reverend Stiles and his vision and push to get us going." Arthur raised his cup and all the others in the diner followed his lead except for Lois Martin and Chief of Police John Bird who sat off in the far corner.

* * *

Early the next morning, Irene spat on her fingers and rubbed at a spot on the front door window. "Kenny, hurry up. I see a small crowd gathering at Doc Thayer's House."

"We aren't supposed to be on duty until ten, and I'm having trouble buttoning this collar."

"Come on down here, and I'll help you."

Kenny whistled at Irene when he came to the last step. She stood in front of him dressed in a blue, full length dress with a hoop skirt. "If you weren't standing in our own house, I wouldn't know you in that old-fashioned dress and pale make-up. The corset makes those breasts of yours look perky." He reached for her.

"Not now, Kenny. Let me help you with that collar. You look just like the photo of Doc Thayer."

The Keenes emerged from their house, Irene on his arm and Kenny with a walking cane. They looked to their left and saw Maida in a dress similar to Irene's, but upon getting closer they noticed a lady's antique timepiece pinned to the bodice.

"Nice piece." Kenny touched it.

Irene took a closer look. "I've never seen it before. Is it new?"

"No, it's one of the government pieces. It must have been a gift for one of the president's wives."

"Well, it's a stunner." Kenny stepped back for a better look.

"Wait." Wally Harris ran across the street. "I need a photo." They posed with the new sign, "The Maida Hobart Alden Clock Museum" in the background.

"Are you two as excited and nervous as I am?" Maida adjusted the timepiece.

Kenny grinned. "We are." He turned. "Look at the line of folks ready to meet the early Massachusetts doctor and quiz him about the ways of early doctoring. We better go."

"Just a minute." Irene fussed with the collar on Maida's dress and whispered. "I still wonder how Reverend Stiles acquired all the stuff for these museums."

"Don't worry and simply enjoy, Irene. I'm sure he and his family have many connections."

Maida picked up her skirts and walked next door to the Alice and Henry Stiles Museum. Barbara and Arthur were standing at the front door and they greeted her in their period costumes. "Barbara, you look elegant."

"I feel rather silly. This tight waistline is about killing me."

Arthur pulled at the neck of his shirt. "You should wear one of these collars to know uncomfortable. Excuse me ladies. I want to make one last run through the house and take another look at my script." Arthur returned to the house and disappeared inside.

"Barbara, did you talk to Chief Bird regarding your concerns about the gun collection?" Maida asked.

"Yes, he's promised one of his deputies would be here to watch over it each time we are open. Since the collection honors the memory of Mayor Sims' son, I don't want anything to happen to it. Do you remember Glenn, Maida?" Barbara asked.

"Oh, yes. A smart boy. And his death, I'll never forget the sadness that gripped the town." Maida tried to adjust the large brim hat that set back on her head, but was making it worse.

Barbara stepped close. "Here let me help you. Are you all set for the tourists?"

"George helped me with the last minute unpacking and rearranging my house. I must admit the collection fits in very nicely with my antiques."

Reverend Stiles, dressed in a frock coat with a black silk puff tie and crimson double-breasted vest, came up the walk to where Barbara and Maida were standing. He stood close to Maida, but kept his distance from Barbara. "You two look perfect for the opening. Irene and Kenny are in their places; the Easley family is over at the new Ironton Corner Walking Trails and Playground; and the Clyde Weaver family is ready to lead tours of the Church. All I have to do is check on Jimmy and Frank and the Ironton Corner Boy Scout Museum." He marched away, head held high.

"He loves this. It feeds his ego and ambition," Barbara said.

"That's true, and it's putting Ironton Corner on the map."

"You sound just like Reverend Stiles." Barbara started up the walk toward the museum.

"I guess I do. Enjoy your day." Maida returned to her house as the first tourists arrived.

At six o'clock the museums closed. The townspeople set up chairs, laid down blankets on the green, and listened to the high school band as they shared stories and picnic suppers until dusk.

Stiles returned to his office.

"Howdy, Reverend. How was your day?"

Stiles focused his eyes. "Leroy, what are you doing here?"

"You promised me a finder's fee right after your opening day for obtaining the letters for the Boy Scout museum." Leroy tossed an itemized bill on Stiles' desk.

Stiles studied it. He walked over to the bookcase and opened the back of the clock that the workers found in the rubble of the Doc Thayer house. He reached in and grasped the object. With a pleased look on his face, he handed Maida's emerald and diamond ring to Leroy.

Leroy's eyes glistened as he held the ring up to the light. "Where did you find this gem?"

"Not for you to know."

"Well, thank you. It will cover most of your debt to me. You are keeping close tabs on the money you are investing in the place, aren't you?"

"Of course."

Leroy placed the ring on his pinkie finger and admired it at arm's distance. "I must be off. I don't want to miss the television news coverage of the museum openings in Ironton Corner."

Leroy started for the door and turned. "Are you going to make an exception to your aversion to TV and watch the opening of the museums?"

"No."

"Don't you want to make this one little exception to see your fine body and that magnificent head of curly hair on television ... and hear your voice? Just thinking about watching your body and voice develop as a teen in my church brings chills to my—"

"Stop. I'm not going to watch. Make sure no one sees you leaving my office." Stiles backed into his desk chair.

* * *

Leroy eased his car out of the cemetery. Just as he was ready to turn onto Main Street, a cruiser pulled up behind him with blue lights flashing.

Chief Bird got out and stepped to Leroy's window and signaled for him to lower it. "Good evening, Sir. You need to turn on your head lights."

"I'm sorry." Leroy reached for the switch and pulled. "After my fine day in Ironton Corner, I've been deep in thought. Each artifact and painting so beautifully displayed. Many took my breath away."

"We have this preacher that's getting us on the map. Did you meet him?"

"I don't believe so." Leroy breathed deeply. "Officer, thanks for reminding me of my lights, but I need to rescue my dogs. They'll never forgive me for being away so long."

Bird released his arms and stepped back. "You come back again. You never know what Reverend Stiles will do next to attract even more people to Ironton Corner. He's revived our town."

Leroy slowly pulled away. He checked his rear view mirror and saw the officer with pencil and notebook in hand.

* * *

Stiles climbed the stairs to his rooms and changed into dark pants and a dark shirt. He crept out of the church and through the shadows around the green, to avoid attention. He stood behind a tree outside Irene and Kenny's window and watched the news.

With his head held high, he strutted through the shady areas to the memorial that stood at its center. He sat on the steps and admired the design of the brick walkways as he had marveled at his image on the television news program. Standing at attention, he clicked his heels together, heard a hiss, and spotted Stella, her back up and eyes glowing in the dark.

She slinked toward him. He reached down. "Good kitty." When she was close enough, he kicked her out of his way and marched across the street to the church.

Opening his office door, he slid into his chair, and performed his ritual with precision.

The Chronicle of The <u>Reverend</u> Matthew Henry Stiles
September 5, 1970

What a day!! Just as I'd planned. This day will be recorded as a transition day in the life of the church and Ironton Corner—all because of me. From the grapevine, I hear the surrounding communities are envious that they do not have a leader with my charismatic personality and drive.

Children and teachers are scheduled for tours through next summer. My historian friend in Williamsburg is bringing a group in November for our Thanksgiving celebration on the green.

Meanwhile now that I have time, I'll be catering to the hundreds of new members and visitors with my innovative ideas about "Mary and the Question of Virginity" for Advent.

The winter months are so dull, I'll need to do something exciting. I'll work on my sermon series, "The Intersection of Popular Culture and the Church." I'll quote from the notes I've taken from Irene's history. She'll be so proud that she won't be bothering me with her tedious questions.

And I'll use my love of film and what they say about religion and culture to educate Joyce. She preached to me a few weeks ago about the movie <u>Midnight Cowboy</u> after I told her I'd gone to Boston to see it. She rattled on and on about the change of its rating from R to X and the influence movies have on teenagers. I'll build on that.

Stiles stopped typing and turned to the skeleton. "Frederic, the ideas are coming. My fingers need to fly over the keys." He turned away from Frederic and focused on the keys and let his ideas roll.

I'll highlight the strange relationship between Dustin Hoffman and Jon Voight—a hustler and a stud as part of the series of sermons. I'll reference the friendship between King David and Jonathan and Jesus and the outcasts. I'll have Leroy dig deep into the psychology of each film. His ideas will touch every heart and soul.

It is going to be beautiful. Through me, the masses will begin to understand the connection between our popular culture and the stories in the Bible.

My research for the series, "Is War ever Just?" is about complete. Those powerful messages will prepare the way for the unveiling of the new monument for Memorial Day 1971.

As he filed his nightly chronicle, Stiles danced through his trinity using the brass-tipped cane from the museum openings.

CHAPTER 27

May 29, 1971

Under the cover of night, Stiles, Leroy, and three of Leroy's hired men wheeled a granite marker to the center of the green. With great effort, they positioned it in front of the Civil War Memorial and the recently erected WWI and WWII commemorative plaques.

Words were carved into the granite.

> Vietnam Soldiers we apologize to You
> For Losing Your Lives Unnecessarily
> In this American Tragedy
> May 30, 1971

The men finished their work and scattered before dawn. Stiles pulled a chair to the window in his bedroom. On a yellow-lined pad, he recorded the reactions of the earlier risers who spotted and read the words on the marker. He called Leroy. "More and more people are coming as the word passes around. I couldn't be more pleased. Maybe some will wake up to the tragedy of the war."

Wally Harris photographed the granite memorial and collected a few of the reactions for the paper. When two townspeople attempted to strike the monument with hammers, Chief Bird and his men grabbed their arms. "Don't make this worse than it is." The men backed off.

WBZ-TV Boston, tipped off by Wally, sent a crew at noon to cover the unfolding story for the six o'clock news. The interviewer moved toward Chief Bird. "Who is responsible for this?"

"I don't know. The first report came to us shortly after dawn from George Lawrence," Chief Bird responded.

"We heard via the wire this morning that other towns were surprised by similar memorials on their greens. Do you think the pastors who have been speaking out against the war coordinated this effort?"

Bird straightened his shoulders. "I don't know, but here comes Reverend Stiles. I'm sure he'll be able to answer that for you."

Stiles whisked by the Chief. Bird frowned at the whiff of Stiles' cologne that filled his nose.

"Reverend Stiles ..." The WBZ-TV crew tried to catch the fast moving reverend. "Are you responsible for this monument?"

Stiles stopped and clicked the heels of his highly shined black shoes together. The news cameraman filled his screen with Stiles' face. "Yes. This is my personal statement about America's involvement in this war." Stiles spoke in a calm voice. "A monument to the folly of war—instead of a monument to honor war. The time has come to build monuments for what men have done to others through war. I am here to tell future generations that not all Americans are proud of what was and is being done in Vietnam— the killing and wounding of innocents and the staggering loss of young soldiers."

"We've heard that other towns have erected similar memorials," The reporter commented.

"They have." Stiles stood at attention.

"Do you feel that you have a right to place this monument on the public green?" The reporter moved the microphone closer to Stiles.

"This is not a public green. It is the property of the church, and I, as the president and treasurer, have the right to use this green as I choose."

"Other pastors these days are being accused by their congregations for bringing too much politics into their churches. Do you feel you are stepping over a boundary between church and state?"

"Absolutely not. Come on Sunday. Hear my words." He turned and walked quickly toward his church.

The cameraman followed Stiles across the street and kept filming as Stiles disappeared into his church office. The viewing audience heard the interviewer's commentary in the background. "There you have it, folks. Reverend Matthew Stiles, who developed the Museums of Ironton Corner and arranged popular summer concerts on the green, admits to placing this monument on the green. You heard his response. This is WBZ News coming to you from Ironton Corner."

Late in the afternoon, Joyce delivered a telegram to Stiles in his office. He fingered the envelope and held it up to the light. He sliced it open with a letter opener, read it and tore it to shreds. He batted at Frederic and marched into Joyce's office. "The First Naval District Band has cancelled their appearance for the Memorial Day Concert."

"You bragged to me how you convinced the band to return to Ironton Corner." Joyce held her hands at arm's length and admired her new fuchsia nail polish. "The cancellation couldn't have anything to do with your monument, could it?" Joyce added.

"You watch on Memorial Day how I'll defend my rights as a citizen to speak my mind. The navy band will regret cancelling on me."

Just before eleven on Memorial Day, Stiles ran across the green and unlocked the door to the Alice and Henry Stiles Museum. He picked up one of the two portable machine guns, marched to the green, and stood at attention in front of the war memorial. When the veterans arrived, he leveled the gun at them. The veterans stood frozen. Chief Bird and two officers ran over and stood between Stiles and the vets.

Bird noticed Stiles' eye twitching. Calmly he said, "Hand over the weapon, Reverend Stiles."

Stiles did as asked. Bird passed the machine gun to one of his officers.

"Reverend Stiles, I'm going to have to arrest you for carrying a firearm and for threatening citizens with it."

"You can't."

"I can." Bird unlocked his handcuffs from his belt.

"I don't think those are necessary." Stiles backed away, a terrible fright filled his face.

"I hope not, but I want you to understand you have committed a crime and will stand before a judge who will decide on the penalty." Bird rattled the handcuffs and returned them to his belt.

"Do I need a lawyer?"

"It depends how you plead."

"I'm guilty of carrying the machine gun, but I never intended to use it." He looked desperate, his face pale and the iris of his eyes enlarged.

"On Monday, you will appear before the magistrate. I suggest you bring Arthur Blankenship with you."

"Blankenship?"

"Yes, just in case you decide to make more of this situation than necessary, I want Blankenship there to advise you."

"You really don't think I'd be inappropriate, do you?" Stiles' voice rose to a high pitch.

"Stiles, I suspect you've done more than a few inappropriate acts. My officers will be keeping an eye on you until Monday."

The stunned group watched as Bird escorted Stiles to the church office. They exited the green in an orderly fashion looking back over their shoulders and shaking their heads.

Stiles slammed the door to his office. He grabbed a yellow pad, hunched over it like a school child reprimanded by his teacher, and scribbled over and over again, "I can't go to jail. I can't go to jail. I can't go to jail." He filed the paper.

He slammed his body into his desk chair. He picked up the telephone receiver and dialed. It slipped from his hand, the cord stretching down the front of the desk. He grabbed the cord and yanked it up. He misdialed again. He banged the receiver down before taking three deep breaths. Picking up the receiver, he deliberately dialed each number. The phone rang once ... twice before Leroy picked up.

All he heard was, "You idiot. A machine gun was not part of our plan."

Stiles banged down the phone, lowered Frederic and pushed and shoved the skeleton against the metal file cabinet. A small piece of bone splintered off and shot across the room. Stiles collapsed on the floor. "I'm sorry Frederic." He held onto Frederic's feet.

CHAPTER 28

May 31, 1971

ON Sunday, Stiles waved the *Ironton Corner Daily News* and the *Boston Globe* as he thundered from the pulpit. "A pastor is to preach and teach and witness against injustice. I've been discussing the so-called 'just war' since some of us returned from marching with thousands in Washington DC. On the anniversary of the deaths at Kent State, May 4, I hung a black flag with a peace sign from the steeple of the church. I insisted the Boy Scouts wear black arm bands to remember the tragedy. To those who say a pastor has no right to have a political opinion, I say you are wrong.

"As I've said before and I'll say again, anything worth talking about on Sunday is political. Jesus, the great liberator, was as political as they come. Vietnam and Kent State are religious topics. When I march and lecture about the injustice of this war, I am raging against the culture as Jesus did. When he dared anyone without sin to throw the first stone at the adulterer, he was warning us about the inability to see ourselves as self-righteous. Killing and war and throwing stones are issues the church should worry about. To say the church should stay out of politics is to say the church should die."

Some listening nodded their heads in affirmation of Stiles' words; others closed their ears to his opinions.

* * *

The usual Monday morning line stretched out the door of the magistrate's office. Stiles and Bird stood at the end and listened to the excuses—a trucker caught speeding through town, three teenagers trespassing on private property, and a woman arrested for DUI.

171

Arthur Blankenship arrived just as Stiles was next in line to see the magistrate. Bird, Arthur, and Stiles faced the judge and listened to the warrant against Reverend Matthew Henry Stiles.

"You have been charged with possessing an unregistered machine gun, using said gun to threaten the public, and not paying the excise tax."

"Unregistered? Taxes?" Stiles shouted.

"Yes. Following your arrest, Chief Bird checked on the registration of the gun and found you had neglected transferring the registration to your name since you are in temporary possession of it on your property. You do own the Alice and Henry Stiles Museum property, don't you?"

"I do, but Mayor Sims—"

"How do you plead?"

Stiles stood tall. "Guilty for letting my emotions about this unjust war get away from me."

The magistrate said, "Reverend Stiles, you are not here for your opinion on the war. You are here for possessing an unregistered machine gun and not paying the proper excise tax and for using it to threaten the public. These charges carry the penalty of sixty days in jail and a fine of $2500."

Stiles gritted his teeth and stood tall. "I plead guilty to the charges."

Arthur stepped forward. "Sir, may I have a few minutes with Reverend Stiles." The judge nodded.

They stood aside. Arthur talked. Stiles listened. Arthur turned back and addressed the magistrate. "My client promises to properly register the guns and pay the excise taxes. He agrees to pay the fine of $2500 to the court, but he asks the court to forgive the sixty days of jail time."

"The jail time is suspended, and you, Reverend Stiles, can pay the clerk of court the fine within seven days. If you have not paid it by then, I'll reinstate the jail time. Do you understand?"

Stiles nodded. The magistrate pounded his gavel. "Next case."

Bird exited through the door marked police station. Stiles and Arthur headed across the green. Stiles stopped next to the bandstand and leaned against the railing. "Arthur, we need to meet to someplace private to discuss fulfilling the next step of my mission. God has put us together, you with your money and me with my vision. Meet me at the first trail split from the parking lot in Findlay State Park with your check book at seven in the morning."

"Why there? Why not my office as usual? That is the exact place where Delbert was murdered."

"Right, and it is a place where I find great peace. I walk there at least once a week. You'll be there, won't you, or I'll have to—"

"I know." Red began to appear on Arthur's neck.

"I will have to reveal more about your lovely Barbara's past and her part in the failure of her father's business. You don't want that, do you?"

"No."

"Your devotion to her makes my little piece of blackmail so easy. Make one check out for the $2500 and another for your usual $1000 monthly gift to me." Stiles walked away with his head held high.

Arthur watched Stiles. He looked like a snake in a position to strike. Filled with despair, Arthur sat on the bandstand steps, head in hand, and cried. He sensed the presence of a person. When he looked up, Joyce was standing nearby.

"Are you okay?" she asked.

"No, I'm totally off track."

"I couldn't help but see Stiles with you from the office window."

Arthur straightened up. "He has me off balance with the monument and the gun incident, but I'll be fine." He glanced at his watch. "I have an appointment, Joyce. Thanks for your concern."

Joyce watched Arthur stumble a little as he walked away.

* * *

The next morning Arthur arrived at the park at the time Stiles directed. He slowly followed the trail to the meeting place. He watched from fifty yards away as Stiles strutted around the spot where they had found Delbert's body. As he grew closer, he noticed a self-satisfied look on Stiles' face. The look initiated a shiver that traveled up his spine. What kind of man is he that can find peace in the spot of a murder? Arthur thought.

"Fine morning, isn't it, Arthur? If you walk quietly, you can hear the birds sing. I think they are getting to know me."

"Don't you picture Delbert's body laying here?"

"No, I never saw it here."

"But there were pictures in the paper. Why doesn't it bother you to be here?

"Time here makes me remember Delbert and his dedication to the church. I see your checkbook bulging in your pocket. Do you have my two checks?"

"Yes, but—"

"But what?" Stiles pulled an envelope from the inner pocket of his jacket. "To Mr. Wally Harris. *Ironton Corner Daily News.* 2 Main Street. Ironton Corner. Urgent news concerning Arthur and Barbara Blankenship."

Arthur grabbed for the letter, stumbled, and tripped backwards over a log. He lay still catching his breath. He looked up and fear gripped him when he spotted Stiles' lips turned into a sneering smile. He watched Stiles lift a foot. Arthur attempted to protect his back by bracing his arms on either side of his body and tightening his abdominal muscles. Arthur muffled a cry of pain when Stiles' foot pushed and his back snapped.

Stiles leaned down and ripped open Arthur's jacket. Buttons popped, flying in different directions. Stiles tugged at the checkbook, ripping Arthur's inside pocket. He tore out the two checks and threw the book at Arthur. He watched it land next to Arthur's right hand. Arthur picked it up and shivered at the inhuman look on Stiles' face as he slid it back into his pocket.

Stiles placed the two checks in his inside jacket pocket, brushed a few leaves from his jacket and pants, and straightened the white handkerchief in his pocket. Arthur watched his pastor pivot and march away.

A short time later he heard the crunch of a twig. He looked up to see Chief Bird.

"Arthur, what happened?" Bird sniffed the air and turned up his nose at the familiar pungent odor of cologne that lingered in the air.

"I was taking a morning walk and fell over this log."

"Where do you hurt?"

Arthur pointed to his back.

"I'm afraid to move you. Would you object if I call for an ambulance?"

"No, don't bother. Just help me up." Arthur grimaced. "Take me home if you don't mind."

Bird braced his legs and assisted Arthur to a sitting position. Arthur's breath became shallow and his face turned pale. "Wait. Let me sit for a minute."

"You need an ambulance, my friend."

"No, but maybe you can drive me home." Arthur braced his hands behind him. His face showed excruciating pain as he moved. Bird slowly pulled him to his feet. He leaned on Bird as they walked one step at a time to Bird's cruiser.

"What made you drive to the park this morning, Chief? Isn't it a little out of your territory?"

"Dick Rogers is away for a few days. I'm helping him out by patrolling the early morning shift. He has others to cover later in the day. Arthur, did you see or hear anyone else in the park?"

"No. I told you I was by myself. There was no one else around."

"From the way I found you, I can't help but wonder how you managed to fall and land on your back. It seems you would have needed a push to get in that ..."

Bird cut his conversation short as he pulled the cruiser into Arthur's driveway. Arthur opened the door. "Leave it alone. I need to protect ... please, John, leave it. I tripped and fell. That's all." He turned to step out of the vehicle.

"Wait, let me help you."

Arthur remained in the seat with pain shooting through his back until Bird helped him out. "John, I want to go inside and get into my whirlpool and forget about this accident."

Barbara walked by the front window and spotted Bird's cruiser pull into the driveway. She wondered why Bird stopped in front of her house until she saw him helping her husband. She ran out the door and hugged Arthur. "What happened? Are you all right?"

Arthur mumbled between breaths. "I fell. I'll be fine. Just

help me in."

Arthur leaned on Bird. Barbara led the way and directed Bird to set her husband in a chair in the living room. Bird looked down at Arthur. "Are you sure you don't need to go to the hospital? I don't want to find out later that you are suing the park."

"I'm not going to sue over a log I didn't see. Thanks for the lift, John."

Bird shrugged. "I hate to see Findlay Park become a place of danger and unexplained events. Call me if there is anything you need to talk about, Arthur. You know I am here for you."

He tipped his hat to Barbara and left.

"Arthur, what can I get you?"

"A cup of tea would be nice."

Barbara headed to the kitchen and returned with a hot cup. She handed it to her husband and pulled a chair next to him. She laid her hand gently on his arm. "Arthur, you said you were meeting Reverend Stiles this morning. Why didn't he help you?"

"He didn't show up."

She studied her husband's face. "You look warm. Let me get you out of your jacket. It is going to need to go to the tailor." She stood up and he leaned forward. She slowly removed his jacket one sleeve at a time and tossed it on a chair. Arthur's checkbook fell onto the floor. She reached down and picked it up. He tried to grab it, but she had it open before he could get a grip. He lowered his head.

"$2500 to the Magistrate. $1000 to Stiles. Why?" She flipped through the check register. "More checks to Stiles—$1,000 ... $750 ... $2,000. How many are there? What are you hiding, Arthur? Did he do this to you?"

* * *

Stiles drove to the bank, greeted the tellers, and deposited the checks in his account. He stopped for coffee at the diner and finally returned to his office. He pulled the "Historic Wall" binder from his satchel, and removed several pages of drawings. He arranged the pages across his desk. "Frederic, now that I'm not going to jail, I need to study these. They are magnificent, aren't they? The historic wall will show all the significant events that have happened in Ironton Corner since its beginning. And see here, a place for them to design something to represent my years. The wall will be another piece that will mark my time here. When I'm the head of all Independent Community Churches in the country, this will be a spot on the tour to show my ingenuity and commitment to the history of the town and not just the church I built here."

Stiles put everything away and leaned back in his chair. "Frederic, I'll contact the artist and have him design a tile for the wall with the words from my statement on Vietnam and one of me holding the veterans at gun point. Years from now, I'll be celebrated as a voice for freedom and justice. It is time to move forward, away from the narrow opinions of this town."

CHAPTER 29

June 14, 1971

Chet motioned Reverend Stiles to come over to the counter. The breakfast regulars hushed, and the ceiling fans clicked in their usual rhythm. Chet leaned over. "Reverend, the town council at the request of Irene Keene has called a meeting at the school to discuss your use of the green to make political statements."

"Really?" Stiles turned to face the breakfasters and announced over his shoulder to Chet. "I'll have my usual and be sure to give me plenty of butter with the muffin." He smiled over the crowd and took a seat at the table in front of the bowling trophies. George and Maida picked up their cups and joined him.

Maida laid her hand on his. "We'll be at the school."

"Good."

"I'm sorry, Matthew," Maida patted his hand, "but we'll be there to support Irene."

Stiles ripped his hand from under Maida's. "Irene's been a thorn in my side since I came here. She's afraid she's losing her power and importance in town."

Maida whispered. "Power? Importance?"

"Maida, you are so naïve. Don't you know your friend wants all the credit for improving Ironton Corner? She doesn't like it that my work has been more important to this town than her role as self-appointed savior of Ironton Corner."

George set his coffee down. "Reverend Stiles, you have my sister all wrong. She wants the best for Ironton Corner. If anyone is a self-appointed savior, you'd better look in a mirror."

Stiles stood up. "You'll eat those words, George." Stiles grabbed his check and turned on his heels. With his posture erect, he marched to the counter. He pulled out his wallet and threw a few bills on the counter. He shoved the door so hard the glass rattled.

* * *

The townspeople filled the gymnasium bleachers. Mayor Sims called the meeting to order. "The town council has called this emergency public meeting to discuss Irene Keene's complaint concerning the political use of the green. First, we'll hear from Irene."

Irene stood to address the crowded gymnasium. "When Reverend Stiles came to town, I protested his construction of the gazebo for band concerts and the walkways. If you remember, I have apologized and I feel the green has been much improved through the work of Reverend Stiles. The Museums of Ironton Corner have brought visitors and revenue to the church and the community for better than a year now. We've all benefited from the pool complex, and we continue to thank Frank and Jimmy Somers for that gift.

"But Reverend Stiles' action over Memorial Day is appalling. Confronting our veterans with a machine gun and his political statement carved into a piece of rock has made the national news. It's not the kind of attention we want or need.

"I propose that due to the abuse of the green by Reverend Matthew Henry Stiles that the town revisit a proposal made years ago that the church transfer the property to the town as many other towns in New England have done." Irene returned to her chair to vigorous applause.

Reverend Stiles stood and addressed the crowd from his seat on the first row in the bleachers. "Over my dead body will the green belong to anyone other than the church, and I am the church." He turned and stalked out. More than one hundred Vietnam protestors, who had gathered outside the school, cheered as Stiles strode out the door. The gymnasium remained pin-drop silent.

Mayor Sims moved toward the lectern. "People of Ironton Corner, the council want to hear your opinions about Irene's proposal. We've placed a standing microphone on the floor. Please use it to share your comments."

More than ten citizens lined up to speak. Most spoke in favor of Irene's proposal, but a few of the new people questioned her motives. Two hours later, the janitor of the school turned out the lights. Irene, Kenny, and Mayor Sims left the building and walked toward the Keenes' house.

"Irene, thanks for presenting this problem to the council. We will begin working with our lawyers and consulting other towns who have procured their greens as public property."

"Thanks, Mayor, for your support. The meeting represented the voice of the people as it should." They reached the Keenes' driveway and bade one another goodnight.

* * *

A week later, the Sterling Fence Company arrived early on a hot summer morning in Ironton Corner. They dug and pounded until four-foot aluminum stakes surrounded the green at eight foot intervals. Halfway through the morning, Irene registered a complaint with the police. The magistrate halted the work and asked for Irene and Reverend Stiles to meet with him in his office.

"Why are you erecting the fence, Reverend?" the magistrate asked.

"You were at the town meeting. This woman," he jabbed at Irene, "is organizing the selectman to take the green away from the church. Until the town acts, I'm doing as I please."

"But you can't do just as you please," Irene said.

"Why not?" Stiles stood ramrod straight.

"The church has bylaws."

"No, it doesn't. Per agreement with Arthur, those were made inactive the day I became president of the church."

"He didn't."

"He did. You think because you quote some early pastor in your book and his promise that the church will never fence the green that it's gospel truth. That quote will not stand up under the law." Stiles smirked.

The magistrate intervened. "If there are no bylaws, no official document, then I can't stop the fence."

Irene stomped off to confront Arthur about the bylaws.

Stiles strolled to the green and instructed the men to continue with their work. At the completion of the fence, the workers installed an extra wide gate directly across from Stiles' office. Reverend Stiles wired signs to the outside of the fence.

Keep Off the Green
Only use by permission of
The Reverend Matthew Henry Stiles
President of
First Independent Community Church
Ironton Corner

Irene ran over to Maida's porch where she was watching Stiles attach the signs to the fence. "See. I wasn't crazy that first day I met Reverend Stiles and tore up that sign. The exact sign is back, and it has multiplied. Look, they are placed all around the green."

"I don't know what to think, Irene. I had such hopes for Reverend Stiles and our town. I don't understand."

Wally Harris snapped a photo of Stiles threading a heavy duty lock through the gate and snapping it shut.

* * *

With one glance at the next day's paper, Jimmy called Bob and Rich Lang. "Did you see the paper? The green's locked up. We need to go see Reverend Stiles."

Jimmy and the boys barged into his office with the newspaper in hand and Joyce right behind them.

"You promised we'd always be able to ride our bikes through the green." Jimmy said.

"I know I promised you, boys."

"I'm mad about the gate," Bob shouted. "And our friends are calling us traitors to America because of your dumb old monument."

"Come in and sit down. Let me explain." Stiles directed the boys to seats. "What is the first Amendment to the Constitution?"

"Freedom of religion, speech, of the press, to assemble, and to petition," the Boy Scouts said in unison.

"So like any other citizen, I'm allowed to voice my opinion."

"You do that from the pulpit over and over again. Why did you have to do spell it out with that ... that monument?" Rich kicked at Stiles' desk.

Tapping his feet under his desk to control his anger, Stiles responded to the boys. "I needed to make a public statement that would stir people to action. That's my job."

Rich squirmed in his seat. "Reverend Stiles, I thought it was kind of weird for you to get the gun and point it at the veterans when you talk about peace all the time."

"I was angry. I acted inappropriately." Stiles pulled his starched white handkerchief out of his jacket pocket and wiped his brow. "I'm sorry. It was an irrational act."

"What about bikes on the green?" Jimmy piped in.

Stiles took a deep breath. "To be honest, in my haste and anger, I forgot my promise. I'll have the men come back and put another gate on the other side. George will open both gates each morning so you and others can continue to ride your bikes through the green to school."

The boys stood and put on their caps and shuffled toward the office door. Jimmy turned back. "You confuse me, Reverend Stiles."

Joyce watched the boys file out the door before she turned toward Reverend Stiles. "You confuse me, too. I've watched you with my boys—with all the boys. They admire you and look up to you. I'm going to the Boy Scout Council about your unpatriotic actions. I will not have you muddying those young minds."

"Get out of my office. I've put up with enough of your innuendos. One call to Arthur Blankenship and that will be the end of you."

"Try it." Joyce slammed the door behind her.

Stiles stepped toward the skeleton, picked up Frederic's bony hands, and played with Frederic's fingers. Noticing the light on the phone, he turned abruptly from his friend. He carefully picked up the receiver and heard Joyce ranting to Irene. He silently replaced the receiver, turned to his typewriter, attentively performed his trinity, and punched the keys.

The Chronicle of The <u>Reverend</u> Matthew Henry Stiles
June 21, 1971

That woman—she and Irene are out to destroy me. I need to look for a way to destroy them.

Meanwhile, I will accommodate the boys so that others

will see that I have their interests at heart. I need them and their parents for all my plans to work.

Stay focused on the next projects. They will bring another segment of the population to the church. They'll be coming to support a pastor who is not afraid to take a stand.

So many churches serve up pabulum. Not me. My new projects will be ready next year.

I'll be away for my much-needed sabbatical this fall. I have a group of the best pastors that I can trust to preach those eight weeks. After my study of church-sponsored schools, I'll slowly introduce the concept. I have no doubt they will buy into my suggestions for the appropriate curriculum for their children to succeed in life.

Stiles completed his ritual and filed the entry. He set his satchel on his desk and drew out the binders entitled "The Vietnamese Village Hut" and "Ironton Corner Historic Wall." Quietly he read and reread every word.

Part 3

Revelation

CHAPTER 30

March 1972

Two large trucks, one hauling a backhoe and the other cement blocks, stopped at Maida's driveway. Maida and Irene, their noses red from the chilly air, broke off their conversation. .

The driver of the first truck leaned over the passenger seat, and rolled down the window. "Ladies, I'm looking for Reverend Matthew Stiles. Can you help me?"

"You'll find him at the church on the other side of the green." Maida pointed to the fenced area in front of her house.

The driver tipped his Red Sox ball cap. "Thank you." He paused. "Funny, I've traveled all over this area of New England, and this is the first green I've seen fenced with warning signs posted. What's up with that?"

Irene put her hands on her hips. "You'll have to ask Reverend Stiles." The women watched the trucks pull away.

"I guess we're in for another surprise." Irene frowned.

"I hope this one involves tearing down the fence. I have to start my wash. I'll talk to you later."

* * *

Kenny heard the commotion from the cemetery and sauntered to the green. He touched the sleeve of Stiles' jacket. "What's up, Rev? What's with the banquet tables out here? Having some sort of lunch?" He pulled off his work gloves and stuffed them into the back pocket of his work pants.

"One of my special projects. Kenny, I'd like you to meet Henry Paulson, a ceramic sculptor." Stiles nodded toward the man.

Kenny pushed his Red Sox ball cap back on his head. "I've seen you in church, haven't I, Mr. Paulson?"

"Yes, Mr. Keene. A while back, Reverend Stiles asked for volunteers to assist with his projects. He contacted me about creating a wall depicting the history of Ironton Corner. With the help of your wife's written history, I believe we've decided on the significant events that best tell the story." Mr. Paulson unrolled a tube of drafting paper and spread it over two tables. "These are the sketches."

Kenny walked along the side of the tables, studying each drawing. Jefferson Post Office. Hobart Mill. Oak Street School. Blankenship Public Library. 1748 Town Hall. At the last drawing, he bent down close. "That's a portrait of our first pastor. You are good. You are really good. This is great. Just what the town needs. When will the wall be completed?"

"In a couple of weeks."

Kenny stood tall. "If you need any help, I live across the green."

"Thanks. I might call on you."

"Reverend Stiles, I hope you're leaving room for future moments in our history." Kenny reached into his back pocket for his work gloves.

"Of course, we are."

Kenny patted Stiles' shoulder. "You've created quite a stir with that monument and the fence the past year, but that wall might redeem you."

Over dinner, Kenny explained to Irene about the wall. "Visitors will see our history right in front of them. Imagine that." Kenny saw a familiar skeptical look pass over Irene's face. "Irene, from the drawings I saw, we'll be proud of it."

"I hope. If we get that fence down and the wall is all that you say, I may have a better opinion about our Reverend Stiles."

In the early morning, Kenny woke to clanking, crashing, and high-pitched truck brakes. He squinted at the clock, 5 a.m. Irene turned over. "What's wrong?"

"I heard a weird racket coming from the green." Kenny climbed out of bed with Irene scooting right behind him. From their front window they watched the scene through the early dawn light: one worker moving cement blocks with a fork lift, two carrying bags and piling them next to a hand-turned cement mixer, and others digging a square trench with shovels.

Irene whispered, as if the workers might hear her. "What are they doing?"

"I don't know. I'm getting dressed and going out there."

"I'm coming, too." They dressed and walked around the green to the gate.

Kenny spotlighted one of the workers with his flashlight. "What's going on?"

"A replica of a Vietnamese hut." The man shaded his eyes from the light.

Irene snapped. "That man is out of his mind."

"I'm sorry, Mrs. ..."

"Keene."

The name tweaked something in the man's mind. "Oh, Mrs. Keene, Reverend Stiles told me to tell you, and these are his exact words, 'to bring your porch chairs over to a watch a piece of Vietnam rising out of the green.' "

"A piece of Vietnam? We'll see about this."

A collection of townspeople gathered inside the fenced green. All day long they came and went; some bringing sack lunches; others thermoses of coffee.

By the time the children were out of school, a six foot long, four foot wide, and five foot high cement block hut stood at the end of the green opposite the band stand. A manufactured thatched pad had been thrown over the top to serve as a roof. Bamboo poles had been shoved under the overhanging thatch creating a porch.

Before the workers left, they stacked clearly labeled rice bags on either side of the small doorway. The electric company came and strung wire from a pole to an electrical box attached to a bamboo stake at the side of the hut.

At dusk a trumpet sounded. The crowd hushed. They turned to see Stiles on the steps of the church with a trumpeter at his side and strangers lined up behind him. The trumpeter marched forward and the masses parted like the Red Sea. Stiles paraded through the pathway carrying a tape reel on a red satin pillow and stood at military attention next to the doorway of the hut.

One stranger marched forward and placed two rickety stools under the overhanging thatched roof on either side of the doorway. Two others placed mannequins of a small girl and an older woman dressed in traditional costumes on the stools.

The trumpet sounded once more, and four more strangers came forward with two large speaker boxes, a professional reel-to-reel tape deck, and a bunch of electrical cords. They marched into the hut as whispers passed through the watchers.

Stiles held up the tape reel above his head. Dead silence filled the green. He disappeared into the hut. After a few minutes, Stiles handed the cord through the window to a worker who attached the cord to the electrical box. As Stiles emerged from the hut, the sounds of low flying aircraft and screaming women and children reverberated through the families and the curious.

While the tape played, another four nameless workers came out from behind the hut. They pounded four-foot stakes around the perimeter of the hut. Unrolling a spool of barbed-wire, they strung it so that the wire surrounded the hut, leaving only a small opening in the back. The tape played on and on. Most of the on-lookers backed away, covering their ears to block out the sounds. A few bystanders marched toward Stiles and shook his hand.

Irene, her auburn hair falling down around her face and her shoes pounding on the brick walk, made her way to Stiles and stood face-to-face with him. "You are despicable. The losses in the war are hard enough without this. When the news gets hold of this ...why do you feel you need to—"

"I need to provoke people like you and the government until the war is ended." Stiles brushed his hair back. He stepped away from Irene and turned to a few lingering bystanders, "As long as the war continues, I'll be making statements. If it goes on and on, this green will be covered with grotesque images of the war until those who have the power to end this carnage, end it."

Kenny stepped into Reverend Stiles' face. "I don't get it. You commission a historic wall and then this. Forget what I said yesterday about your redemption. I'll be with Irene when she demands the town council take control of the green."

Stiles stiffened to attention and stared dead-eyed at Kenny. "I'm not afraid of you or this town. I have plenty of people supporting me—plenty who share my dreams for the church of the future. It's time for churches to do more than pray silly little prayers asking God to change things. Bold action is what we need."

"We are capable of bold action, too." Kenny marched off.

CHAPTER 31

AFTER weeks of putting up with the continuous noise, Kenny, in a fit of frustration, ripped out the electric box under the cover of dark.

The next morning Chief Bird knocked on the Keenes' door. "Kenny, I've had a complaint from Reverend Stiles."

"What kind of complaint?" Kenny held the door open.

"He says you ripped out the electric box of the hut."

"I might have."

"If you did, I don't blame you, but it's my duty to inform you that it's a misdemeanor. Reverend Stiles isn't pressing charges this time, but the next time he's going to. You'll have to appear before the magistrate, and Stiles will sue for damages."

"What is it with that man?" Kenny stepped out and let the screen door slam behind him.

"He's slick. I've been watching him since he arrived here five years ago." Bird leaned on the porch railing.

Irene called from inside. "Anyone for a cup of coffee?"

"It's too nice a day to come inside. Come out and join us." Chief Bird opened the door for Irene. "As long as I have you both here I want to ask you something. Arthur looks like he's aged ten years, have you noticed?"

Irene stood silent for a moment. "The change started when Stiles came to town. Remember when Arthur collapsed at the diner."

"That morning was my first introduction to your Reverend Stiles. Chet told me Stiles and Arthur had words, and then ..." Bird stopped mid-sentence. He narrowed his eyes while a look of awareness spread over his face as if pieces of a puzzle were falling in place.

"And then what?" Kenny nudged Bird.

"Never mind. Irene, you and Arthur have been friends for years. If anyone can get him to open up, it would be you. I'm really worried."

"I wonder—" Irene straightened her posture.

"You wonder what?" Kenny turned to face Irene.

"Nothing ... I need to think."

The chief left and the Keenes lingered on their porch, Kenny leaning on the railing, Irene in her rocker.

"Our daffodils need attention." Irene rocked forward and got up. She stepped off the porch, stooped and stood repeatedly, plucking wilted flowers as she worked her hands and her mind.

A little while later, Irene joined Kenny on the porch. "I'll invite Barbara and Arthur over for dinner in a couple of weeks."

"Why wait?" Kenny asked.

"Each time I've asked him about his health or Reverend Stiles, he's changed the subject. I need to figure out how to approach the discussion so that he cannot dismiss my questions."

* * *

Barbara linked her arm into Arthur's as they climbed the Keenes' porch steps on a beautiful May night. She felt a new tremor in his arm and worried that his health was crumbling over the stress of their personal secrets and the responsibility he carried over the hiring of Reverend Stiles.

Kenny pushed the front door open. "Welcome." He shook hands with Arthur and kissed Barbara on the cheek. "Irene's in the kitchen."

Irene wiped her hands on a kitchen towel. "We're making this an informal evening and eating in here. Kenny, take Barbara's jacket."

"Smells good. You said you weren't going to fuss."

"I didn't. Just my standbys—meatloaf, potatoes, green beans, strawberry salad. Sit. Sit. Kenny, offer them wine. The glasses are on the table." Irene grabbed two hot pads and pulled the meat loaf and potatoes from the oven.

Kenny poured their favorite wine, Blue Nun, in the glasses. He stopped and tilted his head. "That blasted noise."

"Reverend Stiles' latest irritation." Barbara unfolded her napkin.

Arthur offered a toast. "Here's to the person who ripped out the electricity and gave us a peaceful day and night." Arthur winked at Kenny.

Kenny smiled, and they touched glasses. Irene jumped up with her usual energy, insisting on filling the plates even though Barbara offered to help.

Barbara leaned over her plate. "Mm ... smells good."

"Watch the cheese. It makes the meat loaf extremely hot inside." Irene took her seat. Kenny blessed the meal and they dug into the food.

"This is delicious, Irene," Arthur said between bites.

"Your meat loaf reminds me. We've talked about doing another church cookbook. Do you think it's time?" Barbara loaded her fork with beans.

"It's been about ten years since the last one."

"I need a project. I'll call some others and see if they are interested." Barbara held her wine glass almost to her lips. She appeared lost in thought as the men good-naturedly argued about the strange concoctions in the last cookbook.

Irene looked around the table. She set down her wine glass and reached for Arthur's hand. "Arthur, you need to tell us what has been going on since you hired Reverend Stiles. You haven't been yourself."

Barbara took Arthur's other hand. "She's right. You've been distant and our marriage is suffering from your silence. At night, I hear you tossing and turning as if wrestling the devil. Please tell us."

Arthur gently pulled his hands away from their grip and leaned forward burying his head in his hands. "It's a long story."

"Let's take our dessert in the living room," Kenny suggested.

Arthur and Barbara sat close on the sofa. Irene and Kenny took the two club chairs across from them. The coffee and cookies rested on the flat-topped travel trunk between them that served as a table.

"This conversation must remain confidential, and Barbara ...," he touched her face and turned her head so he could look directly into her eyes, "along with my mistakes, I must tell our story, too."

Tears filled her eyes, and she nodded. He leaned forward and attempted to objectively share the situation that had controlled his life for the last five years. The words tumbled out of his mouth in relief, but Irene, Kenny, and Barbara could feel the misery that lay beneath them.

"Years ago, as an employee in her father's business, Barbara was invited to listen to those who wanted to modernize her father's business. The group convinced her that her father's conservative procedures limited the company's growth and prosperity. Young, naïve, and with her strong drive to be a success, she went along with the defiant employees. Her father, a thoroughly ethical person, watched and waited. He hoped his daughter would see that what she and they were doing was illegal and come to him. They didn't. He tried to talk sense into Barbara, but she resisted. With his reputation at stake and his worry for his customers, he called in the law."

Barbara sat forward and spoke using a soft voice, not her usual clear and articulate one. "I helped to create the system, knowing it was edgy, but to my mind not quite illegal. We could walk that thin line between legal and illegal. After all, others before us had straddled that edge. Dad turned me in along with the rest. A business friend recommended Arthur Blankenship to represent me." She hugged onto Arthur's arm. "He did all he could, but I was sentenced to jail." She looked around at the faces of her friends. "I needed a lesson. I didn't know how much of a lesson I'd have to learn."

Arthur pulled her close. "She was given a thirteen-month sentence that would be reduced to six months with good behavior since she had no prior run-ins with the law. After her first month in Framingham Women's Prison, a guard attempted to rape her. Taller than the man, she swung hard at his head. He hit the bars just right and later died of a massive hemorrhage. The prison charged her with manslaughter."

"Why? The guard attacked—" Kenny stood up and paced.

"It was her word against the word of another guard who witnessed the brutality."

"What's wrong with our system? Blaming the women and girls." Kenny continued to pace.

They listened to the hum of an electric clock and the crunch of cookies until Kenny returned to his chair and nodded for Arthur to go on.

"I represented her again, but the system worked against us. The jury found her guilty. She served three more years in the house of correction. I visited her every weekend. That's when we fell in love."

"And to protect Barbara," Irene said, "you've kept this quiet."

"I'm surprised that we didn't read of it in the *Boston Globe*," Kenny said reaching for the plate of cookies.

"The prison wanted as little publicity as possible, so only a few paragraphs ever appeared in the Globe, for which I was angry and grateful. Angry because the system has the power to cover up its own criminal action, grateful that Barbara's name was not in the headlines."

Arthur looked deep into his wife's eyes and swallowed hard. "When Matthew Henry Stiles met George, and then George introduced him to me, the young man had done his homework. He had studied our community and found that I'd run a large law practice before the accident with my back. He learned I served on a committee that reviewed thousands of manslaughter cases.

"Irene and Kenny, manslaughter cases continue to be a gray area of the law. Both charges and convictions are murky and depend on who is involved and what judge hears the case. I still serve on the committee, and we continue to attempt to sort out the fuzzy lines and issues. It's a mess." He paused to sip his coffee.

"I don't know how, but Stiles knew about Barbara and her history. He threatened to expose her if I didn't cooperate with him. I couldn't let him do that." Arthur hung his head.

Barbara squeezed closer to him, as a flood of sadness filled her heart. "You should have told me. We've been here long enough that the community would have talked and gossiped for a while, but those who knew me would have understood. We could have—

" She held back tears of anger mixed with embarrassment over her brash conduct as a young woman proving her way in her father's business. "I was naïve and caught up in the need for success," she said.

Arthur pulled back. "Let me continue, I have to tell you the rest. It's eating me away, emotionally and physically, as you've noticed. Stiles insisted that I support him in the amount of $1,000 a month, even before his first year contract was signed."

"You mean before he came here, you had given him over $4,000?" Barbara attempted to control rage coming from a place deep in her soul.

"Yes, and he has come back for more and more. Remember, Barbara, the night he came to my home office. He wanted another check. I told him that was the last. And he did leave me alone until ... until he called me needing money to pay his fine from the machine gun incident. I argued with him on the phone, but he insisted I meet him at Findlay State Park.

"At the park he harassed me by waving letters addressed to Wally Harris of the *Ironton Corner Daily News* and the editor of the *Boston Globe* with copies to Mayor Sims and the selectmen exposing Barbara's background. He threatened to mail them unless I gave him a check to cover his fine. When I grabbed for the letters, I lost my balance and fell over a log. He reached down, tore the checkbook from my pocket and ripped out the check which I'd foolishly written out and signed because no matter what I did, he always won. I lay there looking at his eyes, filled with such fury, I feared for my life. Stiles' lips turned into a sneering smile as he pushed me harder against the log. I felt a snap and cried in pain. He laughed that high-pitched laugh of his like Frankenstein." Arthur's face reddened and his shoulders slumped in anger and shame.

A mix of emotions tumbled through the hearts in that room until Barbara whispered, "Why didn't you go to the police?"

"Funny, I had my chance because Chief·Bird found me and took me home. Instead of telling the truth, I told him I'd fallen. I wanted to protect you, Barbara."

Irene, who'd been unusually quiet, said, "Now I understand

why you pushed so hard to ordain him and let him be president and treasurer of the parish. But he's assaulted you. It's time to tell the truth and get rid of that man." She grabbed a cookie and took a big bite.

Barbara held Arthur close. "Arthur, you didn't need to protect me. Call a meeting and we'll share the truth together. I know these people will—"

"Barbara, we'd have to leave the area. It's better for me to try to handle it."

"But—" Irene said.

"I know what you're going to say. You'd all love Barbara anyhow, but you haven't seen what I have. Innocent people whose lives have been ruined. Church-going people who point fingers, gossip, and shun when the truth comes out. People say it's no problem, but the suspicion, the looks and the asides wear you down. During my law practice, I've known several who couldn't take the public innuendoes and have chosen suicide. I couldn't risk that for Barbara."

With those words, Arthur collapsed against Barbara. The color left his face. It took all her strength to hold him. Kenny helped Barbara support Arthur. "Irene, get my purse. In it is a bottle of pills the doctor gave Arthur for these spells."

Irene did as Barbara asked. Arthur swallowed the pills with cold coffee, hints of color gradually returned to his face. All remained huddled around the sofa and silent, processing what they had heard.

After several minutes, Irene stood. She set her face. "I need to find George. He hinted that he knows something about Reverend Stiles from his Akron days. It's time that he shares what he knows. Arthur, I'm sorry Stiles put you in such a spot. We'll get through this. Count on it."

Arthur smiled a weak smile. He knew by the look on Irene's face she'd get to the bottom of all the lies and deceptions. Now that the truth was out, relief tinged with fear washed over him.

"Honey, I'll drive you home." Barbara supported Arthur to the porch. Irene hugged Barbara, and then she held Arthur for a long time.

Arthur folded himself into the car. Barbara shut the door and walked to the other side. She gave a slight wave over the roof of the car before she slid into the driver's seat. After she started the engine, her free hand reached out for Arthur's.

The Keenes watched until their tail lights disappeared. They breathed in the fresh night air trying to relax their bodies after the tense evening.

* * *

Stiles unbent from his position behind a sign on the green, pulled his dark jacket around his shoulders, crept low across the street, and slinked into his office. With only the light from a street lamp, he held Frederic's bony finger. "I wonder what that was about. Arthur is looking weak and old. Do you suppose he is about to tell on me?" Frederic's bones rattled.

"Right. I shouldn't worry. The hundreds of new church members have pledged their allegiance to me and my programs. And God called me here. No, God insisted I come here to save this place! The new people won't listen to those stuck in the 50's. They will side with me not the old guard."

CHAPTER 32

May 9, 1972

"GEORGE, this is your sister," Irene announced.

"Really, you don't think I recognize your voice over the phone yet? What can I do for you?"

"We need to talk."

"I have my fishing gear packed to go to the pond. According to the fish calendar, they should be biting today.

"Sounds good. How about if I go with you? It's a beautiful day, and I can have my rod and gear ready in a jiffy."

"What's this about?"

"Reverend Stiles."

"I should have known. I'll be around in fifteen minutes. I hope what you have to say doesn't spoil a good fishing trip."

George piled Irene's gear in the back of his truck. They drove to the pond with his flat-bottomed fishing boat hitched to the back. George backed the trailer into the shallow water ramp, a few hundred feet from the entry to the Tavern on the Pond, and hopped from the truck.

"Irene, move to the driver's seat. Pull the truck forward at my signal," George shouted.

Without any grace, she climbed over the gear shift to the driver's seat. He unhooked the boat and signaled her to drive forward. George tied the boat to the dock while Irene parked the truck. Dressed in jeans and one of Kenny's denim shirts, Irene carried their gear, handed the poles and a cooler to George. She climbed aboard and settled on the front bench facing George.

"You all set?"

George removed the cellophane wrapper from a cigar and wet the end in his mouth before pulling the cord to start the motor. He motored to the east end of the pond and dropped the anchor near some lily pads. George opened a can, and they baited their hooks with earthworms. "Are you here to discuss that infernal screaming all day from the green?"

"No."

"So, what's so urgent?"

"George, I need to know what you discovered about Matthew Henry Stiles from Ruth's relatives." She cast her line in the water near the plants.

"Why do you want to know?"

"Because of two people we love and care about."

"Might that be Barbara and Arthur?"

"Yes."

"He hasn't looked so good the last few months. And every time I see them, Barbara hovers over him like he's going to die, and that isn't like her."

Stalling for time to organize his thoughts, George flashed a grin at his sister. "You've lost your worm. Hand your line here, and I'll fix it for you."

"Wipe that grin off, George Lawrence. I don't need help." She fished a fat worm out of the can. She squeezed, stretched, and wove the worm over and back and through the hook, making the letter S.

George cast his line again. "Well, I best start at the beginning. Apparently his family had a pastor that held such a tight hold on young Matthew that he began to walk, dress, and talk like the man. One of Ruth's cousins said that Stiles even tried green contact lenses to see if his eyes might match the pastor's. Sick, huh?

"During Matthew's sophomore year in high school, the police arrested him for jewelry theft. My cousin said Matthew befriended two wealthy boys long enough to learn when their parents were traveling. He planned and executed a break-in to steal their jewelry—antique emerald rings and diamond brooches. Through an out-of-court settlement, his father arranged for Matthew to be released into his care. Another relative said that the father was known to be verbally abusive so that must have been a double sentence for Matthew.

"Not six months later, the police arrested Matthew a second time. They charged him with armed robbery, possession of a deadly weapon, and assault on the owner of a jewelry firm near Akron. His mother pleaded for him to be released into her care, but with the escalation to armed robbery and assault with a deadly weapon, he was sentenced to two years in the local juvenile detention center.

"He refused to see his father. He accepted calls only from his mother and daily visits from the weird pastor. I'm told he completed his high school studies while in detention. He followed manslaughter cases with great interest, since he came ever so close to that charge. According to rumors, he bragged about how he would have used the gun, if the jeweler had given him any more trouble."

George reeled in his line. "Think I'll pull up the anchor and move us over toward that willow tree. I'll bet the fish are under those branches waiting for us."

With the anchor in place, they tossed their lines. After a nibble and a tug, Irene pulled in a small sunfish. She unhooked it and tossed it back. "The juvenile record must be why the Unitarians refused to ordain him. Your information fills in important gaps in the story." Irene tossed her line and it landed in the weeds. She tugged hard and broke her line. "George, does Stiles know you know all this?"

"I don't think so. I believe that my sources were very discreet." George pitched the stub of his cigar into the pond.

"If the Unitarians found out and you found out, that means he might figure out the connections and the leaks. George, be careful." Irene restrung her line. "I need to think about what you've told me."

They fished for another two hours, and with their limit met and the stringer full, George pulled up the anchor.

As they came near the shore, Irene said, "Must be time for the Tavern to open for lunch. I see the valet's lemon yellow Chevy racing into the parking lot."

Chip screeched to an abrupt halt when he noticed George coming into the dock. He jumped out of the car, leaving the door wide open, rushed over, and helped secure the boat. "Mr. Lawrence. Mrs. Keene. Did you catch anything?"

"Yes, a stringer full." George held up the fish.

"I see you're running late, Chip."

"I had a late night."

"A girlfriend?"

Chip's face flushed with embarrassment.

"Are you young people still parking out along the entrance to the Revere Forest Reserve?" Irene prodded.

"Yes."

"Some things never change." George shrugged.

Chip smiled good-naturedly, but added a comment in his defense. "It's not just kids that hang out there. I saw your Reverend Stiles creeping around out there a few times over the past couple of years."

"Really?"

Several cars pulled in and Chip ran over to assist.

CHAPTER 33

May 10, 1972

STILES drove to Revere Forest Reserve and knocked on the cottage door. Leroy swung the door open wide and pulled Stiles inside with a motion that turned into a short dance. "Welcome, my friend. Why are you stiff as a board? Something weighing on your mind? A glass of my homemade wine is guaranteed to lift your spirits." Leroy flashed his eyes. "Sit down and make yourself at home."

Stiles relaxed on the wool plaid sofa that smelled of age and cigarettes. Leroy set the bottle of wine and two glasses on a shabby maple coffee table and filled them. With a glass in his hand, he held it to the light. "Look how the light plays in my wine." Leroy twirled the glass and followed its dancing glow.

"You are crazy. Sit down before you spill it."

Leroy let his gaunt frame fall into a low over-stuffed chair. Lifting his long skinny legs, he rested his heels on the edge of the sofa. Chalk white skin shone between his pant leg and the top of his short black nylon socks. A look of disapproval came from Stiles. "Pull your pant legs down. Your white skin is an ugly sight."

Leroy kept his legs where they were. Irritating his friend was one of his favorite sports. "You told me you've added another eighty members to the church. Hopefully, a number have money because by my count, you're running low on funds."

"I'm not concerned about the money. My concern is the Keenes and the Blankenships. Irene had them over for dinner the other night. I saw them go into the kitchen, then into the living room. The Keenes never use their living room. So I wondered why. I watched them say goodnight. Irene's hug showed more affection than I thought she or any New Englander was capable of."

"You don't suppose Arthur told them about the little arrangement between you two." Leroy dropped his legs to the floor.

"If he was going to tell anyone, it would be Irene." Stiles sipped his wine.

"Matthew, you need to slow down."

"I can't slow down. I need another hundred new families. I won't be satisfied until I have four hundred families using the church facilities. I must succeed. God has chosen me. God wants me to show my father that my gifts are as important as his."

"Slow down. Enjoy your success. The rest will come."

"No, it won't if suspicion is mounting."

"Who else are you worried about." Leroy watched Stiles fidget.

"George. He's here, there, and everywhere in the church and the basement."

"Hum, now there is something to worry about. Remember your father told you that George had lived in Akron during his early marriage. You need to find out what he knows about your early life. It didn't take much for you to bump into Barbara Blankenship's record. If he knows the right people, he can find yours." Leroy lighted a cigarette.

Stiles pitched forward. "If you had not—"

"Now, now, now." Leroy preened and leaned back against the chair. "You were predisposed to your behavior by watching your father walk over people and use their weakness to his advantage." Leroy inhaled and smoothly exhaled. "And then you invited me and only me to work with you in the detention center. My talks and mentoring have brought you to the place you are now."

"You helped me and then you deserted me. No one could find any trace of you." Stiles sulked.

Leroy blew smoke rings and draped his long arm over the back of his chair. "Stop your whining. I didn't desert you. I waited for the right time. I watched you at Harvard. I knew exactly when you would need my guidance. If you run into trouble here, I promise, you and I will disappear and wait for the right moment to begin again."

He took a deep draw on his cigarette and puffed slowly as

smoke rings floated over Stiles' head. "Maybe a movie will relax you—take your mind off your worries. The classics allow us to achieve such purity of thought. I've watched your endeavors. Like Victor Frankenstein, you refuse to accept the limits put before you. God has bestowed you with the task of opening the eyes of those who follow you. Maybe there is another of life's lessons to learn from the film. Shall we watch *Frankenstein*? "

"I'll get the screen." Stiles headed to the bedroom.

Leroy opened the hall closet door. He pulled out a projector and sound box and along with a crate of sixteen millimeter film reels. Placing the projector on a sturdy table and the sound box on the floor, he stretched out two cords, connected the empty reel in its place, and snapped the first of two film reels in its position. He fed the film through the sprockets, while Stiles worked with the screen. With the lights off, Leroy hit the switch, the test pattern filled the screen, and then, the film began. Leroy and Stiles lounged at separate ends of the sofa and lost themselves in the story.

The movie over, Leroy slid forward and turned off the projector. He leaned back and twisted his body to face Stiles. "See, Victor doesn't let anything get in his way. He stifles his feelings. He transgresses all boundaries and creates something new like you are doing with this church. Some will celebrate your victory; others will want you locked up. It's the chance we, who seek to surpass ordinary human abilities, take."

"I don't know if you are Victor and I'm the monster or if I'm the monster and you are Victor." Stiles said.

"My role is to guide you to complete your dreams and ambitions, not make you into a monster. Matthew, you are meant for greatness, and this church is the start. You'll be the president of a new denomination of churches world-wide before we are through. Remember Victor Frankenstein's words, 'I will pioneer a new way, explore unknown powers, and unfold to the world the deepest mysteries of creation.' "

"Sometimes I feel like a puppet and you are the puppeteer."

"My dear boy, isn't that how your father raised you? You'd be his puppet, if you were not mine. Don't blame me. You are better than him. You are one of God's favored ones. If you continue to follow my guidance, the heavens will be ablaze in our glory."

"I need to go." Stiles stretched up from the sofa and started to lower the screen.

"Leave that my friend. I'm going to watch the movie again. Go with my blessings." Leroy settled back and flipped on the projector.

Stiles made his way to the door in the dark.

The Chronicle of The <u>Reverend</u> Matthew Henry Stiles
May 10, 1972

Leroy irritates me and calms me. The best characteristic about Leroy is that he believes in my vision and eventual success. Without him, my dreams might be simply dreams, instead of concrete realities.

Wally Harris' photographic spread of the historic wall will be in the paper tomorrow. For the dedication, I've arranged for a descendent of the local Indians to perform a traditional dance and for the Daughters of the American Revolution to provide a reading.

The local school teachers, at my suggestion, prepared a booklet for each grade level to hand out to the students. The dedication will mark another milestone in my ministry here.

After that, my energy will be focused on the final preparations for the sixty who are traveling with me to Germany and the Black Forest.

CHAPTER 34

June 14, 1972

On a hot afternoon, two Greyhound buses lined up in front of the church. Six Scouts, nervous and excited about their first trip out of the country, assisted the drivers in organizing luggage for the storage areas. At the sound of a high-pitched bell rung by Reverend Stiles, the Weaver family sang, "Climb Every Mountain" from The Sound of Music. The well-wishers applauded, and the tourists, some with cameras hanging around their necks, others with carry-on luggage draped over their shoulders, lined up to board the bus.

Reverend Stiles stood in the well of the first bus. Picking up the microphone, he said, "We're on our way for two weeks in the glorious mountains and forests of Germany. May our trip be safe, and may we return full of energy. Frank Somers is in charge of this bus. Address any questions to him."

Stepping into the second bus, Stiles set his brief case behind the driver and clapped his hands together. "Settle back and enjoy our adventure. I've planned this experience to amaze and intrigue you and engage your imaginations." The buses beeped their horns three times in unison as they pulled away from the curb.

On the ride to Logan International Airport, Stiles gazed at his reflection in the tinted window and remembered the nightmare he had faced six weeks ago. He had received a call from a supervisor at Pan Am. The bland voice on the phone said, "Your check of $52,000 for the remainder of the airfare and tour expenses was returned to us for insufficient funds."

"That just can't be."

"I'm afraid it is. I am sorry, but if we don't have the money in forty-eight hours, your trip will be cancelled and the deposits will not be returned per our contract."

"Yes, yes, I will have the money."

He recalled scrambling through the museums, making lists, and drawing diagrams. He relived Leroy's tongue lashing as he stood in his mentor's house shamed, yet aroused by the unexpected drama.

"You idiot. You and your reckless spending. I warned that you were moving too fast, but you didn't listen. No, no, no, your ambition blinded you. Do you have any records of what you've spent? Why didn't you know that you had drained all the accounts dry?" Leroy paused for a breath. "What did you do with the second mortgage you took out for the museums? I'll never understand how the banks gave you that mortgage without a signature from someone else in the church. You are ruining your climb to success."

"Stop, stop, Leroy. I'm humiliated enough. I need you to deposit $52,000 in my account now."

"Is your account completely empty?"

"Yes."

"You spent it all?"

"I don't have time to argue with you, I need the funds to complete the payment for the tour."

"If I lend you the money, how do you expect to repay me?"

"I've made a list of the most valuable items in the museums and drawings to help you locate them. Take only the ones I've listed and fence them through your usual contacts. Those specified items will bring you about $60,000. That will bring you a generous $8,000 for your work."

"I need to think this through over a bottle of wine."

"I don't have time for wine."

"Sit with me while I look at my accounts and make the necessary calls to arrange my funds placed in your accounts."

The bus braked hard and the driver's voice blasted over the PA system, bringing Stiles back to the present.

The driver announced, "We've arrived at Logan International Airport. Look around and gather your belongings. You will not be returning to this bus for two weeks. Enjoy your trip."

Stiles breathed deeply to calm his nerves, hoping there would be no unexpected surprises on the trip or upon his return.

The drivers unloaded their cargo, the skycaps tended to the luggage, and the vacationers followed Stiles inside the terminal. Stiles opened his briefcase and handed each person their tickets. "You'll need these and your passports to check in. After we are all checked in, we'll go to the gate."

At the gate, Stiles distributed a packet to each person. "In addition to the other guides and information sheets, I'm giving you a little something to read on the plane. As you recall from our preparatory meetings, I'm fascinated with the sinister, yet comical tales about sorcerers and wizards said to live in and about the Black Forest. I've copied a few of those stories for your reading pleasure."

Maida slipped the packet into her purse. "This trip is going to be the best because of you, Reverend Stiles. Thank you."

With the announcement of their flight, the group filed onto the plane and looked for their seat assignment as they inched down the long aisle to the back. The men assisted the women in lifting their carry-ons, placing them in the overhead bins before taking their own seats. Stiles looked over the travelers. Satisfied they were all comfortable, he took his seat, buckled up, and nodded off dreaming of Leroy back in Ironton Corner.

* * *

Leroy turned off his headlights, slowly inched his dark blue Ford station wagon up the blacktop driveway behind the Alice and Henry Stiles Museum and parked. Carefully he opened the car door. He listened for any human sounds. Not hearing any, Leroy, dressed all in black, stepped out of his car and walked to the backdoor.

With a set of small tools that he pulled from his side pocket, he fiddled with the lock and pushed the door open. He returned to his car, carried a load of blankets inside, and placed them on a table in the foyer. Climbing the stairs in his shoes with no tread, he went directly to the gun cases. He used his tools again to spring the locks. After making several trips down the steps carrying the weapons and placing them on the sturdy table, he wrapped each gun in a blanket.

He lugged the bundles to the back of his wagon, stacking them to one side. He pulled a new dust mop from the wagon bed, walked back inside, wiped down the stairs and the entry, backed out of the museum while still mopping, and locked the door.

Throwing the mop into the back seat, he climbed in the driver's seat and moved his car. Before stepping out of his car behind Maida's house, he studied the drawing of the layout of the interior that Stiles had given him. He jimmied Maida's back door and located the clocks. He read the accompanying description of each clock and whistled at the suggested value of each. In an orderly fashion, he collected not just the clocks Stiles had on the list, but all the clocks and carried each one to the dining room table.

He went upstairs and removed all the blankets from Maida's linen closet. Downstairs, he bundled the clocks, carted them out one by one to his car, and stacked some in the back of his wagon and others on the back seat. He returned to the house and located her jewelry boxes, packaged them, and carried the bundle to the front seat of his car.

Returning to the house with the dust mop, Leroy cleaned everywhere he had stepped. He leaned on the handle of the mop in front of Maida's hand-hewn clock in the hall. It was as exquisite as Stiles had told him. As he removed one glove and touched the clock's irresistibly handsome finish, he saw the lights of a car passing by and ducked. He jumped when the mop handle made a loud noise as it struck the wood floor. He pulled the glove on and rubbed the spot where he thought he had touched the cabinet of the clock. Picking up the mop, he moved to the back door using it behind him. He locked Maida's door, looked to be sure no one was about and moved to his car. He sat in his car catching his breath.

The paved alley behind the Scout Museum and Doc's Apothecary Museum was sheltered by trees and had no occupied homes on either side. Leroy wiped his sweat-soaked hands before replacing his gloves and moving out of his car. Working the lock on the Scout Museum, Leroy removed the most treasured letters from

Lord Baden-Powell. With great care, he placed them in a cloth-covered portfolio to protect them from harm and laid the port-folio on the back seat. Finally, he went back inside with his dust mop.

At the Apothecary Museum he unlocked the glass display cabinets. He carefully removed each of the antique doctor's instruments that had been borrowed from the American Medical Association and neatly placed them into individual soft cotton bags. They filled the last bit of space in his car. He again did his dusting routine.

With no headlights and with as little engine noise as possible, Leroy drove away. He breathed a sigh of relief when he reached the highway. By dawn, Leroy had unloaded his car. He worked the remainder of the day removing the government markings from the borrowed pieces. By noon next day, he had made contact with all of his customers.

Over the next two days, he met buyers in alleys and on back roads. In suit and tie, he returned the $52,000 he had withdrawn from his accounts to cover Stiles' debt. The evening of the third day, he organized the remaining money—his profit—into neat piles of like bills, on the dining room table. He surveyed his take ... $42,000. "Leroy, the risk you have taken for Matthew has netted you a nice little profit to be deposited into my special account. Now, I deserve to open my best bottle of champagne."

With a towel around the bottle, he popped the cork and smiled a crooked smile. Sitting at the table, he sipped and played with the piles of bills, counting and recounting. After draining the last of the champagne into his glass, he placed the bills into a brief case and spun the combination lock.

At ten sharp, he heard a rap on the door. "Courier service," a voice announced. He opened the door and handed the case to the courier. The uniformed man gave Leroy a receipt. Leroy tiptoed to the phone, removed it from its cradle to silence it, walked into his bedroom, and stretched his lanky body on his water bed. He slept the night and the next day away like an innocent child.

CHAPTER 35

June 17, 1972

WHEN Irene and Kenny finished using The Art of Making Love that morning, he returned the book to its drawer. He used his hand to flatten his mussed hair. "The travelers are in the Black Forest today."

"I bet Maida comes back with more than one cuckoo clock."

"Why do you say that?" Kenny reached over to touch her one more time.

Irene pushed his hand away. "Because she studied the photos Stiles supplied her with over and over until the pages were well-worn. Kenny, she's the oldest traveler, do you think she will be able to keep up?"

Kenny stretched. "I mentioned that to Frank. He said not to worry, that he and Jimmy will keep track of her."

"I promised to check her house every three days. I'll go over right after breakfast."

"Do we have to move from here?" Kenny attempted to pull Irene close.

She gave him a kiss on the forehead. "Yes."

Irene dangled her legs over her side of the bed, ran her fingers through her hair, picked up the comb on the night stand, and teased her to hair to its full height. Wrapping her nude body in the robe that she pulled down from the corner post of their bed, she batted her eyes down at Kenny. "I'm going to shower. The oatmeal and coffee will be ready in thirty minutes."

After cleaning the dishes, Irene stood on the steps and enjoyed the smell of late lilacs that surrounded her porch before she stepped across the driveways to Maida's house. She unlocked the door and stepped inside.

Taking one glance into the parlor from the hall, she stopped her forward motion. "What? This can't be! No, it can't be!" In a daze she walked through the parlor and dining room. The empty spaces stared out at her. Where were the clocks? At the sound of the front door slamming, she ran toward Maida's kitchen.

Kenny caught her arm. "Irene, wait. It's me. What's wrong?"

"Someone has stolen the clocks."

"All the clocks?"

"Yes."

Kenny guided Irene to a chair at Maida's kitchen table. "Sit."

"My legs are rubbery. Please check upstairs." She took a couple of breaths, trying to settle nerves.

"The thief cleaned out her linen closet and took the clock from the hall table," Kenny called as he came down the stairs. Returning to the kitchen, he rubbed Irene's shoulders that were up around her ears in fright.

"I can't believe we didn't hear something." Irene's shoulders visibly relaxed slightly.

"With all the jabber from that thatched house, the steeple could collapse and we'd never hear it. Did you call the Chief?"

"No. Please call him and George."

Kenny made the calls and returned to Irene's shoulders.

They heard a rap on the door and footsteps. "It's George and me," Chief Bird called out. Irene and Kenny joined the men in the hall.

George clutched his sister. "Who would do this to Maida?"

Almost in slow motion, Chief Bird walked through the rooms. He noted the empty spaces and picked up the small signs that described each clock and placed them in his pocket. "What about upstairs?"

"I went up there, but I didn't touch anything, not even the handrail. The thief cleaned out her linen closet, too."

"What about her jewelry?" Bird asked.

George ran up the stairs. Bird reached to stop him, but he thought better of it. He understood George's worry and concern over Maida.

"All of it's gone," George called as he slowly descended the stairs.

Chief Bird turned to Irene. "Could she have taken it with her?"

"No, she told me she packed two inexpensive necklaces and earrings to match. She said she didn't want her good pieces to be stolen on the trip." Irene, visibly weakened by the losses for Maida, leaned against Kenny.

Chief Bird paced through the dining room and parlor; he stopped in the hall admiring the tall clock like he did every time he visited Maida. "This crime is likely to be the work of one person. If there'd been more than one, they would have taken this. Its value is close to six figures."

"Wait." George opened the front of the tall clock, pulled on a hidden drawer and felt inside. "Her diamond and emerald ring is gone." His face sagged and tears welled up. "Maida's ... her family ring ... she'll be crushed."

Bird leaned against the newel post at the bottom of the stairs. "My crime crew will dust for prints. If you don't mind, will you drop by the office and give Bernice, my secretary, descriptions of Maida's jewelry? She needs to post all the information as quickly as possible."

"We will." Kenny answered for Maida's shocked friends.

The Chief started for the door. "Let's check the other museums before I call my guys to dust for prints and gather other evidence."

"We'll be careful not to disturb anything," Kenny said.

"I know you will. George, I assume you have the keys." George locked Maida's door and led them two doors down from Maida's house.

They turned left onto the decorative zigzag-patterned brick sidewalk that led up to the door of the Alice and Henry Stiles Museum. George opened the door and pushed it back. The four of them walked through the first floor looking for any missing seascapes. None were missing.

Stopping at the bottom of the steps to the second floor, George turned to his friends, "I'm surprised that the paintings are all here. I checked and the collection is valued at well over $75,000."

"The thief may not have had a way to fence those." Chief Bird followed the group up the highly polished stairs to the second floor. Reaching the top, their jaws dropped at the sight of the empty gun display cases. "The Sims will be devastated. How could anyone steal the collection dedicated to the memory of their son is beyond me."

Kenny walked to the corner of the room and picked up a photo of the Sims boy. "The thief evidently threw this into the corner." He ran his finger down the crack in the glass. He handed it to Irene.

"I'll return this to the Mayor and his family. This is ... I don't know, but—" Irene's face crumpled into tears and Kenny helped her down the stairs.

Chief Bird remained upstairs studying the crime scene. From the top of the stairs he watched the three friends huddled, looking at the photo. He knew what they felt—their trust had been violated by an unknown thief. Houses would be locked tighter, and he'd be patrolling more often until they felt safe again like he did after the murder of Delbert Martin.

The foursome walked to the Scout Museum. George unlocked the door. He held his breath as he pushed the door open. The others followed behind and immediately spotted the open cases where the valuable letters had been laid out for the public to appreciate the history of the Boy Scouts. "Well, I'll be," George said.

"Damn, damn, damn," Kenny mumbled.

Irene read the sign that posted the names of the Boy Scouts printed on it. She touched each name. "The scouts will be devastated. It's going to feel like ...," she hesitated, "I hate to use the word ... rape to those boys." She pounded her hands against the case.

Chief Bird stepped next to Irene. "You're right. The entire town is going to feel the impact of this crime."

George stood still and took a brief mental inventory of the room. "This person knew what he wanted ... what was valuable. He must have cased the museums."

Chief Bird made some notes in his notebook. "Let's see what is missing from the Doc's Apothecary."

They crossed the beautifully manicured green yard to Doc's. Colorful zinnias and tall yellow summer daisies clamored for their attention, but no one noticed. George handed his ring of keys to Kenny. "Kenny you unlock this one. I'm tired of being the first to see the damage."

The empty cases blackened their spirits even more. Bird collected the information cards and placed them in his pocket along with his notebook.

Irene spotted the fatigue on Bird's face. "Come over to the house and I'll put on a pot of coffee"

George and Bird followed Irene and Kenny across the street and down the block. The chief waved at a few passing cars. He glanced at his watch—eight-thirty, Saturday, 6-17-72 the dial read. The town is wakening from its peaceful sleep to this, he thought.

Gathered around the Keenes' kitchen table, George pulled a well-chewed cigar from his pocket. "Reverend Stiles will be shocked. Do you think we need to call him?"

Chief Bird stirred half of the cream in the pitcher into his coffee. "Let's wait. I want to do some investigating. Unless I find out something he needs to know and could do something about, we'll let him enjoy the trip."

"What can we do to help you and your men?" Irene asked.

"Will you contact Wally Harris? Ask him to use his influence to get WBZ to announce the theft and the temporary closing of the museums."

Bird rose from his chair and placed his coffee cup on the drain board. "Excuse me. I need to get my team busy. See you later." They watched the chief walk out the door.

Irene stood at the sink washing and re-washing the same cup. "My, my. Once the news is out, there will be questions and questions. I need to rest before I can face the barrage of phone calls."

"When the travelers arrive home one week from Saturday and see no lines to view the museums, they'll know something is wrong. We'll be repeating the story." Kenny spilled a bit of his coffee into his saucer, lifted up the saucer to his lips, and slurped the hot beverage. It soothed his spirit.

* * *

For a week, the green swarmed with reporters seeking stories and information about the robbery, while Chief Bird tended to the investigation. He informed the appropriate federal agencies. He checked the finger prints from the information cards. They contained too many partial prints and smudged prints to make any kind of identification. Frustrated, he remembered the large "Do Not Touch" signs on Maida's hall clock. He had his men return and dust the tall clock for prints. There was only one. An officer followed that print through the system. The officer informed Bird that the print matched a long dormant case of robbery. With this unexpected knowledge, Bird awaited the return of Reverend Matthew Henry Stiles.

CHAPTER 36

June 26, 1972

FAMILIES, friends, and colorful helium-filled balloons greeted the Greyhound buses as they rounded the corner and parked in front of the church. The drivers jumped out, pulled luggage from the compartment, and piled it on the curb. After collecting tips from the tourists, they drove away tooting their horns.

The greeters hugged their returning friends and family members. Some enthusiastic tourists pulled postcards from their purses and handed them around the crowd; others opened bags and showed off their souvenir German hats and beer mugs.

George turned on the record player he had installed in the window of Stiles' office per Stiles' instructions. German dance music blared from the speakers. Starting with Stiles, everyone danced around and up and down the church steps, celebrating the safe return of the travelers. One by one, exhausted from their travel and the welcome home party, the tourists rounded up their luggage and headed home, except for Joyce. She stood on the steps tapping her foot. "I wonder where your grandmother is, boys."

"She probably had to find her keys. She always misplaces them." Joyce's eldest son quipped.

"Here she comes," said both boys in unison. Joyce's mother climbed out of the car with her usual grace and gave the boys big hugs. The boys loaded luggage in their grandmother's trunk, and settled into the back seat with bags of souvenirs piled on their laps.

Joyce hugged her mother. "Mom, thanks for getting the boys. As I told you in my call from the airport, I want to check the office to see what waits for me tomorrow. I'll be along in a short while."

"No problem, Joyce."

Irene called from her place on the church steps. "Joyce, did the boys really enjoy the trip?"

"They did and we did. Reverend Stiles seemed distracted at times. Other times he made me shiver at his creative telling of German folktales. He relished in the evil characters." Joyce joined Irene and Kenny on the steps and pointed. "Reverend Stiles is doing his last schmoozing with that wealthy couple that joined us for the tour. He catered to them every day. He's coming this way. Maybe he'll thank me for picking up all the details during the trip like checking us in and out of the hotels and making sure the luggage was correctly labeled."

Stiles marched up, hands on hips. "What's wrong here? This should be a big weekend for the museums. The war tape is silent." He furrowed his brow. "Kenny, if you cut the electricity again, I'm going to press charges."

"You have more to worry about than me cutting electricity." Kenny stood and moved close into Stiles' personal space. "While you were away, someone stole all the government property you borrowed for the museums, along with Maida's clocks, as well as the clock your grandmother gave you that you prized so much."

"My grandmother's?" Stiles stepped back from Kenny.

"Yes, it's gone." Kenny joined Irene on the steps.

"And Maida's jewelry is gone, including her emerald and diamond ring," Irene added clasping Kenny's arm.

Stiles collapsed on the church steps and Maida rushed over. "What's the matter Reverend Stiles? You look like a ghost."

"Maida, dear, didn't you hear anything Kenny said?" Stiles mumbled.

"No. George was taking a peek at the old cuckoo clock I purchased as my souvenir. I can't wait to see how it looks with my other antiques. Each time it sings, it will remind me of our spectacular trip." Maida clapped her hands together like an excited child.

"Maida, please sit. I'm afraid that we have a problem." Stiles patted the place next to him.

Maida sat, pulling her skirt over her knees. "What?" she asked, looking from one friend to the other.

"George, tell her. I can't." Irene squeezed her friend's hand.

George stood in front of Maida and reached for her hand. "Several days after you left, Irene went over to check your house. She found that all the clocks except the tall clock had been stolen along with your jewelry."

"My clocks? My jewelry? George, they didn't find my ring, did they?"

"It's gone."

Maida took a deep breath. "Does Chief Bird have any idea who? They'll be returned, won't they? Only you and I knew where I kept my ring ..." She stopped and studied Reverend Stiles.

"Maida ..." George reached down and tapped her shoulder. "Are you okay?"

"I'm fine." She fussed with her skirt again. "My property will be found and returned, won't it?"

Chief Bird, who had been standing a few steps away to give Maida's friends the opportunity to share the sad news, stepped closer, and looked down at Maida with that familiar compassion reflecting from his eyes. "I doubt we find any of it. I'm sorry. A theft like this one has all the marks of a professional. He steals the stuff one day and has it fenced a day or two later. It's a real racket."

"I can't believe it. We don't have this kind of crime in Ironton Corner. My rings ... my clocks ... the family history ... all gone." She struggled to her feet and leaned soul-crushed against George. "I need some quiet to absorb all this," Maida whispered.

Maida and George crossed the green with Irene and Kenny carrying her luggage.

Joyce stormed toward Stiles. "This must have something to do with you. If you are responsible for Maida's losses—"

Chief Bird stepped between Stiles and Joyce. "Joyce, we're all upset. Go home and be with your boys."

Joyce turned on her heels. Bird caught the flash of temper and disgust spreading over Joyce's face as she dashed off.

Stiles turned to the chief. "Thank you. Joyce is just tired from the trip. Did the thief touch the other museums?"

"They stole the entire gun collection, five letters from the Lord Baden-Powell collection, and the most valuable medical instruments from Doc Thayer's place. The thief knew his business.

My men have dusted for fingerprints and footprints. We found smudges of finger prints on the information cards, but nothing we could identify. The thief cleaned the floors and surrounding areas thoroughly, so we found no footprints either. But, as thorough and professional as he was, he made one mistake."

"What was that?" Stiles whitened and started to pace.

"We found one fingerprint on the tall clock at Maida's."

Stiles fussed with the black curls that had fallen over his forehead. "Did you find a match?"

"As a matter of fact, we did. "Reverend Stiles, I'll let you rest tonight, but at ten tomorrow morning, I want you in my office."

"Can't you see I'm devastated? Can't our conversation wait a day or two?"

"No, it can't. Be there or I'll send a squad car to pick you up."

* * *

George unlocked Maida's front door. She walked in and hugged her arms around her body. "It feels cold in here." George guided her into the living room. They sat on the sofa. Kenny carried her luggage up the stairs.

Irene set the cuckoo clock box on the dining room table and headed to the kitchen. She returned with a bottle of sherry and four small glasses. "Maida, this will help." Irene poured, and they drank in silence.

"This is hard. Such a wonderful trip, and we had to be welcomed by—" She looked around. Her eyes filled. "And Reverend Stiles ... I need to be alone."

George reached for Maida's hand. "Do you want me to stay with you tonight?"

"Thanks, George, I'd appreciate that. The guest room bed is made up. Let's talk tomorrow when I've rested."

Irene and Kenny hugged Maida. They let themselves out the front door. "I need a walk," Kenny said as he guided Irene down the steps.

"I'll join you." They walked around the green and noticed a small light in Stiles' office. "He must be trying to understand it all, too."

* * *

Stiles punched at Frederic. "Sloppy, sloppy, sloppy. How could you be so careless, Leroy? How could you be so careless?"

He dialed and redialed Leroy's phone number. No answer. He struck Frederic harder. "Leroy, you said you'd leave nothing incriminating behind. What happened? You lusted after that clock, didn't you? And now, because of you, they want me at the police station in the morning."

He dialed again. No response. Disgusted, he stomped up the stairs to his room.

CHAPTER 37

June 27, 1972

DRESSED in a freshly-cleaned black suit with a crisp white shirt and Harvard tie, Stiles marched to the police station promptly at ten to avoid the attention of a squad car picking him up. Joyce watched him. standing well back from the window of her office.

Inside the police station, he bowed when he greeted the chief's secretary, Bernice.

She looked up and flashed a quick smile. "The chief will be with you in a few moments. Please take a seat."

Instead of sitting, he picked up a magazine, thumbed through its pages, threw it down, and plucked up another. The intercom buzzed. Bernice said, "He's ready for you, Reverend Stiles."

Stiles walked to Bird's office door and rapped.

"Come in."

He pushed at the door. Chief Bird came from behind his desk and offered to shake Stiles' hand.

Stiles folded his fingers around his jacket lapels. "How long am I going to be here? I have a sermon to plan for Sunday and paperwork to catch up on after being gone for two weeks."

"Please sit down, Reverend Stiles. I have a list of items to go over with you." Chief Bird returned to his desk chair; Stiles sat ramrod straight in the chair opposite him.

"What have you discovered about the thefts?" Stiles asked.

"You'll find out later."

"This is sounding serious. Do I need a lawyer?"

"You might before this is all over. It depends."

Bird handed Stiles a packet of papers stapled at the corner. "This is a list of everything that was stolen."

Stiles studied the lists. He raged inside. Leroy stole more than what I listed. I shouldn't have trusted him. He lusts after anything shiny and valuable. Stiles slapped the papers on Bird's desk. "I'm sorry about the government items, but I'm grieved about the loss of Maida's family clocks and her jewelry. You could have delivered these papers to my office. Chief, why am I here?"

Bird produced a folder. "These are the papers you signed when Mayor Sims' family allowed you to display the gun collection." Bird opened the folder. "It says ..."

"It says that I am responsible for its safety, for registering the guns each year, and for paying some kind of ridiculous tax on them," Stiles recited from memory.

"You never paid the tax or registered the guns each year."

"I haven't had time to do that. I've been busy building up this town and church. I've had to keep on top of Sunday worship, the clubs, and budget. I have the Department of Education of Massachusetts ready to grant me a license to start a private school in our building. It has taken the department over two years to recognize my genius and the ways my special school will benefit the entire school system. Do you know how much work it takes to get these people to understand God's dream for this church and this community, even for more innovative education? The Scouts want more from me. The Travel Club needs me to organize more events. They've asked me to preach a series on the stories that relate to the Black Forest. Do you know what that requires of me? Aside from this ... this unfortunate event ..."

"Event? The theft of the government pieces and Maida's personal property is not an event. It's a tragedy. You need to think about your responsibility for its restitution. I believe you've told the community, if I may quote, 'the museums are my financial responsibility.' "

"They are and I'll deal with that. I still have my money in my trust. An appointed prophet of God does not shirk his responsibilities."

Bird buzzed his secretary. Out of the corner of his eye, Bird caught a mixture of hate and disgust flash from Stiles' eyes. "Bernice, ask my officers to escort the prisoner in."

The officers pushed a hand-cuffed Leroy Roach into a chair opposite Stiles. They stood at alert on either side of the prisoner.

Stiles turned his eyes away from Leroy's penetrating stare. "Who's he?"

"Reverend Stiles, don't. We know about your Akron days and your visits to his house."

"To his house ..."

Leroy released a sly smile. "Matthew ..."

"What?" Stiles snapped.

"Remember the yellow Chevy?" Leroy sang.

"What yellow Chevy?"

"You know the car—the one that belongs to the valet at the Tavern on the Pond." Leroy crossed his legs and leaned his bony elbows on one knee like some reptile looking pleased after a delicious meal.

"He's making all this up. He's crazy. Have you looked at his record, his background? You'll find out he's a chameleon."

Bird studied each man and then focused on Stiles. "Reverend Stiles, we've had ten days to investigate the robberies. One of my officers found the link between you and Reverend Leroy Roach through the valet."

"That boy. You can't believe that boy." The tic in his left eye went out of control. His right eye remained wide open.

"Calm down," Chief Bird ordered.

Stiles stiffened his posture. "Why is Leroy here?"

"Unfortunately, even though he wore gloves, he couldn't resist removing one and touching Maida's handsome hand-hewn tall clock."

"You idiot." Stiles jumped out of his chair and lunged toward Leroy. The officers shoved him back.

"Reverend Stiles, I have signed testimony from the former Reverend Leroy Roach implicating you in the robbery."

"You ...You ..." Stiles repeated. "You weasel, out to save your own skin. I suppose you've made some kind of deal."

"Reverend Stiles, before you say any more, we need to inform you of your rights. You have the right to remain silent. Anything you say can and will be used against you in a court of law. You have the right to an attorney. If you cannot afford an attorney, one will be appointed for you."

"I waive my rights. I've done nothing wrong. My father will ..."

"Reverend Matthew Henry Stiles, you are under arrest for initiating the robbery and advising the illegal sale of all the government artifacts in the museums, as well as the illegal possession of two machine guns and selling the Sims collection of fire arms. You are further charged with initiating the robbery and the selling of the personal property of Maida Hobart Alden."

"You can't ... Leroy engineered all this ..." Stiles charged toward Leroy.

"Sit down, Stiles," Bird ordered. "Cuff him."

"No." He threw himself at Bird. The officers slammed him back in the chair. "No. No. No." Stiles' body slumped, but as if he heard a sharp order, he immediately straightened his back. "Call Clyde Weaver. Have him notify Arthur Blankenship and my father."

Chief Bird studied the two men. He'd heard of dishonest pastors, but these two were the worst. "We are through here for the time being. Officers, escort Reverend Stiles to his cell and then return for Leroy Roach."

One of the officers took a tight grip on Stiles' elbow. Stiles tried to rip away. The officer gripped tighter, led him out of Bird's office, and down a cement block hall. Another officer unlocked the steel door to the cell block. Stiles balked and screamed. "No. No." He squirmed, and the officer lost hold of his arm. One officer took his bully clubs from his belt. "Stiles, do you want me to use this?"

"No," Stiles shouted.

Each officer took one of Stiles' arms and pulled him into the first of three cells. Stiles fell forward and crumbled onto the thin mattress. The chains that anchored the metal bed to the wall clanked together. The officers locked his cell.

He removed his white cotton handkerchief, wiped his face, and breathed deeply. He appeared composed until the steel door opened, and the officers escorted Leroy in the cell block. The guard unlocked Leroy's hand cuffs and shoved him into an adjacent cell.

Stiles jumped up and grabbed the bars. "You have betrayed me, you son of a bitch."

"Matthew, I had no choice. After they discovered my finger-print on that damn clock, and that valet came forward, they had me. I won't spend the rest of my life in prison, even for you."

Stiles tapped his ring against the metal. "What else did you tell them?"

"I told them about your problems in Akron and your incarceration."

"You ... you promised ... you taught me ... you can't betray me."

"I can. It's called survival." Leroy's green eyes sparkled from the power he derived from implicating Stiles in the plot.

Stiles covered his ears. "I'll get out of this. You'll see."

"Your sloppy bookkeeping and messiah complex got you into this situation." Leroy eased down on his cot and relaxed.

"Me? You and me, don't forget. I'll tell them how you manipulated me—no, how you brainwashed me—in high school. Yes, that's what I'll tell them."

"Matthew, admit it. You have willingly followed the devil to get what you wanted." Leroy turned his face to the wall away and immediately fell asleep.

Stiles spent the night staring at the ceiling of his cell praying and yelling at God, "I have not followed the devil. I have followed you. Why have you forsaken me? Find a way out for me. I've worked for you, not the devil. It is time for you to show your power."

CHAPTER 38

THE law offices of Clyde Weaver and Associates occupied a two-story brick building across from Chet's Diner. Clyde had returned from lunch and was sitting at his desk when his phone rang.

"Oh yes, Chief Bird."

"We've arrested Reverend Stiles."

"What? On what charges?" Clyde scribbled notes on a yellow pad as Bird talked. He underlined federal, robbery, and Maida Alden.

"Reverend Stiles wants you to call his father and Arthur."

"I'll do that. When can I see him?"

"Whatever you can arrange will be fine."

"I'll clear my calendar, Chief. Tell Reverend Stiles I'll be there late this afternoon."

Clyde called Arthur, and asked him to come to his office as soon as possible. He turned his chair and studied the gallery of photos behind his desk: Stiles at the vigil for Martin Luther King, Stiles marching in Washington D.C., and Stiles at the opening of the Museums of Ironton Corner dressed in top hat and cane. "What have you done to yourself, Matthew?"

Clyde turned his chair, picked up his yellow pad, and studied his notes. He shook his head as if to make the charges sink in. He reached for the phone and with the help of Akron information he found the number for Henry Stiles. Dialing the number, he wondered how Stiles' father was going to react to the news. "Mr. Stiles, Clyde Weaver from Ironton Corner, Massachusetts. I am a member of your son's church, sir."

"Yes. I recall. It's hard to forget the only colored family in his church. I have many colored—"

Clyde let the comment slide. "Mr. Stiles, your son asked me to call."

"I told him 'No' the last time he called for money. He's a ..." Clyde held the receiver away from his ear during the barrage of expletives.

"I'm not calling about money. At the present time, Matthew is in police custody in Ironton Corner. He is charged with federal and state crimes."

"What's he accused of doing this time?" Clyde heard the disinterest in Henry's voice.

"Initiating the robbery of the property of the federal government. Illegal possession of firearms. The theft of the personal property of Maida Hobart Alden ..."

"What does he expect me to do?"

"Matthew wants you to come."

"You tell him he's on his own."

Clyde heard the call disconnect before he could utter another word. He kept the receiver to his ear, shaking his head. He wondered how anyone could disown his children, no matter what they'd done. He loved his own too much.

A rap on his door startled him. "Mr. Blankenship's here," his secretary announced.

"Show him in." The men pulled chairs around the small conference table.

"Clyde, you look like the starch has been knocked out of you."

"I just got off the phone with Henry Stiles."

"I can imagine what that was like. At Matthew's ordination, he took me aside and gave me an earful of his successes. But you said Matthew told you to call me. Is the situation more serious than the machine gun incident?" Arthur asked.

"Plenty. Here's a preliminary list of the charges against Reverend Stiles." Clyde shoved the pad toward Arthur.

Arthur read the charges and read them again. He straightened his back and felt the throbbing pain that had persisted since Stiles held him down against that log in the Findlay State Park. "I'm not going to be able to help you."

Clyde looked puzzled. "Can I ask why?"

"I don't want to prejudice you against a person who might be your client."

"That damaging?"

"Quite possibly. It deals with his character. If the case lands in federal court, the federal prosecutor, Fred Schumacher is a stickler, so it's best I don't share more with you. I am sorry." Arthur stood and touched Clyde's shoulder. "I don't envy your job." Arthur left Clyde's office.

Clyde sat back in his chair, stretching his long legs out as he reread his notes. He shook his head at the charges. Informing his secretary that he'd be out meeting with a potential client, he left his office for the short walk to the police station.

"Hi, Bernice, is the Chief busy?"

"He said for me to send you in when you arrived."

The two men shook hands and the Chief closed the door to his office. "Have a seat, Clyde. Here are the official arrest papers."

"All of this is hard to take in." Clyde fanned the stack of papers.

"Our investigation has been thorough, and we feel we have a good case. Reverend Stiles needs your help."

"It will only be my help. Arthur says he cannot be involved for personal reasons. His father has no interest in coming or helping. He said he's had enough of bailing his son out of difficult situations."

"Clyde, I need to tell you about his accomplice."

"An accomplice."

"Yes. Reverend Leroy Roach." The Chief filled Clyde in on the details of their investigation which included Roach's history with Stiles.

"What a mess. I better see Reverend Stiles now."

An officer escorted Clyde to Stiles' cell. "Did you talk to my father? Is he coming? Where's Arthur?"

"Calm down."

"Get me out of here." Stiles screeched as he gripped the bars.

"Wait. Officer, open the cell." The officer unlocked the cell. Clyde guided Stiles to the cot. He opened his brief case.

"Is Father coming? If the arraignment doesn't go well, I'll need his money."

Clyde placed his large hand on Stiles' back. "I talked with your father. He wants me to keep him informed."

"Is that all?"

"For now." Clyde kept his hand on Stiles' back.

"And Arthur?"

"He's declined to help."

"He told you that. He can't, he's under my ..."

Stiles stopped. A look of disbelief crossed his face. "How long do I have to stay locked up?"

"We'll see. For now, I need to hear the truth from you."

Leroy, listening to the conversation, shouted from his cell. "What is truth?' Pilate asked Jesus."

"Who's that?" Clyde asked.

"I'm The Reverend Leroy Roach. I've known this young man since he was in the sixth grade. Isn't that right, Matthew?"

"Shut up, Leroy." Stiles jumped up and grasped the bars again.

"We really got acquainted while he was in high school. Matthew, you'll tell him why, won't you? Don't forget the good parts."

"Guard," Clyde Weaver called.

"Yes, Mr. Weaver."

"I need a private room to continue my interview with my client."

The guard unlocked the cell and handcuffed Stiles.

Leroy taunted. "Be sure and tell the truth, Matthew. That is, if you can sort out the truth from your lies."

Stiles strained at the handcuffs as the guard led them down the hall. "You have to get these things off me."

Inside the conference room, Clyde said, "Officer, please remove the cuffs." Clyde held Stiles'eyes with his. "He'll behave."

The guard removed the cuffs and stepped back from Stiles chair.

Clyde tapped his pen on the table as he watched Stiles settle. "Reverend Stiles, you face serious charges."

"I'm being framed by that man. If you look into his green eyes, you will see the evil plans he has designed. Get me out of here."

"Take it easy. After we talk for a while, you will be released in a few days until your preliminary trial."

Stiles drew in a breath and relaxed.

CHAPTER 39

July 2, 1972

OVER the next few days the headlines in the *Ironton Corner Daily News* and the *Boston Globe* read: "The Reverend Matthew Henry Stiles Arrested." "Stiles Held in Connection with Museum Thefts." "Pastor Stiles Faces Federal Charges." "Who Can We Trust, if Not Our Clergy?"

Barbara scanned through the *Boston Globe,* stopped suddenly slamming the paper on the table. "What's this all about? 'Retired lawyer Arthur Blankenship to speak at First Independent Community Church of Ironton Corner.' You didn't tell me! What can you say about that evil little man?"

"Maida and George talked, and she called me."

"And who can turn down Maida, let alone George. What are you going to say?"

"My thoughts are coming together, but I know I want the church to understand the charges so that the rumor mill doesn't exaggerate them. I've asked Chief Bird to answer questions after the service. Remember all the erroneous and vicious talk around Delbert's murder."

"How could I forget?" Picking up the newspaper, Barbara knocked over her coffee. Arthur jumped up as the hot liquid came running across the table aiming for his lap. He grabbed a towel and mopped the table and the floor. Looking up, he found Barbara laughing. "Remember our first meeting when you spilled water on my prison clothes."

"How could I forget? I was so smitten by you that my fingers were all thumbs."

Still laughing, they held each other until she started hiccupping, a physical reaction to the laughter and the release it provided. Walking arm in arm to the screened porch, they sat on the white wicker sofa. Barbara cuddled close to her husband. "We needed that. The tension's been building and building since the robberies."

* * *

On Sunday, the Blankenships were met outside the church by sign-carrying, silent demonstrators. One carried a home-made model of a hot air balloon with the words, "Stiles = Hot Air" written on it. Two veterans held a banner that stated, "It's About Time Stiles Gets His Due." One man wore a sandwich board that read, "Time to Reclaim the Green." A young woman carried a sign that read, "Reverend Stiles, you changed my life. Thank you."

Inside packed pews greeted them with a full choir filling the balcony. Arthur escorted Barbara to her seat and climbed the steps to the pulpit. He stood with his hands poised on each side of the lectern. He swept his eyes over the worshippers before he spoke. "This is a sad day for First Independent Community Church of Ironton Corner. Our pastor, Reverend Matthew Henry Stiles, has been charged with initiating the robbery and illegal fencing of government artifacts, the illegal possession of two machine guns which includes the charge of fencing the Sims' gun collection, and the robbery and fencing of the personal property of Maida Hobart Alden.

"Our pastor, who breathed life into our dry bones, has spent most of this week in a cell. He was released late last night into the custody of his lawyer, Clyde Weaver, until his trial.

"Rumors and accusations are flying around town, over the airwaves, and in the paper. Reporters have interviewed many of you and others in our community. Some have already crucified Reverend Stiles; others are willing to wait until the due process of law determines his innocence or guilt.

"As you know, Maida Alden's house was invaded by the perpetrator and her personal property has been stolen. She has requested that you reserve judgment, be careful with the gossip, and pray for Reverend Stiles and Clyde Weaver.

"To demonstrate Maida's request, she is going to come forward and light a candle for Reverend Stiles and Clyde. I'm going to light a candle to represent our church."

Maida walked up to the front. Arthur joined her. They lit the candles. The choir sang,

> May nothing evil cross this door
> and may ill fortune never pry about these windows;
> may the roar of rain go by.
> By faith made strong,
> the rafters will withstand the battering of the storm ...
> though these sheltering walls are thin,
> may they be strong to keep hate out and hold love in.

Holding Maida's hand, Arthur turned to the congregation. "We need the strength of those words to withstand our present storm. I have candles at each of the doors and copies of those words and a prayer. If you like, please take a candle and the readings and light the candle each night and pray the words to the song."

A profound silence passed through the congregation as Maida and Arthur walked to the back of the church.

On the church steps, Maida hugged Arthur. "Thanks, Arthur. You touched their hearts."

Frank and Jimmy Somers stopped on the steps. "Thanks Arthur, Maida. By the way, why aren't you representing Reverend Stiles with Clyde?"

"It's a long story. One day, if it's necessary, it will come out, but for now my reasons must stay buried. Jimmy, how are you doing with all this?"

"It's tough. If he's guilty, he's betrayed everything he talks about in Boy Scouts." Jimmy jingled the car keys in his pocket. "Let's go, Dad. I want to be with my friends."

* * *

Late in the afternoon, Stiles changed into his pajamas and lay in his bed. Restless, he reached for his glasses and struggled out of bed. He crept downstairs to his office and locked the door behind him.

"Frederic, I'm back." He released the pulley and lowered the skeleton so its toes brushed the floor. He laced his fingers through

Frederic's fingers as young lovers might do, palm to palm.

Releasing Frederic, he walked around his office, straightening the edges of pictures and dusting off his collections with the sleeve of his pajamas. He stopped at the empty place his grandmother's clock had occupied, and ran his hands over the bare wood.

Back at his desk, he typed for a while, tore the sheet out, and began again. On his fifth start, he completed his chronicle entry. Standing, he opened the file drawer three times, pulled out the file, and placed this entry in front of all the others.

Reaching for the phone, he dialed his parents. "Mother, it's me."

"I know, son. I'm ..." Stiles heard a crash. "Mother—"

He heard the receiver drop on the wood floor, a whimper, and "No."

"Mother."

"Your mother can't talk now." His father now had the phone receiver.

"Father? What happened to mother?"

"She's distraught and disappointed about your arrest. She simply fainted and pulled the phone table to the floor. Son, I'm furious. I thought you had learned your lesson. What's wrong with you? I tried to knock sense into you when you started your 'playful indiscretions,' as you called them. And now, you have added federal charges to your list of crimes. What were you thinking?"

"I tried to tell you I was in a bind, but you didn't listen."

"I told you I wouldn't bail you out, and you went right ahead and made your plans. And, then, to hear that you are still under the influence of Leroy Roach."

"I thought I heard Mother's voice."

"She's a little disoriented that's all. She's sitting up now."

"Will you put her back on the line?"

"No, she's too weak to talk to you. What do you want?"

"I need you to be here for the trial, and I need the remainder of my trust."

"The rest of your trust? You depleted that a long time ago. You aren't the son I trained you to be. Good bye, Matthew."

CHAPTER 40

July 2, 1972

STILES struggled with the vision of his mother bruised and scared and his father demanding her silence. His stomach turned and he grabbed the paper basket. Only dry heaves came. Shaking his head to rid it of that vision, he turned on his record player. As he listened to "Chopin's Funeral March," he stared at Frederic. "Well, my friend, the work starts now. I will not spend another day in jail. I'll find a way to lay the charges off on Leroy. I haven't done anything wrong. I've followed the will of God. If I have done anything wrong, God is guilty along with me. I have sacrificed a stellar career in education for God and this community. I'll show them that the guilt lies with Leroy."

Slam. Thump. Thump. Stiles looked at his watch. 8 p.m. He thought, that must be Joyce getting a head start on the newsletter.

Stiles stretched. "Frederic, the music soothes me." He returned to his typewriter and, over the next two hours, outlined a series of sermons on the intrigue of the Black Forest of Germany and another series on the pitfalls in the criminal justice system. Switching off the light over his desk, he wished Frederic goodnight, and unlocked the office door. Joyce's door was ajar. He pushed it open and saw his special boxes torn open on her desk. Rage consumed him.

"What are you doing?" Stiles demanded, slamming the tops of the boxes shut. "Nobody was to touch them. They are my private property. Did Irene and Kenny put you up to this?" His left eye twitched violently. He reached for the cotton handkerchief in his jacket pocket and held it to his eye.

Joyce stood eye to eye with Stiles, her black eyes flashing. "I've been suspicious of your way with the church money for a long time. Before your trip, I began my own investigation. Tonight I found fifteen checks from the Hobart Trust and Lawrence Endowment accounts, signed by you for museum expenses. You told us that your trust was paying for the museums."

"You can't do this. This is my private property." Stiles reached toward Joyce.

Joyce blocked his reach with a karate-like chop. "I tore open other boxes and found checks for magazines subscriptions, for payments on your car, for your personal travel, and I don't know how many notices for unpaid bills. The church must be a year or so behind on electric and gas bills. And, if that was not enough, I found two letters from the bank threatening foreclosure."

Stiles didn't speak. Joyce stopped, breathed deeply to regain her strength. She reached down without losing eye contact with Stiles, pulled open her top desk drawer, and plucked out a cancelled check.

"And this one from April 16, 1969 is the only one where you didn't record anything on the memo line." Stiles tried to grab the check. Joyce stuffed it down her blouse and into her bra.

She patted her front. "This check is made out to a Leroy Roach in the amount of $20,000."

Stiles turned white.

"The check is dated around the time of Delbert Martin's murder."

Stiles stammered. "You ..." He charged toward Joyce. Joyce stepped back, but tripped on her desk chair and fell backwards.

Stiles grabbed Joyce's letter opener and lunged as Joyce struggled to get free from the chair.

A strong arm seized Stiles' arm. "Put that down," Kenny Keene ordered. Kenny clutched Stiles by his shoulders, pulled him back, and pushed Stiles to the floor, holding him down with his knee.

"Boy, I'm glad to see you." Joyce thrashed about to release her body from the chair and struggled upright.

"I saw your light, looked at my watch, and decided it was very late for you to be in the office. Then I spotted Stiles' car and no lights in his upper rooms, and so I let myself in."

"I'm glad you did. If you could have seen the look in Stiles' eye."

Stiles struggled under Kenny's knee. "Stay still," Kenny ordered.

"I've found a stash of cancelled checks and unpaid bills. All the checks have been written on the Hobart Trust and the Lawrence Endowment. They must be empty by now. We need to call Chief Bird."

"No, you don't. I'll explain." Stiles screeched.

"Joyce, call Chief Bird."

A few minutes later, Bird and two men clambered into Joyce's office. The officers took over restraining Stiles. Joyce pointed to boxes and told of her long time suspicions and recent discoveries.

Each time Joyce paused, Stiles screamed, "I have done nothing wrong. I have the right to sign checks and spend the church's money as I please."

"We'll see about that. Meanwhile I am arresting you for an attempted assault on Joyce Lang with a lethal weapon."

"Call my lawyer."

Officer Daniels and Carter led Stiles into his office where Bird batted Frederic to one side and placed a call to Clyde Weaver.

"Clyde, I'm sorry to wake you. There's been another development with Reverend Stiles. We need you at the church office."

"Now?"

"Yes, now."

Ten minutes later, Clyde arrived, his coat hanging off one shoulder. "What's happened? Where's Stiles?"

"Reverend Stiles attacked Joyce with her letter opener. Stiles is in his office with two of my officers."

Clyde looked into Joyce's office where Irene Keene tried to calm Joyce. Bird accompanied Clyde into the room. Clyde touched Joyce's shoulder. "Joyce, I'm sorry. Are you all right?"

"Yes. He exploded with rage. I've never been so frightened."

"I had a hard time keeping Stiles nailed to the floor with my knee," Kenny admitted, pacing the perimeter of Joyce's office to control his anger.

"What happened, Joyce?" Clyde ran his fingers over the top of a stack of three boxes on her desk.

"Before the museum project, I became suspicious about the church's finances because I had a few calls from the electric and gas companies about our bills. Stiles fumed when I told him. He said those companies were sloppy with our accounts and he'd handle it. When he announced the museum project, I asked him how it was being funded. He said his trust fund. I didn't believe him and mentioned it to Irene and Kenny. The museums were such a success that I put my suspicions away.

"Before the Black Forest Tour, I noticed that he spent an unusual amount of time in the basement filing papers in these boxes. On our return and the news of the robberies, I decided that it was time for me to go through the boxes. I told Irene and Kenny what I was doing and for them to watch when they saw a light in my office late in the evening. I worked furiously through the boxes while Stiles was jailed. Tonight I found more cancelled checks drawn from the church's trust accounts and signed by Stiles and another made out to one Leroy Roach, dated the day after Delbert Martin was murdered. I waved it at Stiles. He grabbed my letter opener, pushed me into to my desk chair, and raised that weapon over his head. Kenny stopped Stiles."

Silence filled the room.

"I need some time with my client." Clyde wiped beads of sweat from his forehead.

"He's not himself. My officers will stand in the hall with the door slightly ajar," Bird said.

Clyde walked across the hall and looked into Stiles' office. Reverend Stiles was disheveled. As he paced, he played with the buttons on his pajamas. "I was within my rights. I have a paper—"

"Did you have a right to attack Joyce?" Clyde asked.

"I wasn't going to hurt her. She's been a problem ever since I came here, always sneaking around. I had no privacy." Sweat broke out on Stiles' forehead.

"We'll sort this out in the morning. I advise you not to say another word."

Bird knocked and stepped inside. "Clyde, since Joyce's office is a scene of attempted assault, my officers will sort through the boxes tonight. Do you have any objection?"

"Those boxes belong to me. You have no right." Stiles jerked, and the officers stepped forward and held him fast.

"Reverend Stiles, I told you not to say a word," Clyde said.

"Chief, I have no objection. I'd simply like a copy of what you find in them."

"Of course. Come on, Reverend Stiles, back to your cell." Bird motioned for his officers to escort Stiles.

"I can't go there. Leroy harassed me every night." Stiles' eye twitched and watered. He seemed to shrink into himself as the officers tried to escort him out of the room.

"I'll have a talk with Mr. Leroy Roach," Bird said.

Stiles pointed to his pajamas. "I can't go to jail dressed like this."

"Clyde, do you mind accompanying your client upstairs?"

"Is that necessary?" Stiles played with his black curls that were now hanging over his forehead.

"Clyde must go with you. You are now accused of an attempted assault with a deadly weapon. That charge limits your rights."

Clyde touched Stiles' elbow. "Come on Reverend Stiles." Clyde led him out the door and upstairs to his rooms. While waiting for Stiles, Clyde studied a pile of Matthew's book on his night stand. Looking up from thumbing through *Frankenstein*, Clyde noticed Matthew preening in the mirror. He shook his head.

Stiles adjusted the white handkerchief in his jacket pocket. "There. The perfect image of success, wouldn't you agree, Clyde?" Stiles pivoted on his heels and marched down the stairs to his office.

Stiles went directly to Frederic. He held the skeleton's hand and whispered, "I'll be back." He turned to the Chief. "I'm ready."

"Wait, Chief," Joyce said. "I want to make sure this check is in your hands." Joyce retrieved the check from her bra and handed it to Bird. Bird studied it. A look of disgust traveled over his face. "Cuff him."

"No." Stiles backed into Frederic as if searching for protection.

"Yes." Officer Daniels cuffed him and the two officers led him out.

"Kenny, my men will be here most of the night. Please inform George so he doesn't become alarmed during his early morning walk."

Bird followed the officers across the green with Stiles held tight between them. As promised, Bird entered the cell block to talk with Roach. Roach stretched off his bed. "What's he doing back in here?"

"He's run into a few more problems."

Leroy sauntered toward the bars and held them lightly in his hands. "What more could you possibly add to his charges?"

"I have a check in my pocket made out to 'Leroy Roach' with nothing on the memo line."

The chief watched Leroy grasp the bars hard until his fingers turned white.

"Leroy, do you want to tell me why Stiles wrote a check to you for $20,000 on April 16, 1969?"

"I need to talk with my lawyer."

Bird shifted his position and leaned on the corridor wall. "If you tell me about this check before you meet with a lawyer, I may be able to help you with the current charges and charges from years back."

"I don't think I want to do that, Chief."

"I've seen how Stiles can manipulate a story. Are you going to trust his version?" Bird took a toothpick from his other pocket.

"You got another one of those toothpicks?"

Bird handed him one. Leroy twirled it between his fingers. "When will you be transferring me to prison?"

"We had you listed for July 5, but with this new development, I don't know. I have a hunch the prosecutor is going to need to talk with you. Good night, Mr. Roach."

"Chief," Stiles said, "you promised to tell him not to taunt me."

"Oh, right. Roach, don't taunt Stiles. Tomorrow's the 4th of July. Officers Daniels and Carter will be checking on you and bringing your meals."

Chapter 41

July 5, 1972

"How did the prisoners do yesterday?" Bird asked the officers over coffee and donuts at their regular daily meeting in Bird's office.

Officer Carter wiped the sugar from around his lips with his hand. "Mr. Roach behaved. Reverend Stiles asked for paper and pencil."

"We gave it to him. He wrote and wrote, then tore sheet after sheet from the pad, ripped each sheet into pieces, and littered the cell floor. When I took his breakfast tray in, I had to catch myself from slipping on the paper. He must have spilled his coffee on some of it," Officer Daniels said.

"Mr. Roach told Stiles to clean it up, but Stiles laughed like some distressed bird. Really strange, wasn't it Daniels?"

"Sure was. What's up today besides watching those two?"

"Reverend Stiles has requested that his lawyer, Clyde Weaver, be present to hear the formal charges against him. I'll need you to escort Stiles to the conference room."

"Yes, sir." The officers emptied their coffee cups and took the remainder of the donuts to Bernice in the outer office.

Clyde arrived and nodded to the officers. Bird pushed through the door from his office. "Thanks for being punctual, Clyde. We're going to meet in the conference room. Are you ready, Bernice?"

"Yes. I'll bring the coffee pot and some cups."

"Good idea. We may need it before the day is out."

The men took seats on either side of the table. Bernice set up the coffee and sat at the end of the table nearest the door, in case she had to do something for the chief. As she placed her pad and pencil on the conference table, Officer Daniels escorted Stiles from his cell and guided him to his seat at the other end of the table, furthest from the door. The officer stood beside him.

Clyde nodded to his client. "Are you doing all right, Reverend Stiles?"

"How can I be doing all right? Me in jail and cuffed when the real culprit is Leroy Roach and his accomplices. Can't you remove these cuffs?"

Bird motioned to Officer Daniels. He removed the cuffs and stood closer, hand on his gun. Bird put his toothpick in his pocket. "Clyde, my men sorted through the boxes all night. An officer will be arriving soon to report."

"You have no right or reason to go through my private papers. I've done nothing wrong," Stiles protested.

"Before we hear that report, I need to inform you, Reverend Matthew Henry Stiles that you are hereby charged with assault with a deadly weapon on one Joyce Lang." Bird focused his eyes on Stiles.

"My client feels that because of the stress created by the situation, his mind was not his own. He'd like that entered into the record," Clyde reported.

"Bernice, you have that in your notes, don't you?"

"I do."

At a light rap on the door, an officer entered the room. "Do you want me to read this report in front of the accused?"

"He's waived all his rights, so proceed," Clyde responded.

"We have totaled the cancelled checks at $477,000. We found two bank notes showing Reverend Stiles borrowed another $100,000 with the church building as collateral. And, we came across several notices from the bank politely asking for payment, before they consider foreclosure on the church."

"Wait, wait. I was within my rights." Stiles motioned to Clyde. "Please show Chief Bird the document." Clyde produced the document.

This is to certify that Matthew Henry Stiles is the president, minister, and treasurer of First Parish Unitarian Church of Ironton Corner having been duly appointed on July 31, 1969, and that he is empowered to sign for and on

behalf of the parish, to incur obligations and debts, mortgage property, sell or buy real estate and securities, and act
for and on behalf of the parish in any business or religious
situation whatsoever, and that he is the trustee of all the
funds, properties, real estate, securities, and all other buildings of the First Parish Unitarian Church of Ironton Corner.

   Signed: Arthur Blankenship, President

"Arthur Blankenship? Bernice, will you please contact Arthur
and ask him if he can join us?" Bernice rose and left. The Chief
read through the words again and folded the paper.

Bernice returned twenty minutes later with Arthur.

"I would have been here sooner, but I've been meeting with the
church leaders." Arthur took a seat next to Clyde.

"The church has no leaders. I'm the only leader." Stiles enunciated each and every word. "Remember I told you that a church
run by committees will fail; one run by a strong leader without
oversight by the congregation will become a church that will make
a difference in the world."

"Matthew, stop!" Clyde placed a hand on Stiles' shoulder.

Arthur looked from Clyde to Bird. "What can I do for you?"

"Stiles produced this." Bird handed it to Arthur. "I'd like you to
explain its origin."

"Clyde called early this morning to alert me to Stiles' copy of
the document." Arthur produced two letters from inside his coat
pocket and handed one to each man. "This will explain the history
of my involvement with Matthew Henry Stiles."

Bird and Clyde read the notarized letter. Stiles tapped his ring
on the table.

"Arthur, you say that you never registered the document with
the court. So this," Clyde held up the document, "means nothing."

"It means everything," Stiles shouted, trying to stand. Daniels
pushed him down.

"Reverend Stiles, Arthur accuses you of blackmail. Did you
blackmail Arthur?" Bird asked, as calmly as he could, still trying
to digest the contents of Arthur's letter.

"Matthew, you don't have to answer that question," Clyde said.

Stiles sat tall. "I'm proud of what I did with Arthur's money."

"Matthew, stop. You're incriminating yourself."

"Clyde, don't interrupt me. I used Arthur's gifts to build the brick walkways and the bandstand. Remember the paltry forty who attended church before I appeared in that hot air balloon? His money paid for that balloon. The use of the balloon was genius."

"Stiles, you used what you knew about Barbara to blackmail me to hire you and to support your ordination. You say God called you to be with us. I'd say your paranoia and ego called you to be here." Arthur attempted to stand.

"I needed to accomplish more than my father. My mentor—"

"Be quiet, Reverend Stiles," Clyde commanded.

"I can't," Stiles continued as if in a trance. "I need to tell you about The Reverend Leroy Roach. He coached me through every step of my plan. It began in high school. He was the only one who understood me."

"Stiles, I warn you, stop!" Clyde stood.

"What I didn't think of, he did. The Vietnamese hut with the attack sounds was his idea, and he helped with the monument about Vietnam. He installed the surveillance camera in the boy's bathroom after the installation of the pool. The monitor is in my—"

"That's enough." Clyde clapped his hands in front of Stiles to interrupt his manic-driven stream of conversation.

"I merely peeked at the boys. I never touched them. Leroy said if I touched them I'd be called a pervert."

"Camera! What camera?" Bird asked.

"The monitor is in the best place."

"Where?" Bird demanded.

Stiles hummed the Funeral March.

"Must be near that damn skeleton," Arthur said.

"Bernice, will you please get one of the officers to examine Stiles' office again? Do you have any objections, Clyde?"

Clyde wiped his brow. "Do you have a search warrant?"

"I took care of that first thing this morning, in case we might need it," Bird said as Bernice left the room.

"Chief, unless Reverend Stiles listens to me and stops this ranting, I'll need to withdraw as his counsel."

"You're excused, Clyde," said Stiles. "I'll handle this myself."

"Let's take a break," suggested Clyde.

"Why? Don't you want the full story of how I saved the church ... the creation of my product ... the church, the campus and activities ... ahead of my time ... the new paradigm?" Stiles pointed his index fingers at Bird. "Besides, I'll never serve time, no matter what I say to you."

"Speaking of serving time ..." Bird handed Stiles a copy of a cancelled check dated April 16, 1969.

Stiles fingered the check. He raised his eyebrows trying to keep his composure. "What did Leroy tell you about this?"

"I talked to him early this morning. He said you paid him to find someone to kill Delbert Martin for you." Bird kept his eyes on Stiles.

Stiles interjected a nervous laugh as he talked. "I knew he'd try to blame it on me. Chief Bird, Leroy doesn't know how to tell the truth. He, in his plans for my success here, planned to do away with Delbert, so I could have sole control of the church money. I had nothing to do with his unfortunate demise."

Bird gritted his teeth and took in a deep breath. "Now, along with initiating the theft and then the illegal sale of private and government property, and unlawful possession and sale of firearms, we are charging you with financial fraud, and as an accomplice in the murder of Delbert Martin. And the federal agents—"

A rap on the door interrupted Bird. He got up, walked to the door, and opened it a crack. A voice said, "It's Officer Carter. I need you in the outer office, Chief."

"I'll be back in a few minutes. Clyde, even though Stiles has dismissed you as his lawyer, you might want to educate him about financial fraud and accessory to murder. I don't believe he understands the amount of jail time he'll serve if he's found guilty of all his crimes. Arthur, come with me."

Stiles jumped up. "As I said before, I won't be serving any jail time." Officer Daniels pushed him back down.

Bird closed the conference room door. He and Carter ducked into the Chief's office. Carter reported. "Chief, we found the equipment, monitors in his office and his private rooms, a camera in the boys' bathroom, and ..."

The chief's office door banged open. Joyce barged in. "I want to strangle that man. He's a pervert. I should have guessed about the equipment. He protected his room and his office from any invasion, always locking and unlocking each door and cabinet."

"Joyce, I need you to leave."

"Not until I have my say. It was shameful the way that man looked at the boys on the trip. I told my kids to stay away from him. He dwelled on the ghosts and werewolf stories while in the Black Forest. Scary and crazy. Where is he?"

"Joyce, right now only my officers, you, and I know about the equipment. For the sake of the boys, I need you to keep this quiet. He'll get his due."

Bird leaned against his desk. "What a mess. I need a minute. Carter, please escort Joyce from the building."

A few moments later, Carter quietly returned to the chief. "Chief, are you okay?"

"I'm thinking about those boys ... I hope they never find out."

Bird took a deep breath. He and Carter returned to the conference room. "Stiles, stand. We found the monitor and camera. Officer Daniels and Carter, lock him up while I talk with Arthur and Clyde."

"You can't do this." Stiles struggled under the grasp of Daniels. He spat at Bird on his way out.

Bird returned to his chair. The men sat quietly, each with their own thoughts, questions, and disgust over the news and how they'd been deceived.

Bird broke the silence. "How was Stiles while I was out of the room?"

"Strange, I'd say," said Clyde.

"That left eye of his gave him fits. He fussed at it, as usual, with his cotton handkerchief. He mumbled, 'What next, Leroy? What next, Leroy?' over and over. At times, I didn't think he knew we were still in the room." Clyde drew in a breath.

A gunshot reverberated through the concrete and steel of the jail.

CHAPTER 42

BIRD jerked out of his chair. "Stay here. Call for the medics." He ran out the door, down the corridor, and threw open the door to the cell block. A second shot and a third one rang out.

Blood splattered over Bird's uniform as Officer Carter slipped to the floor at his feet. "Stiles got my leg. Did I get him? What about Leroy?"

Bird looked and watched Stiles slide down the wall of his cell with an eerie smile on his face, a gun at his feet. "Looks like you got Stiles. Blood's gushing from his chest. Leroy's slumped over his cot."

"Where's Daniels?" Carter pointed to the cells.

Bird stepped into Stiles' cell and found Daniels on the floor. Struggling to get up, Bird gave him a hand. "Are you all right?"

"I'm sorry. With all that paper on the floor, I slipped. Stiles overpowered me and banged my head on the bars. I felt him grab my gun. I'm sorry, so sorry. Who got Stiles?"

"I did." Carter leaned against the doorway to the cell, blood seeping through his pants and his face chalk white. Bird grabbed Carter just as he collapsed and laid him on Stiles' cot.

Bird entered Leroy's cell. He leaned in close and checked the wound on the side of Leroy's head.

Leroy groaned. "That maniac tried to kill me."

Medics rushed into the cell block. Bird yelled, "The serious one is in that cell." He pointed. "This one can wait."

Two medics pushed into Stiles' cell. They saw the pool of blood around him. "This one's hanging on by a thread." They stabilized him and then loaded Stiles on a gurney and rushed out.

Another of the medics checked Carter. Carter said, "I'm okay. It's my leg." He faded out again.

"This one is in shock. He's going to go with us."

"Carter, I'll be over as soon as I can," Bird said to his officer.

"What about me?" Leroy whined.

Another two medics checked Leroy. "You are lucky. The bullet just grazed your head. You need attention for at least overnight."

Emotionally exhausted, Bird and Daniels sat on the cot in Leroy's cell. "This is my fault," said Chief Bird. "I shouldn't have had you remove Stiles' cuffs."

"I'm to blame for allowing Stiles to overtake me." Daniels hung his head then lifted it up. "Chief, what can I do to help you?"

"Call the State Police. Ask Captain Rogers to get their crime unit out here. Tell him since the shooting involved my staff, I want an outside group to study the scene. Then go to the hospital and supply the hospital staff with any information they may need. Ask hospital security to have an officer stationed in ER until we get this sorted out. I want Roach and Stiles to be guarded at all times."

"Sure thing."

Bird walked into the outer office. Bernice was giving coffee to Clyde, who sat slumped in a chair in the corner.

Wally Harris flew in the door. "Chief, what gives? Rumor is there was a shooting. Was Stiles the shooter?"

"Rumors already?" Bird gave out a sigh.

"Yes, you know the locals listen to those scanners all the time."

"Captain Rogers is coming over with his crime team, Wally. You'll get the details as soon as I do."

Wally understood and left. Bird looked at Clyde. "How are you?"

"Still catching my breath," Clyde said. "I heard one of the medics say that Stiles is fighting for his life."

"Yes, I'm not sure if I'm hoping he lives or dies." Bird wiped his forehead.

"What can I do?" Clyde asked.

"Call your Church council and inform them, if they haven't already heard that there's been a shooting involving Stiles and two of my officers. Tell them we'll get the details to them when we know them."

Bernice interrupted. "Chief, they need you at the hospital. They're losing Stiles."

* * *

Dr. Johnson met Bird at the door to the ER. "In a moment of consciousness, he said he wanted to see you."

Bird picked his way through the jumble of emergency and life support equipment. The doctor instructed Bird. "Say his name close to his ear."

Bird did as Dr. Johnson instructed. Stiles' eyes opened a slit and closed again. He mumbled. "Did I g-g-et Le-roy?"

Bird glanced at the doctor for guidance. Johnson mouthed, "Leroy's going to make it."

"No, he's going to make it," the Chief whispered.

Stiles' mouth changed into a small smirk. "File ... letter ... office." Stiles drifted back to unconsciousness.

The doctor and Bird stepped away from Stiles as a nurse checked the monitors. "Doc, have you contacted his parents?"

"Yes, they're on their way. They want us to keep him on life support until they arrive. His father's hired a private jet. They've arranged to have a car waiting for them at Logan. They hope to be here by ten p.m."

"What about Roach?"

"He says there's no one to contact on his behalf."

"Can one of your aides call me and let me know when Reverend Stiles' parents arrive?"

"Sure."

"What's Roach's condition?"

"He's stable. We'll keep him overnight, and then I presume that we'll send him back to you."

"Yes. Let me know, and I'll send an officer to pick him up. Is it okay to see Officer Carter?"

"Sure that's fine. Just realize he's a little groggy from the pain medication and shock."

Bird took the elevator to the second floor and found Carter's room "Carter, you look good for taking a shot." Bird stood near the bed.

"It's not too bad, Chief. They stopped the bleeding and will do a little surgery tomorrow."

Bird shuffled his feet. "I need to tell you that Stiles is on life support until his parents arrive."

Carter turned his head away from Bird. Bird remained quiet.

"If Stiles dies, this will be my first." Carter moved his head back to face Bird.

"The first is hard. They're all hard. We'll set you up with a psychologist as soon as you're feeling physically better. When this happened to me, I thought I didn't need a shrink, but it turns out he helped me in more ways than I knew."

Bird pushed a chair to the side of the bed and stuffed his body in it as comfortably as he could. "Do you feel like telling me what happened?"

Carter nodded and adjusted his bed to a more upright position. "I opened the cell block for Daniels and turned to walk back to the office. A couple of seconds later, I heard a shot. I jerked the door open and saw Stiles holding the gun. I yelled, 'Put the gun down.' He turned the gun on me. He got off a shot at the same time I shot him. That's when you came in."

"We'll need to get your story on record at the station."

"Right," Carter said. "How's Daniels?"

"Beating himself up for allowing Stiles to get an upper hand."

"Who would have thought that weasel man had such strength?"

"I think he knew his game was up and acted out like a cornered animal." Bird pushed his body out of the chair and patted Carter's arm. "Take it easy. You are one fine officer."

* * *

Captain Dick Rogers joined Chief John Bird and Officer Daniels in the conference room at the station. "Daniels, will you repeat your story for the Chief?"

"Chief, it seemed like a simple escort until he rammed his elbow hard in my gut and neck. He beat my head against the bars. I lost my breath and felt him tearing at my gun. I tried to stop him. Then he jabbed his elbow in my throat. In a haze I saw him aim the gun at Roach and heard Stiles scream, 'You'll no longer have control over me,' and then I lost consciousness. The next thing I knew, you were standing over me."

Rogers held a clipboard. He flipped through the papers. "From what my men and I have learned from the crime scene, your story supports the evidence. I'll write up the report and have it to you in the morning, Chief. I've had a gnawing feeling about Stiles since we investigated Delbert Martin's murder, but I didn't think it would come to this."

"Me, neither." Chief Bird leaned back in his chair.

"How's Stiles?" Daniels asked.

"He's on life support and his parents will be here around ten."

"And Roach?"

"He'll be released tomorrow. My officers will bring him back here. I'll talk to the prosecutor and ask Roach if he, now, wants legal counsel."

Bernice tapped on the door. "Reverend Stiles' parents have arrived."

"Bernice will you make me a copy of Captain Rogers' report?"

"Chief, do you want me to go along with you?" Roger asked.

"You know, that might be a good idea. Thanks. Daniels, get some rest."

CHAPTER 43

TWO officers stood at the emergency room entrance. "Have you met the parents, Chief?" Alden asked.

"Yes. They were here for their son's ordination a few years ago."

From the doorway, Bird and Rogers watched Alice and Henry Stiles standing like statues next to their son's bed. Two security officers stood a few steps away. Alice turned.

Henry Stiles pivoted and jabbed his stubby finger toward Bird. "You ... you are responsible for this." He started for the Chief.

Rogers jumped between Bird and Henry Stiles. "Mr. Stiles, please don't make matters any worse."

"Any worse ... one of his officers shot my son."

Alice Stiles reached for her husband. He pushed her away. She steadied herself with one hand on the edge of the bed as the other was in a sling. Bruises covered one side of her face. When she attempted to move to a chair, she limped. Chief Bird went to her side and assisted her. She nodded her thanks, as she dropped her head to the side trying to hide the bruises.

"Mr. and Mrs. Stiles, this is Captain Dick Rogers of the State Police. We're so sorry for this situation."

"Sorry ... you'll be more than sorry when my lawyers get busy," Henry said, setting his jaw.

A stifling silence filled the room. Mrs. Stiles found her voice. "We talked with our pastor."

"There was no we, Alice. You talked to your pastor." Mr. Stiles gave her a dark look.

"Yes, Henry, I did, and then the doctor." She straightened her posture and glared at her husband. "And I will not prolong his life with these machines. Dr. Johnson said when we're ready, he'll turn them off. He's not expecting Matthew to stay with us but a few minutes." She pulled a flowered handkerchief from her sleeve.

"Woman, I said we are keeping him alive until my lawyers look into the shooting."

"Henry Stiles, we are not waiting. You are not in control of this decision. The doctor said only one of us needed to sign the papers, and I did while you were parking the car." She folded into a chair like a balloon losing air.

Henry Stiles marched out of the room. The two officers made eye contact. Captain Rogers followed him.

Mrs. Stiles struggled to get out of her chair. Bird offered her his hand, and she leaned over her son and tenderly touched the curls on his forehead.

"Is there anything we can do for you, Mrs. Stiles?"

"No. If you don't think the town or church will mind, I'd like to bury him here in Ironton Corner in a private ceremony." She ran her fingers down the side of her son's face. "Will you contact Kenny Keene about that, Chief?" Bird nodded.

"And please call George and Maida. Matthew spoke so highly of them. Ask them to box up Matthew's personal belongings for me." Her voice wandered off and returned a few moments later. "I don't expect he has many personal things except that skeleton. He found great delight in Frederic. I never understood it, but I guess we don't always understand our children, do we?"

Alice leaned close and kissed her son. "Later, Chief, I want to sit with you and hear the details about what he's done. I wish I could have helped him, but between his father and Leroy Roach, all I could do was love him. And at times I didn't do that very well."

Bird remained a quiet presence, observing the intense pain of a grieving parent.

* * *

In the hall, Mr. Henry Stiles stood at attention. "What prompted the shooting?"

Rogers kept his voice level. "Your son pushed the escort officer against the bars and elbowed the officer in the neck. He grabbed the officer's gun and shot Mr. Roach. Another officer yelled 'Put the gun down.' Reverend Stiles turned the gun on that officer, shot him in the leg. The officer returned fire."

"He thought he had a right to do whatever he pleased." Mr. Stiles stepped away from the cooler and stared into the room at his son. "I'm just sorry he didn't kill Reverend Leroy Roach. That man ruined Matthew's life." He brushed at a few pieces of lint on his jacket.

"Mr. Stiles, your threat about lawyers, I think it is a little too late for that."

"Fuck you." Mr. Stiles pivoted on his heels and charged into his son's room. "Alice, let's get this over with."

Softly Alice replied. "I'll do this when I want."

The sounds of the machines ticked away as the two parents stood there, each with their own thoughts.

Mrs. Stiles touched Bird's arm. "Will you get the doctor now?"

The doctor entered the room and gave a gentle hug to Mrs. Stiles.

He tended to the machines. She watched her son's face and held his lifeless hand. They watched the machine flat line and listened. The doctor squeezed Alice's hand and whispered, "It's over."

Alice kissed Matthew again. "I'm sorry I wasn't stronger for you." Her body swayed, and the doctor held her up.

"Woman, how am I going to explain this to the people at my club and to the executive board—that our son was a common thief, and maybe more?"

"Escort that man out of here. I don't ever want to see him again." Mrs. Stiles held her head high. "Please give me some time with my son. Chief Bird, will you ask for the chaplain to come?"

"You take your time. I'll send George and Maida over to pick you up."

Mr. Stiles swaggered out of the room with Bird following. "Get my car," Mr. Stiles demanded of a security guard.

"Yes, sir."

Bird and Rogers headed back to the station. "What's with his father? Hate, anger, or arrogance?" Rogers asked.

"Those and more, I'd guess. Talk about Leroy Roach ruining his son, I don't think I want to know what all that man did to him, let alone what he has done to his wife. Thanks for your help with the crime work, Dick." Bird turned into the police station.

"I'm happy we could help. The newspapers are going to have a field day when all this comes out. Those church folks sure had high hopes, didn't they?" Rogers said as he opened the car door.

"Yes, they believed Matthew Henry Stiles was the answer to a dying church and for that matter a dying community. I'll call Irene and Kenny in the morning and ask them to gather the church tomorrow evening. I'd like to be the one to explain the details before the rumor mill completely takes over."

Instead of returning to work, Chief Bird walked around the green to the church and let himself into Stiles' office. He reached into the file drawer and pulled out *The Chronicle of Matthew Henry Stiles*. Bird backed into the desk chair and read for an hour. He read the last entry a second time.

The Chronicle of The <u>Reverend </u>Matthew Henry Stiles

If this letter is being read to you, either I've disappeared or I'm dead.

If Delbert Martin had cooperated with me, if Arthur Blankenship had registered the letter giving me complete control over the monies of this church, if Irene Keene had kept her suspicions to herself, if every person had increased their pledges to the church as I had demanded, my dreams for First Parish church would have been fulfilled.

I had the right dreams for First Parish Church. I had the enthusiasm and the energy to build First Parish to be the model church of the century. I had you pointed in the right direction, but you kept stumbling and disappointing me. You forced me to stoop to other, less than orthodox, means to keep my dream alive. You people have disappointed God.

I imagine that you will tear down the fence and the thatched house and then work on transferring the ownership of the green to the town. I am sure the museums will be permanently closed, and the church will fall into disrepair.

You'll try to sell the museums to recover some of the

money I spent on them but they won't sell. The greater community will consider them tainted. You'll return to the small homey group of forty that you were before I came, but without the church building, because the bank will take it away from you.

I am sorry for nothing. One request: if I'm dead, bury Frederic beside me and don't forget to think of me when you hear Chopin's "Funeral March." I'll be humming that piece as you bury your church.

Don't forget to include something about me in the historic wall.

The Reverend Matthew Henry Stiles

Bird studied the hollow eyes of the skeleton. "Tell me, what did Reverend Stiles find in your dry bones and hollow eyes?"

Bird secured the file under his arm and stepped outside the office door. As he shut the door, he listened for Frederic's rattle.

EPILOGUE

August 1973

A YEAR of negative publicity followed Stiles' death. Reporters from all over the country arrived to interview citizens of Ironton Corner and tried to dig out every morsel of detail regarding The Reverend Matthew Henry Stiles and Delbert Martin's murder. The Saturday editions of the *Ironton Corner Daily News* included announcements and invitations to the festivities for Labor Day weekend in the "Newly Resurrected" Ironton Corner. Of course, the announcements included photos and detailed stories by the award winning journalist, Wally Harris.

August 4. Come and witness the transfer of the deed for the church-owned green to the town.

August 11. Be present for the reopening of The Museums of Ironton Corner, under the leadership of Maida Alden with the financial support of Alice Stiles and the Massachusetts Arts Council.

August 18. Irene Keene's new history of Ironton Corner, *Lest We Forget*, will be available. Irene will be present to personally sign your copy.

August 25. Be sure to notice the new addition to the historic wall—the hands of a skeleton. Maida Alden says that she expects many questions about why the council has included the skeleton's hands. She told this reporter that she will respond with, "How much of the story do you want to hear?"

September 1. You may remember the speculation that the church in Ironton Corner would be foreclosed and the historic building destroyed, but when you arrive in Ironton Corner you'll see a sign on the church that reads:

This Church is still in business.
The people are its ministers.
Clyde Weaver the Pastor

Made in the USA
Charleston, SC
03 February 2013